if
on a one-way street
you chance

if
on a one-way street
you chance

Merle Colborne

In Memoriam

Brian Creagh-Barry

First published 2022
by Tin Mug Books
14 Sprowston Road
Norwich UK
NR3 4QN

tinmugbooks@hotmail.com

The right of Merle Colborne to be identified
as the author of this work has been asserted
by her in accordance with the Copyright,
Designs and Patents Act, 1988

ISBN 978-1-3999-0784-2

Cover by **www.studio-medlikova.com**

Designed and typeset by benstudios.co.uk

"No one is born hating another person because of the colour of his skin, or his background, or his religion. People must learn to hate, and if they can learn to hate, they can be taught to love, for love comes more naturally to the human heart than its opposite."

Nelson Mandela

1

He's pushing his supermarket trolley down into the street now, the scrap metal man, just as he did the day I died. And he's whistling the same four notes above the steely screech of the wheels and the scuff of laceless boots on hot, hard tar. He is wearing a wide-brimmed lady's pink hat and a khaki string vest. He's pushing against the traffic that comes occasionally around the one-way street that wraps about the kwaZulu hill where black-masked monkeys maraud and green snakes slide. His brinjal-black arms, taut with muscle, gleam with effort and sub-tropical humidity.

Time changes rhythm. Drifting and wobbling and looping back on itself, accelerating and spinning and hurtling forward, bunching and swelling and bursting in all directions, it is a dandelion clock whose blown seeds fall through cracks as narrow as the synapses over which omnipotent messages leap in unbroken continuity with unimagined consequences.

Washed by the same cold currents, icebergs rather than islands, even to ourselves unknown, we live largely unaware of the continual shifting and creaking, the breaking and melting, beneath and all around us.

A centipede is crossing the street on a Mexican wave of eyelash legs. A spider whirls on the steel-bright bungee cable she extrudes from her belly.

A bird watches.

But don't be deceived: life's events spring not from a simple crosshairing but the random convergence of a trillion tiny incidents. It is only in novels and movies that disparate lives plait neatly together. In ordinary life, outside of our intimate relationships, most human contact is extraneous and in defined contexts. We barely recognise the supermarket assistant out of uniform and feel uncomfortable seeing the chap from up the road at our doctor's.

The grass on the verge has grown back and been cut several times since. The stain on the tar has faded. The hadedas have left their nest in the wild fig tree. The chained puppy is fully grown.

The people who live in the houses, they too have got on with the everyday business of living and dying: the Indian family in the purple house, the widow looking for mail from Australia, the old Afrikaans man and the Coloured family who live in the house where the big gate, still, is left open. Number 42 remains unoccupied. At number 29 all is much as it was. The trowel lies where I dropped it though now it's hidden beneath the weeds that have overrun the lower garden. The lettuces have bolted and gone to seed. The mealies have been scavenged.

Hearing the scrap metal man's signature whistle and the screech of the trolley above her radio, the Indian lady in the kitchen of number 95 lifts the wooden spoon from the hissing pan and, twisting the gold bangles on her slim brown arm, sucks her lips in, praying the front gate is locked.

Splayed nostrils briefly enticed by the aroma of spices splitting and popping in hot effervescent oil, the scrap metal man pushes his trolley down past the purple house. There is no sign today of 'The one who walks around and around', the one whom people indicate with the twirl of an index finger. What none of us knew was that he puts food out for the birds, that he can name them in English and in Latin, that by a simple tweet-tweet or a bizztkizzkizz or a gertchargertcha he can outline the shape, colour the nape and rump and wing coverts, bend the toes, angle the head, ignite a bead of light in a small round eye.

#95

Son of a Great Soul

He had started walking around the house, keeping always the purple walls and turquoise roof tiles on his right, the marigolds, bougainvillea and hibiscus on his left. Around and around, his spare frame erect his arms metronoming from bare shoulders round and smooth as apples. It felt to him that with each circumnavigation he was winding another length of bandage firmly around the wound, numbing the pain.

To the woman inside the house it felt as though he were binding another length of rope fast about her, keeping her captive. However much she turned up the radio, however much she occupied herself with her chores, wearing a pinafore over her sari to clean the brass, or polish the imbuia, or braise the onions with garlic and ginger, coriander and cumin, fennel and mustard seeds, or whatever combination of aromatics she was using for the evening meal, she was aware of him, his immaculate shaved scalp, brown as a pecan, passing like clockwork by the kitchen window, the fall of his bare feet on the cement path, his shadow approaching and receding as it reflected in the glass of the gold framed picture of Sai Baba.

Around and around, day after day, he went. Sometimes when he caught the sweet scent of lighted incense wafting through the net curtains, a small frown creased his brow for he could see her – vermilion *bindi* on her forehead, palms pressed together – at the lighted recess in the hall, the smoke, like soft fibres of cashmere, mingling with her hair, her lips shaping persistent prayers to Ganesha, son of Shiva, whose capacious elephant head contained all spiritual wisdom, whose supple trunk could remove any obstacle. But she would not speak to him about what he so needed to know. It was this that caused him such pain.

What distressed her most was that, though he could see how much this walking, walking, always walking, upset her, he would not stop. What would the white lady who had bought the wood and iron house down the street think, him walking around and around the house? She wanted to scream but it felt as if something heavy was pressing down, crushing her ribs, suffocating her. Some mornings she felt too drained to get out of bed and just lay there under the brushed nylon cover, listening to the tendrils of a high pitched female voice twining around its male counterpart on Lotus fm. Lay there with her hands folded under her slackened cheek, staring at nothing, reliving that long ago afternoon in the cane fields.

It had fallen to her, Anisha, the only girl among five brothers in the extended Clare Estate family to look after Rabi when he came into the world ten years after her mother had borne the last boy. He had cried a lot as a baby but, with the guidance of her debilitated mother who had retired to her bed after his birth, Anisha managed well enough, occasionally even getting some quiet pleasure holding the baby boy in her arms, as he sucked at his bottle, his big brown eyes never leaving her face.

When her mother passed a couple of years later, Anisha was distraught. She had lost the only person she could turn to and though she performed the proper mourning rites she feared she might have overlooked some detail or that the spirit in which she performed them was not pure enough and that her mother's soul would have no strength and so would be swept away into the unknown vastness.

People whispered that it was Anisha who had hastened her mother's death; that she had got what she deserved; that, subservient to her broken-hearted father and her brothers, it was only right that all the household duties should fall on her wicked, young shoulders.

Anisha managed to keep the household running but found it hard to cope with the extra demands of the growing boy. She had shown him a hundred times how to gather his fingertips together and curve his palm to scoop up the food, instead of simply smacking the flat small hand he'd submerged in yellow dhal against his face. She had shown him a thousand times how to thread his skinny, obstinate arms into his sleeves. It seemed to her that he was wilful, that he had deliberately set out to annoy her: wetting the bed, dirtying his clothes, always crying. One day when he had soiled his pants again and she, screaming, had yanked him, shrieking at the top of his small lungs, to the outside toilet, and shaking him, had sat him down, his little heels drubbing the wood surround, his bare bottom perched over the black hole where bluebottle flies buzzed, it was all she could do to stop herself from shoving him down into the steaming stench until he stopped screaming, stopped breathing. It was the woman next door who, hearing the commotion saved both the small boy whose cries turned to silent gulps and the overwrought young woman who burst into uncontrollable sobs.

It was after this that people said Rabi had the devil in him. The other boys paid him little attention. The bereaved old man, known to everyone as 'Daddy', just sat on the stoep, chewing betel nut and drinking the sweet, milky tea his daughter served him throughout the day. He chastised the child constantly for the trouble he caused his sister. Couldn't he see how much she had to do?

The boys teased Rabi: in the next life he would come back as a cockroach. He had seen the cockroaches scuttle out from under the sink, seen how fast they disappeared again as Anisha tried to whack them with a rolled up newspaper, how she sometimes laid poison, told him not to touch. But he did touch. One day he coaxed an ailing cockroach into a Chilli Bites carton and played with it for hours, poking its date-brown body, enjoying the soft tickle of its long cottony feelers on the tips of his tiny fingers.

And then he was called away and when he went back later to find his friend, the cockroach and the carton were gone.

People said he was odd, not like other children.

'You strange boy? Where you coming from?' one of the men keeping Daddy company on the stoep asked.

'From under the Elephant's Ear!' laughed another.

Rabi had crawled in under the big broad leaves of the *colocasia* that grew at the side of the dilapidated old house and had seen nothing to support this notion.

Wherever he came from, whatever he had been in a previous life, Rabi was determined not to come back as a cockroach and spent long hours looking for alternative incarnations: hiding in the long grass gawking at locusts in their green armour-plating, or lying on his stomach on the concrete slab next to the dustbin gazing at swift ants lugging crumbs larger than themselves, or watching the bees alighting on the hibiscus.

People said that he was slow.

'Why you not talking?' they would ask and, staring at him with close, commanding eyes, would say 'Da Da…Ma Ma', exaggerating the movements of their jaws, exploding the sounds in his face, making him cry. But there was only one word the boy would utter: '*Ramanama.*' He would say it over and over again. '*Ramanama. Ramanama.*' And people would look at each other and ask, 'Where he get that from?'

Others remarked that they had heard him imitate the birds. He had an ear for their calls: the way that one would snick the silence, short, sharp, like the snip of hedge clippers; the way another would flute sweet soaring melodies. He observed the swallows sitting with locked claws on the electric lines, the wind lifting their tail feathers and exposing the soft warmth of their tiny beating bodies and how they shuffled along regripping the wire. And he watched the hadedas, the *kankane*, in the mango trees teaching their bulky offspring to fly.

It wasn't until he was nearly four years old that Rabi began to speak. Suddenly, overnight and in whole sentences. And started asking endless questions.

It drove Anisha to distraction but the little boy's curiosity amused the older uncles, two or three of whom were always there on the stoep.

'What's an essteedee?'

'Little pitchers have big ears!'

'What's pitchers?'

'Same as jugs?'

'What's jugs?'

The men roared with laughter.

'Alla time you be saying What? What? What? Me, I am giving you nicky name,' said one of the uncles.

'What's nicky name?'

'You see this man here,' he gestured towards an elderly gentleman who visited the house occasionally. 'He name Chintaharan but he knowing everything so we giving him nicky name, "Walking Encyclopaedia."'

'What's cyclopaedia?'

'What? What? What? From now on you no more Rabi. From now you "Hundred Watts."'

'What's hundred watts?'

'Come I'll show you,' said one of the older aunties scowling at the men. She took him to the standard lamp, stood him on a stool and pointed to the number and the writing on the bulb, then she clicked the switch and the light came on. 'See: 100 watts, very bright.'

Rabi was fascinated by the delicate insect with its silvery antennae and its crystal-clear body that lived in the glass egg, how, shivering slightly, it sprang to life when he pressed the switch. It was much nicer to be 'Hundred Watts' than to be a cockroach. He clicked the switch over and over and sometimes the wiry insect made a buzzing sound and then it made a popping noise and then it wouldn't come alive anymore and, because he had killed the insect in the glass egg, he would be frightened and droop his shoulders and draw his thin body in, waiting for the battery of smacks.

'How many times I'm telling you not to play with electricity?' Anisha would scream, 'Globes don't grow on trees!'

But grown-ups lied. Rabi knew they did.

He had had seen a whole treeful of light bulbs when one of the aunties had taken Anisha and all the children in the Toyota to see the Christmas Lights at the beachfront and shown them the hotel where one of the uncles worked.

They had stood on the pavement next to the verandah and watched uncle in his shiny black pants and short, red jacket, balancing a silver tray of brown bottles on the tips of his splayed fingers, circling the tables and smiling, smiling, smiling, his gold fillings gleaming in the white expanse of teeth.

'Hurry up coolie!' the white men had called. And he had smiled and smiled.

'What's a coolie?'

'I'll wash your mouth out with mustard!' Anisha had said.

But the next day when the men were sitting on the stoep talking 'Walking Encyclopaedia' said, 'Khuli is Hindi word and it is meaning "working man."'

'Like Uncle?' asked Rabi.

'Yes, like Uncle!' they laughed.

He had seen, too, the white men on the verandah making jokes about the black man sweeping up the glass they had smashed.

'What's Kaffir?'

The men guffawed.

'Kaffir is Arabic word,' said 'Walking Encyclopaedia', 'and it is meaning non-believer.'

'Nonsense!' said one of the men, 'it is meaning lazy bastard.'

'What's bastard?'

'What you teaching this child?' Anisha shouted, dragging him off by the arm, smacking his bony bottom on the way.

And then, as suddenly as he had started, Rabi stopped asking questions.

After her mother passed Anisha added Lakshmi, the goddess of wealth and prosperity, to her prayers. Before serving her brothers their meal she always offered a small portion to the deity's image and prayed to her to send a man of light complexion in a Mercedes, gold in colour, with a brass tissue box on the back window ledge, to rescue her and buy her armloads of gold bangles. Preferably 18 carat.

One afternoon when Rabi was six or seven, he picked up bits of conversation which lodged in some corner of his mind from where they would occasionally rise and disturb him.

An auntie whom they hadn't seen for some time had come to visit. She had had her hair cut and was wearing long shorts and a T-shirt.

'What's happened to you?' asked Anisha who had come out onto the stoep where the men were.

'I have given myself to the Lord.'

'And who you did you give yourself to, Anisha?' one of the men asked. A look of terror had flashed across her face and she had fled inside.

'That wasn't very Christian!' scolded the auntie following her into the house.

'Christian!' shouted one of the uncles turning to the other men, 'Don't talk to me about Christian! Who brought us out from India to work like slaves on the sugar plantations because the black bastards were too lazy? Christians!'

'They weren't lazy. This was *their* country. They weren't going to be forced to work for the British invaders, all of them Christian!'

'Yes, and thanks to them, the Christians, you're not sleeping in the streets of Calcutta, defecating in the gutter and all!'

'And who giving us hassle till kingdom come calling us all same name, one time – Naidoo, Moodley, Pillay – not to be wasting time writing Poovalingam, Pramjeet and Periasamy?

Christians! And who broke our houses down with their "Group Areas"? Christians!'

'And who sent the Jews to the gas chambers?' called another.

'And who killed Jesus?'

'And Jesus himself a Jew and all!'

'Always Christians claiming all good is Christian and all bad unchristian.'

'No matter,' said Chintaharan 'Many streams to one ocean. Many paths to God. *Vasudhaiva kutumbakam.* The world is one family.'

Rabi had trailed into the house to Anisha's room where the bedroom door stood ajar and saw Anisha curled up on her divan, sobbing. The auntie was sitting beside her, stroking her and, with eyes closed, repeating the same thing over and over: 'For I am the way, the truth and the light. No man cometh to the Father but by me the Son.' Then she stopped and said, 'Anisha, one day you must tell Rabi the truth.'

And Anisha prayed harder to Ganesha to help her through these dark times and harder still to Lakshmi to find her a husband who would give her a beautiful *mangalsutra* made of such special beads that it would silence the whisperers and that he would take her to live in a five bedroom mansion with wall to wall carpeting and built-in cupboards and a girl to do the cleaning. In Reservoir Hills.

The auntie came often to visit. Her safari-suited husband would drop her off and then drive away in his new yellow Ford Zephyr 'to attend to business matters.' The uncles said that many Indians forgot about the law of karma and living according to *dharma* or the rules of good conduct and they became Christian so they could get better success in life, better *artha*.

'They think they say "I'm Christian!" they get more respect from whites, better opportunities.'

'Yes, even the biggest crooks say "I'm Christian!" and give their businesses English names like *St George's Refurbishing* or *Windsor Fashion Fabrics* and then wait for doors to open.'

'And they do!'

'Yes, Mercedes doors and all!'

The auntie told Rabi that Jesus had died on the cross for his sins. And she told him that the Lord, Son of God, born of the Virgin Mary, would one day come back to earth and everybody should prepare for the Second Coming and that he must be a good boy and pray to Jesus and be born again. 'No, not as a cockroach!' the auntie laughed reassuringly when he asked.

Rabi asked Jesus to send him good karma. A Toyota or a Ford Zephyr. But nothing happened and then he heard the uncles say that the Karmann Ghia was very good so he prayed for that instead. But no car came. And Rabi wondered if Jesus had died because he dirtied his clothes and asked too many questions and couldn't do anything right.

What he wanted more than anything in his next life, Rabi decided, was to be able to fly. He had once observed a flying cockroach in the outside toilet and he saw one hot summer night that even ants could fly. Hundreds and hundreds of them came tapping at his head, flying with their long white wings towards the insect in the glass egg which lit the stoep at night. But in the morning they had disappeared, leaving their white discarded wings like mourning dress on the red cement.

He often held an arm out stiff and straight hoping that some flying creature would think it a branch and alight. A butterfly did once settle on his forearm and he was startled by the power of its muscled grip, astonished that such fragile beauty could have such strength.

One day Rabi climbed up into the mango tree, spread his arms and held them so taut that his muscles ached. Then he jumped. Anisha gave him a good scolding and put ice on his sprained wrist. The uncles changed his name: 'Forty Watts', very dim.

Rabi's teachers said he was a dreamer, that he had too much imagination, that he didn't apply himself, that he didn't relate well to his peers. But he loved books and spent long hours in the school library feeling a current of excitement and anticipation every time he pulled out one of the old maroon volumes with the 'The Book of Knowledge' embossed in gold letters on its spine and unfolded the coloured plates and looked at the rows and rows of birds and butterflies, insects and moths.

It was in religious instruction one day that Rabi discovered to his shame that karma had nothing to do with Karmann Ghias or any cars at all but was the thing that decided what you would come back as and had something to do with your soul which was like a sticky surface where all the bad things you did got stuck. Rabi thought his soul must be like the thick yellow length of paper that hung in loose twists from the kitchen ceiling and was full of black flies. But he also learnt that if he was very good some of the flies would drop off.

He tried to do good deeds. He had learnt to read remarkably well and would read aloud to Daddy but the old man got irritated and told him to go away. He would help Anisha dry the dishes but he was too slow she said. When he tried to go faster, he dropped things and once he broke a cup and she told him he was useless and to get out of her kitchen. He tried to help her dust but she would always find the one place he had missed and hold up a telling forefinger: 'Can't you do anything properly?!' Rabi wondered what he could do that wouldn't get him into trouble and would help the flies drop off his soul and so he decided to save the sweeties people sometimes gave him and put them next to Anisha's teacup or on her pillow. She smiled at him and said thank you the first few times but after a while it seemed to annoy her, this little thing he did to please her, and she started shouting: 'You think you can just give me sweeties, Rabi, but…'

Yet every July or August at *Raksha Bandhan*, held to celebrate a girl's bond with her brothers and to protect them against evil, Anisha – just as she did for all the boys in the family – tied the red thread around his wrist. And Rabi cherished the thin, crimson chord which made him feel that he must be alright after all.

And then, quite suddenly, Daddy passed. For many days the men grew their hair and didn't shave and they ate only boiled food but Rabi was not sad that Daddy was late. Now Anisha wouldn't have so much to do, always making him tea. Now she mightn't get so cross. He knew that it was wrong, that it was bad to feel pleased that Daddy had passed. But he couldn't help it.

He prayed to Vishnu for forgiveness, and, just in case, to Jesus too. But he worried: people said that if you were really bad, the bad things would stick to your soul not like flies that could drop off, but like barnacles.

He dreamt that he was covered in barnacles and that people yelled and ran away when they saw him. And some people turned on him and threw stones. And sometimes he would scream and wake up. And Anisha would shout at him and tell him not to be so silly.

Occasionally the uncles took him fishing down at the harbour and he saw, through the bottle green water where the minnows looped in bands of light, the harbour wall encrusted with barnacles. He took a stick once and tried to scrape them away but the stick broke and the barnacles didn't budge.

Things did get easier for Anisha after Daddy's passing, but though the lines on her forehead faded, the sorrow in her eyes remained. And then one day even the sadness seemed to have lessened.

It was at a family wedding that a matchmaking auntie introduced her to Krish. He was dark-skinned and much older than she but he had a kind face. He ran his own business doing fitted kitchens and built-in cupboards and lived with his mother in a brick house in a better part of town and drove a Nissan bakkie with a radio/cassette.

When Krish started courting Anisha, Rabi went along as chaperone. He would sit in the back of the bakkie and feel the wind on his face and then they would park at Blue Lagoon and he would watch through the rear window of the cabin. He saw how Anisha would talk and talk in a way he had never seen her talk to anyone else and, once or twice, he saw her crying and, more than once or twice, Krish took her in his arms and kissed her. And sometimes when the moon was full, the ocean silver and the fishermen's faces were washed in light and the sound from the radio/cassette breathtakingly beautiful, Rabi could feel something like a sad sort of happiness seeping into him.

When Anisha and Krish got married it was taken for granted that Rabi would move with her into the house Krish shared with his mother. He settled into his new school, which had an excellent library of books (mainly gifts from deceased estates) but remained essentially a loner. Having the unheard of luxury of a room to himself, with its own separate entrance, he would read till all hours of the night and then spend his days sitting listlessly at his school desk.

The atmosphere in the home, however, was not pleasant. The two women found it very difficult to share a house; Krish's mother was always complaining. One day when Rabi came home from school a little earlier than usual he heard her shouting:

'You think you can come here with that bastard of yours…'

'You be careful what you say!' Anisha had yelled back.

Rabi had slipped out and walked for miles and then sat on a swing in the park, a thin boy in a too-big school blazer. When, eventually, he came home, both women turned on him.

'What time do you call this?' Anisha shouted.

'See, he no-good boy!' the old woman chimed in.

It was then that Rabi began to think of The Second Coming and how Jesus too had been scolded for coming home late. Since the time that Anisha had lain sobbing on her divan, the words the Christian auntie had said, 'One day you must tell Rabi the truth,' had frequently surfaced in his mind. He spent many hours thinking about it: Krish was not his father but he was married to Anisha. Joseph was not Jesus's father but he was married to Mary. Krish was much older than Anisha. Joseph was much older than Mary. Krish was a carpenter. Joseph was a carpenter – though Rabi doubted whether he would have done fitted kitchens but you never know, he had read about central heating in the ancient palace of Knossos.

One day he asked the Christian auntie who, like all the family, came to visit still, if Mary's husband Joseph would have known how to make kitchen drawers and things.

'What kind of a question is that, Rabi?' she laughed. Later when Anisha told her that Rabi was behaving more strangely than usual and that she suspected that he might have overhead things he shouldn't have, the Christian auntie said 'I think maybe he thinks he is the Son of God.'

It was not long after that that Rabi heard Krishs's mother screaming at Anisha: 'Take your bastard son and go!'

'You have no business…'

'You think I don't know…!'

'You know nothing!'

'Huh! I know damn all!'

And Rabi had covered his ears and locked himself in his room. It was Krish who brought his food to the door.

Rabi went out early and came back late. He didn't go to school. He sat in the bushes and hid behind the toilets in the park and when some of his school mates cornered him and asked why he wasn't in class he told them he had things on his mind.

He had always known there was something wrong, that it was not just because he was so much younger that he had all along felt so different to his brothers, that there was something strange about his relationships with other family members, something that he had never been able to put his finger on.

He thought long about when and where he could raise the subject with Anisha and then one day when she again asked him how come he was so clumsy, he said 'Must be hereditary!' and, seizing the opportunity, asked 'Is it true?'

She started: the moment she had so long dreaded. 'Is what true?'

'That you are not my sister?'

'Rabi' she said reaching out towards him.

'Don't touch me!'

'Rabi I know you're upset…'

'But if you are not my sister why did you give me the *rakhi* every year?'

'It's not just for brothers.'

'But you pretended!' And he snapped the band from his wrist.

'It was for the best.'

'What does that mean?'

'It was best that you didn't know.'

'Didn't know what? That you weren't my sister that you were...' But he couldn't say the word.

She reached towards him again.

'Leave me alone! You lied to me! My MOTHER,' he snarled, 'my MOTHER lied to me!'

'Don't Rabi!'

'How do you think it makes me feel?'

'I'm sorry Rabi...'

'When were you going to tell me?'

'I don't know...'

'You let me believe that granny was my mother...That's why people said "Anisha killed her!"'

'Who said that?'

'Everybody... I heard them.'

'What did they say?'

'You worry about what people say. Not about the truth! About me!' He ran from the room, slamming the door.

They knew! Everybody knew except him. Was he then too undeserving to be entrusted with the truth? No wonder he had always felt like an outcast. No wonder people always kept their distance. They were protecting the family, protecting her.

They talked about him behind his back, whispered about him. They had betrayed him, every single one of them. They had purposefully deceived him. They had all failed him, every last one of them. Damn her! Damn them! Damn them all!

The next morning he accosted Anisha again. She knew what was coming. It was what she most dreaded.

'Who's my father?'

'I can't tell you!'

'Why not?'

'Because I can't!'

'Why not?'

'Because I just can't!'

'Why? Because you had so many men? Is that why?!'

This time it was Anisha who fled the room in tears.

At first it felt to him as though the earth itself had shifted on its axis and then he began to feel that all the things that had been swirling about in his heart, playing games in his head over the years were settling on slightly more solid ground. Now he knew what he suddenly realised had been slowly dawning on his conscious mind, knew rationally what he had always at some subliminal level felt, that she, Anisha, was not his sister but his mother.

He could now not speak to her at all and began playing an elaborate charade: getting up and leaving the house without saying goodbye, going for long walks, talking to the birds, locking himself in his room, helping himself to food only after everyone else had gone to bed, eating just a little from each of the many Tupperware containers stacked in the fridge, being careful to leave everything just as it was, hoping that no one would notice he'd been in the house. But while his withdrawal saved him embarrassment it only increased his anguish.

When the many family members came to visit, the men sitting on the three piece suite watching TV, the women sitting on the stoep, nudging and glancing and muttering, they'd ask

'Where Rabi?'

'He's gone for a walk.'

'Why always walking. Where's he going with all this walking?'

'India probably!' And they all laughed.

And so Rabi managed somehow to continue living his tightly controlled life. The house remained sprung with tension.

It was only after Krish's mother passed and Rabi, for his step-father's sake, had helped to attend the body and accompanied the ashes down to the Umgeni River to be scattered on the water, it was only then that Rabi felt his spirits lift a little, the atmosphere in the house ease.

But not a day went by that he didn't wonder about who his father was, what he looked like, what he did. Perhaps he was a doctor, a lawyer, perhaps he was someone famous. Perhaps there were other half brothers and sisters. Perhaps they lived around the corner, perhaps halfway around the world.

Sorting through a fresh donation of books in the library one day, Rabi opened a copy of *My Experiments with Truth* by Mohandas

Karamchand Gandhi. 'From my sixth or seventh year up until my sixteenth I was at school being taught all sorts of things except religion,' he read. 'I may say I failed to get from the teachers what they could have given me without any effort on their part. And yet I kept picking up things here and there from my surroundings.'

When Rabi read those words it felt as though he had written them himself.

And he read too that Gandhi often used to ask one of his cousins questions and 'he sent me away with this answer "When you grow up you will be able to solve these doubts yourself. These questions ought not to be raised at your age." I was silenced but not comforted.'

Rabi had seen many pictures of the Mahatma with his bald head and his little glasses but now he found a photograph of Gandhi as a younger man when he had lived in Durban. He had thick black hair. He had ears that stuck out. He had kindly brown eyes. Rabi looked in the mirror and smiled at his own image: thick black hair, protruding ears, brown eyes. He willed them to warm.

Then he read that as a small boy Gandhi used to repeat '*Ramanama*' to comfort himself, that he had gone for long solitary walks, that he was shy, that he had scraped through Matric. Could it be? The son of the son of Gandhi? It was not entirely impossible. The idea grew on him. It was not impossible at all.

'But one thing took deep root in me – the conviction that morality is the basis of things, and that truth is the substance of all morality,' Gandhi had written.

Rabi stared at the woman in the sari who sat with folded arms in the lounge. She knew the truth, and wouldn't tell him. For that he loathed her. And suddenly it seemed that everywhere he looked in newspapers and on television all over the world there were people just like him wanting to know who they really were; children of all ages looking for their fathers. There were always stories in the papers about the importance of identity, of genetic influences on one's physical appearance, on one's mental capacity, one's talents and personality, even on the little things one did, like sitting knees together shins splayed. There were items about the advances in science that could give irrefutable proof of blood, about the developments in psychology that showed how people like him needed 'closure' to feel whole. For some searchers there were happy outcomes, for others there was heartbreak, for people like him there was just a huge void, a sense of nothingness.

One day he shaved his head and started wearing small round glasses and began walking around the house. He read and reread what Gandhi had written about self-realisation, about knowledge of self.

'Truth became my sole objective. It began to grow in magnitude every day, and my definition of it also has been ever widening.'

Rabi thought about these words a great deal.

Then one night he sat cross-legged on the floor of his room staring at the candle he had lit and as time passed he began slowly to concentrate on the flame that flared like a mitre from the wick. And gradually it came to him that there was a part of him that was absolute, beyond the make-up of his cells, innocent of hereditary, untouched by the things that had from the moment of conception perhaps, been imprinted in the deepest layers of his being.

For what he was, above and beyond body and mind, more than personality, more than character, was pure soul far removed from anything that the little god of science could yet explain, beyond any powers of the reason to fathom, something that simply was. He knew that if he could free himself from the concerns that had so skewed his life and accept himself just as he was, he would feel a flowing outward to all of creation and merge with the universe and feel a wholeness and a oneness far beyond anything that he could ever have envisaged.

Rabi stayed staring at the candle until it burned down, its flame consumed in molten wax, and he felt a great sense of peace and lay awake until he heard the small birds shirring the paling silence and called to mind that in some ancient traditions the bird is seen as born twice, once into the shell and once out into the unbounded sky.

And he felt invigorated and got up and walked out into the day and watched the sun leap over the hill and saw the mango leaves suddenly golden lit, and saw the air thick with rampant life, and saw glory in the grass. He had never felt so free, so unfettered, and what was most astonishing was how effortless it had been.

And then he came back to the house and began his walking around, only now he was walking in the opposite direction, keeping the house with its purple walls and turquoise roof tiles on his left, the marigolds, bougainvillea and hibiscus on his right.

Anisha inside the house was listening to the morning news. And there it was again:

The unutterable word, the unthinkable act that was everywhere now. Screaming from international headlines or tucked away among local news items, heading out of war zones and schoolyards, out of old age homes and children's nurseries. It was used about women dressed in voluminous robes and about women not dressed at all; it was used about octogenarians and infants. And each time she saw the word in the papers or heard it on the radio or TV it was as though her body, picking up the vibration, relived, in some small way the terror of it all… the pressing down on her eyes…on her mouth…the stalks of harvested cane poking into her back…the rip and tear of clothing…the forcing apart of her thighs…the smell of soiled trousers…of blood…of salt…of shame…and always the sound of the wind blowing wild in the sugar cane.

And now, walking around the house in the opposite direction, it felt to Rabi as if the bandages with which he had tried to numb his pain were being unwound. His step grew lighter, his feet more fleet. A small smile played on his face and the words of the Mahatma came to him: 'I began to understand more and more the infinite possibilities of universal love.'

And hearing the soft fall of his feet on the hard cement it dawned on the woman inside the house that he was going in the opposite direction. She suddenly felt as though the rope that had been pulled so tight around her was now unwinding, that she was being set free, she felt the heaviness lift, her spirit lighten. She went outside and sat cross-legged on the grass, holding her face to the morning sun, feeling its warming rays stroke her skin.

And Rabi came and sat beside her cross-legged on the grass, and held his face too to the sun.

And there was peace between them.

2

Like his fellow 'entrepreneurs', the scrap metal man stores his supermarket trolley at the scrap yard on the main road below and collects it when the gates of Utopia Scrap *open at 6 a.m. At that hour, with the small hard wheels of the empty trolley lightly singing in the still sharp air before the heat rises and the traffic thickens and the noisy road works begin, the scrap metal man, alive to the moment, cranks hope up a notch, clicks it into happy anticipation, and, as the day settles in, radiates a sprung cheeriness that causes the more materially advantaged pressing down hard on their hooters to wonder how a man in a string vest and a lady's pink hat, pushing a dilapidated trolley into the oncoming traffic can be so buoyantly sure that life is essentially wonderful.*

Though the scrap metal man no longer works underground in the mines, there are hazards enough on the roads above: drivers who gleefully threaten the lives of those at the end of the pecking order believing somehow that this will affirm their own tenuous place further up. And dogs.

Now the ubiquitous four-legged guards picking up his scent begin to bark. Down along both sides of the street where I lived thoroughbreds, cross breeds and motley mongrels streak, full-bellied and self-important, to their front gates worrying at the grilles and lifting their heads to emit a menace of pitches and timbres and reverberations that cut into one another and loop over each other and roll down the street like the unfurling of suddenly released razor wire, through which the scrap metal man advances, whistling, still, his four bright notes.

The postman has already been so the woman at number 87 comes out now to see whether it is the meter reader, the junk mail deliverer, the broom maker, the samosa seller, the mealie hawker, the woman who swaps vegetables for second-hand clothes, the man with the weed-eater looking for piece work, the man with nothing looking for a bit of bread, the opportunist looking for a chance or merely a stray cat that is causing her two dogs to bark so persistently. Amused by his mother-of-the bride hat she smiles at the scrap metal man and feels again inside her letterbox in case she has missed something, a card perhaps from Australia. What would Mark say if he could see the old Pyott's Assorted *biscuit tin one of the labourers had turned into a letterbox for her?*

#87

Going nowhere

The face bent over the work was slack-skinned, like an easy chair whose slipcovers had worked loose and, for all the expensive emollients patted on with butterfly fingertips, the creasing beneath the astute blue eyes marked, the magnification wrought by the reading glasses, unfortunate.

She held the crochet hook in her right hand pushing it under and up with a sideways whittling movement. The bright yarn, passing through the shuttle of her flying fingers, made a soft shushing sound. The dog lying heavy in a warm curve at her feet looked up from under the eaves of his brow, his moist eyes alert to her mood. Her mouth, drawn tight across clenched teeth, was tucked in at the corners.

Five chains, slip stitch, four trebles. Meredith sighed. Mark was nagging again. He had, naturally, come over for the funeral and stayed a week afterwards to 'tie things up' and find 'a little something' to take back to Australia to remember his dad by. He had taken Stan's golf clubs, top of the range, recently bought after extensive research, and the framed poster Stan had always hung in his den wherever they had lived. It was an old-fashioned linocut of men standing at the dockside watching a large locomotive fall into the water. The caption read: 'Oh shit!' Meredith knew that Mark had seen it as a comment on his parents' marriage. She also knew that he had no idea how right he'd been.

'Don't be concerned about the future, Mom,' Mark had said. 'Dad and you were going to come over to Oz in a few years anyway so just bring it forward. Why not? Nothing for you here. Almost everyone you know has left. Sell up. Come and live in New South Wales. There's hardly any crime, no AIDS issues and thousands of South Africans. You can make new friends. Watch your grandchildren grow up.'

She had said nothing.

'Mom?'

'Mmm?'

'You'd like that wouldn't you?'

Her smile was bleak. The idea of yet again standing powerless on the sidelines (in raising their son, as in almost everything else, it was Stan's wishes that ruled), the idea of watching her grandchildren being shaped to grow up to be the kind of adults she abhorred, appalled her. She had not seen a great deal of them, or their blonde Australian mother, but already they disturbed her. Those loose indulgent mouths, those large rapacious eyes askance with entitlement. She must love them, she supposed, but suspected she loved her dog more.

Blue had taken to sleeping on the bed, leaving hair all over the little folded tartan rug which Stan had kept at the foot of the bed to warm his long cold feet. She had often wondered about those cold feet. Though everyone seemed to see him as decisive, she knew better. Whether it was buying a new car or hanging a picture, he had lived by the code of 'informed decision'. And he would inform himself exhaustively and not just about the obvious things like the prices of various cars and their resale value. He would find out what inherent weaknesses there were in a particular model, how much replacement parts, both original and pirated would cost, how much labour would be involved in, for instance, reaching the gear box of one car as opposed to another, which paint colour was more durable, which one cheaper in the event of a respray… And so it went. By the time he had come to a decision she had lost all interest and felt utterly drained.

'Well, aren't you happy?' he would ask patting her knee as they sat in 'their' new car, or standing, head tilted, in front of 'their' new picture and then glance at her with a questioning lift of an eyebrow and a dash of smugness about the mouth.

It was the same with his triple bypass. He had planned it meticulously: date, insurance, surgeons, hospital, ward, bed, back copies of the *Financial Times* reports. He hadn't forgotten a thing. Except to say goodbye.

When Meredith ran out of crochet wool (wool shops no longer sold wool, only 'acrylic, 100%!' as one assistant had joked) she simply unravelled her work by the vehement arm length, rolled the curly result into tight bright balls and started again. It wasn't that she was making anything, it was simply that she was *doing* something. People seemed to want her to *do* something and she found that she didn't need, and curiously didn't want, a sense of accomplishment, that all she wanted was to be occupied in some kind of mechanical process. It was the very repetitiveness of the task that calmed her, the way someone else might find comfort in the rituals of the rosary beads.

It was normal that she should be indecisive about what she wanted to do, people said. It was barely three months since her husband had died. It was perfectly natural that she should feel stranded and bereft.

The truth was she felt neither. What was paralysing her was something else entirely: astonishment. Something akin to what a small boy who has stumbled onto a Christmas party might feel when confronted with a pile of presents waiting to be unwrapped and a table full of glorious food and then finds it's all just for him. A sense of freedom and excitement reined in by apprehension, easing perhaps into mere caution now. And guilt. Well, just a little guilt. In one way she felt her life was just beginning. Or perhaps she was simply picking it up at the point she had left off when she had met Stan.

She is leaning on the white railings of the *Windsor Castle*, her long auburn hair whipped by a cold wind, watching the white cliffs of Dover diminish and disappear as the big white liner swans its way back to Africa. She had come to Europe in her

1960 varsity holidays and had stayed on teaching English and au pairing. Her parents hadn't objected: the situation in South Africa was worrying, the economy in the doldrums. (Which to her shame now, and to all whites like herself then, was the most significant thing about Sharpeville when 69 unarmed black people were shot dead while marching to protest the forced carrying of ID passes at all times.) Her parents hoped she would meet a nice young chappy and settle down in good old England where Cliff Richard was tunefully encouraging the young ones not to be afraid.

But she hadn't, and was now coming back to continue her architectural studies at university. She was looking forward to seeing friends and some familiar things again but she would miss the sense of history in the air, the old buildings, the uncensored books and films (on Sundays too!) and, if not in England, then certainly across The Channel – the food, the wine, the men with Marcello Mastroianni eyes and cognac in their voices.

She is aware of a fellow a few years older than her, hands in pockets, tallish.

'Going home?' he asks.

'Ja!' she says.

'Me too,' he says brightly, 'economy's picked up…better standard of living…sunshine! I'll miss telly though!'

'Yes, no! I'd forgotten! Television…' she says adopting an Afrikaans accent, 'will be the end of civilisation as we know it, the break-down of the moral fibre of *die vaderland*.'

And so they slip into conversation, sit in low canvas chairs on a cold deck, snuggle under tartan rugs and sip Bovril. Looking back she realised that she couldn't really remember what he had looked like at the time.

Mark was starting to put the pressure on: 'It's what Dad would have wanted,' and 'We worry about you,' and, more cunningly, 'Just out of interest, get an estate agent in. You'll be surprised how much the property is worth. You might even get the purchaser to take over the dog.'

'It'll be snapped up!' said the agent, Cindi-Lee, as she clattered across the white Italian tiles in see-through high-heeled sandals and tapped a silicone nail on the granite kitchen surfaces. 'Got everything going for it: good area, close to churches and schools, state of the art security, en-suite bedrooms, top of the range kitchen, utility room, remote-controlled garage door, and…' she fluttered a handful of ring-encrusted fingers at the slate patio where two small lollipop trees and a couple of cacti provided the only greenery, 'low-maintenance garden. Very sought-after.'

Meredith stretched her lips wide, but her eyes abandoned the attempted smile. Cindi-Lee – my god where do they get these trailer-trash names! – had just listed everything she disliked most about the cluster housing 'lock up and go' unit Stan had insisted on buying some years ago and which she had never managed to call home.

'Selling the table too?'

'No!' Meredith snapped. Though God knows she had no intention of shipping it off to Australia. In fact she'd been actively discouraged from sending anything more than a couple of boxes of personal effects.

'Well, never mind,' Cindi-Lee patted the freckled back of Meredith's hand. She was used to these old people being a little tetchy selling up.

'You're so lucky, moving to Australia, close to your grandchildren! I'd give anything to have my kids grow up there. Things aren't what they used to be in South Africa. At least crime was under control before.' Meredith felt her jaw tense.

'Yes, under the control of the government that perpetuated it.' She hadn't intended to say that, it had just somehow come out.

Cindi-Lee glanced at her uncomprehendingly. What was the old bag on about?

Never mind, she had already figured out how many thousands of Rand she would get out of the seven and a half percent commission the agency would earn out of what she believed the property would go for.

'Really! That much?' Meredith exclaimed. Mark was right, the place was worth a lot more than she had anticipated.

Within a very short time of Cindi-Lee sticking her stilettos and a 'For Sale' board with a pin-up of herself into the lawn outside, she telephoned in her whiny, high-pitched voice:

'Want the good news or the bad news first?'

Meredith hated the phrase. Attaching strings never allowed one to feel fully one thing or the other.

'Doesn't matter.'

'We have an offer to purchase!' Meredith baulked at the '*we*'.

'The bad news is they don't want the dog. But I'm sure we'll come up with something. I know several people who did the humane thing: had a vet put their dog down. I can give one or two a ring if you like.'

Meredith was shaking.

'It's alright,' she hissed and replaced the receiver.

Mark was delighted.

As for 'the dog' to whom he had been introduced for the first time a few months ago and who seemed to have a proclivity for mating with his leg, well of course she could try and find a home for him. Otherwise there was always the SPCA. Anyway it wasn't important. The important thing was that she had got her (*her!*) price.

He was pleased too that it would take three months for the transfer to come through; time enough for everyone to get used to the idea of 'Granny coming over'; time enough for her to organise herself, that's if she could manage to do so on her own – he could perhaps arrange to come over and help.

Meredith was sorting through her books, some of them old orange Penguin and turquoise Pelican originals. There was nearly all of D.H. Lawrence, and all four of Durrell's *Alexandria Quartet;* there was Joyce's *Portrait of the Artist as a Young Man* and her student books: *Architectural Principles in the Age of Humanism* and ah! She pulled out Nikolaus Pevsner's *European Architecture*, the little book she had opened in cathedrals all over Europe.

She turned to the introduction and the paragraph she'd heavily underlined: 'Architecture is not the product of materials and purposes – nor, by the way, of social condition – but of the changing spirits of changing ages. It is the spirit of an age that pervades its social life, its religion, its scholarship, and its arts.' And what she saw in her mind's eye was London's Millennium Dome – a vacuous, unintentional memorial to hubristic cock-ups – and the two-fingers, up-yours thrust of the New York Twin Towers which had collapsed along with the human values for which the World Trade Centre never stood. She read the scribbled note in the margin: 'You make the environment – then the environment makes you.' Today tourists were given guided tours of shopping malls, and school children taken around pizza factories.

With the books sorted into piles 'Take' and 'Donate' Meredith started on the task that had remained a dull ache in her mind. 'My mistress is going away and leaving me…' she began drafting the ad. No, that sounded as though she were being deliberately cold and mean. 'My mistress has to go away and leave me…' That seemed to suggest she had been committed to some sort of institution. An asylum or a prison perhaps. She tried another angle 'I will guard your property…' No that wasn't right either. She was certainly not going to give Blue to people who wanted him just to do a job of work – there had to be mutual affection. In the end she settled for a simple straightforward 'Relocating'.

She had only one response: a fellow called Charlie who was looking for a companion for his dog, Lassie.

Blue would love that Meredith thought.

'Has Lassie been spayed?'

'Yes, yonks ago…why, your chap a bit of a goer is he?'

'Well…' Meredith laughed.

'Hope he won't wear the old girl out!'

Meredith asked for his address and said she would think about it and give him a call.

The house was in a part of town she didn't know so she took a map, put Blue in the car and set off to check it out. She found the area just up from a busy main road where extensive road works were impeding the flow of the traffic – mainly trucks, buses and minibus taxis. Children of different races were playing cricket in the one-way street. 'I'm Ntini!' she heard a white boy call. Then she saw the little place. Like a child's eyes and nose drawing of a house: two small windows and a door, the upper half of which was glass, with a border of red and blue rectangular panes; a chimney, where in another season a wiry line of Crayola grey may have been unravelling; corrugated roof and walls; a thick scribble of bush. In places the sides of the house showed the bluish tinge of raw corrugated iron where the paint had flaked like blue gum bark. Here and there the red roof paint had boiled and burst; periwinkles had taken root in the gutters. From under the house, perched on several brick columns, a ginger cat emerged and stared at her through sliced kiwi-fruit eyes. For the rest, the property had succumbed to a voracious alien creeper and now lay heavy and still in the early afternoon light. The double gates were chained together. There was no bell, just a sign 'Beware of the Dog. *Passop vir die Hond*' and at that moment a black and white collie, Lassie she presumed, came bounding up the drive, barking. Blue leapt to the front seat. Barked back.

'Hulloooo!' Meredith called, getting out of the car.

When she was a child you simply clicked open the gate, walked up the path and knocked on the door which invariably would have been opened to you – if you were white. Which of course going to the front door you would have been. Things weren't quite so open and welcoming at the back door then, but over the years suspicion grew on all sides and little garden gates had frequently been replaced by locked grilles set in high surrounding walls topped with shards of glass.

She called again. Lassie barked more loudly. The cat stretched, arched its back and slunk around to the other side of the house. This time she thought she saw the slight movement of a curtain.

'Anyone home?'

Meredith knew that she should just accept that either Charlie was not at home or didn't want to be disturbed. It was rude to insist. But making some contact with this place, this instant! became suddenly supremely urgent. She felt like a drowning person straining to reach the proffered rope.

The door was wrenched open and a man of around her age thrust his head out and glowered from beneath unkempt eyebrows.

'Jehovah's Witness?'

'No,' Meredith laughed, 'I'm so sorry.' She felt as guilty as she had as a child when a cricket ball had gone through a neighbour's window.

'It's about the dog.'

'Oh!' he said, 'so that must be Blue! Should have told me you were coming.'

'I know,' said Meredith, 'but I just sort of found myself here.' She hadn't really meant to spy.

He opened the door and came up the driveway in what he would have called 'PT pants' and a torn T-shirt. ''Scuse the appearance,' he laughed and jiggling sinewy shoulders as he unlocked the gate, started singing, 'If I knew you were coming I'd have baked a cake, baked a cake…'

'Haven't heard that song in years!' she smiled.

Seeing Blue in the car he began another, 'How much is that doggy in the window?…'

'If I had a dog I won't be lonely…' Meredith joined in, the words she'd never given a second thought to, suddenly seeming so very significant.

It was years since she had felt so light-headed. 'Giddy' Stan would have said.

'Well Lassie, what do you think about getting a boyfriend? Or should I say live-in lover?' Then turning to Meredith 'I'm afraid I'm a bit of a softie. Let the old girl sleep inside…' Meredith smiled.

'Would you like to see the place? Bit of a mess but what the heck!'

'Love to!' said Meredith, buoyed by an odd feeling that she had stumbled into her future where he had an important, but passing, role to play.

The house, solid enough with its oregon tongue-and groove walls and ceilings, was a tip, but in her mind's eye Meredith was already removing the pelmets and built-in cupboards, ripping up the filthy fitted carpets. She could see her precious table, with a blue jug of yellow irises on its polished surface in the spacious kitchen, bunches of lavender hanging upside down from the ceiling and, in the recess of the brick-built extension, Blue dosing in front of the old black coal-stove. Of course one wouldn't use the stove all the time but wouldn't it be good occasionally to smell wood smoke and the yeasty baking of fresh bread in scoured loaf tins.

'Ever thought of selling?'

'Every day!' said Charlie, 'Mentioned on the phone… daughters are in Darwin; keep begging me to go over.'

'Well why don't you?'

'Go tomorrow, if I could sell. Had it on and off the market for a couple of years. But it's hard to get a bond on these old places and anyone with cash wouldn't want something like this. About eighty years old. Nearly as old as me,' he winked at her. 'Need special permission to be pulled down.'

'Pulled down?!'

'Ja, they buy these old houses for the land and then demolish them and build a modern place with a granny flat they let out to pay the mortgage.'

'Such a shame!' said Meredith.

'That's what the heritage people say too. So here I sit not getting any younger either!'

Before she left Charlie had told her the suggested asking price.

'We've got some thinking to do, Blue,' Meredith said getting into the car.

One could see the Indian Ocean from the top of the ridge: a broad band fixed to the edge of a pale high sky. Even though, like the unremarked shops or the traffic lights, or the tree at the end of the road, it was there in the same place every day, Meredith thought the sea always seemed to call attention to itself and made people tell each other how lucky they were to live near it and how they really ought to appreciate it more. She would give Blue a special treat.

'Beach!' she called.

He was beside himself with joy at the sound of the word, teetering on the edge of ecstasy, his mind's eye fixed on the prospect of stretched muscle on wide sand, of cool wetted fur.

She parks in the empty lot. Opens the passenger door. 'Beach!' Blue scrambles out falling over his own wayward limbs, his claws clattering on the concrete, and then in long, looping bounds heads for the spine of dunes where sparse marram grass grows. A black cut-out, stark against the white sand, he stands for a moment looking down at the wind-shredded sea. The ragged fur on his long legs whips out like the fringe on cowboy chaps. Then he turns to look at his mistress wading towards him through the spun glass sand and grazing wind that whips her pale shins. And now Blue is off, his cantering weight leaving momentary paw prints on the yielding sand.

Meredith bends to pick up a stick, thick as a thighbone. Canine memory regroups, firms into anticipation. Blue stops abruptly, compresses his long body into a charged accumulation of tensile muscle and obedient bone. He snaps his ears upright, freezes his focus, clamps the tip of his tongue between the ice white peaks embedded in his black-lipped jaws. These are teeth that can kill. Or smile. In their own way and only for food. His neck is masted against the wind, his paws bolted to the faltering sand. Coiled for the trigger moment, he is alert to every shift of intention. Meredith smiles, for a swift second contemplates a teasing change of mind. Sensing the threat, Blue cocks his head, upbraiding her. Meredith is beguiled. Turns to fulfil the promise. Throws.

Before the stick has peeled off her fingers, Blue bounds into the sea, leaping in long undulations over the advancing criss-cross of waves. He moves forward buoyed by the deepening water pushing beneath his belly. Now his paws lift off the sea bed and he starts the steady dip and pull of long alternate legs through the heavy, wet tug of the sea, his chin resting on the water, his eyes clamped to the bobbing stick as the sea toys with it, sending it into sudden unexpected paths. He hesitates. His quarry disappears in the rush of water. Then suddenly it is spat up and out and bobs on the swirling ocean. He paddles towards it measuring the distance, judging the tide's vagaries. And then he is upon it. He snaps his jaw open, locks it about the sodden wood and pulls himself around. He lowers his neck so that the stick is floating steadily on the water and swims towards the pale two-legged marker there on the shore. His paws touch sand and he rises from the sea. As the water drops from his body and the stick comes up into the air Blue, discovering its sodden weightiness, adjusts his grip to realign the balance and bounds up the beach, his wet fur sluicing the sand as sea water sheets off his startlingly slender body. Wagging a wet triumphant tail, he drops the stick at Meredith's feet.

'Good boy!' she massages the hollow at the back of his damp happy head. Blue braces himself on four taut legs and swings his long furred body vigorously from side to side, sending bright necklaces of water arcing up into the air, unfurling the wet matted fur, making it lift and glisten in the light. More! But she is taking a brief break now so Blue thinks to dig around the stick to move it. The compliant sand flares up between his fast propelling paws. And now he turns kicking his back legs and, caught by the high bright light of the sun, the sand showers down in a falling mop of sparkles, each descending loop intertwining with a rising arc in a spinning helix of action.

She is in awe of him, his utter livingness, his total occupation of each tiny sliver of time. She had once been a little like that.

And then she had met Stan and what she had seen as simply a bit of a shipboard fling had turned out to be a premature finale. Over the days, they slipped from deck chairs and rugs into cabins and narrow bunks and early one morning with the cold Atlantic sloshing against the slippery wet glass of the porthole, the condom had burst. 'Oh shit!' It was in fact *she* who'd bought the famous poster.

She had occasionally thought of leaving Stan but he had been kind enough to her and had been a good provider; their son had gone to excellent schools and a good university. Stan had bought him a brand new car as a graduation present and with an MBA 'under his belt' he had landed good jobs and was 'doing very well for himself' as Stan always proudly said. She often wondered why this statement had, invariably, to do with money and possessions.

The time she had most thought of separation was when they had immigrated to England at the end of 1976. The South African economy had again 'hit the rocks'. This time it was 'Soweto', the uprising led by black schoolchildren many of whom were shot dead, and 'The Violence' which was growing. Stan had got a good position in a pleasant town in the North West and, despite the fact that a semi-detached house was considered down market back home, had found one with central heating and a burglar alarm. Crime had crept into the UK too – 'all these immigrants' the estate agent had said, oblivious of the irony. When he came home from the office Stan was perfectly happy to sit in front of the telly, in a Marks & Spencer cardigan and check slippers, sipping *The Famous Grouse*, which secretly, he had started calling his wife.

Meredith had hated it all: the endless rows of identical houses (single storeys were 'bungalows', double storeys were 'houses' she was curtly informed), the driveways with their new show-off cars bearing the current year's alphabetic registration letter, the long narrow backyards where the 'womenfolk' were always dashing in and out between showers to hang out or bring in the washing (those flannel nighties, those ribbed tights hung brazenly, gussets to the sky) the metal grilles on the Off Licence, the Co-op, the boring food, the drinking, the lace curtains ('Peeping Poms' young Mark had quipped), the insularism. 'It *is* an island!' Stan had said. 'With an erstwhile empire!' she'd retorted. Then too, her body feta-white in the bath. Stan. How she longed for joyous people, smiling faces!

It was largely because of the improvement in the South African economy and the daily taunts of his desk calendar –

'It's sunny today in the RSA!' – that Stan decided they should return.

Back home she had not had the courage to talk of separation. Was she now again going to fall into the trap of putting other people's wishes ahead of her own, of not wanting to hurt anyone and thus impairing her own happiness. Was she, simply for Mark's sake (but did they *really* want *his* mother, *her* mother-in-law to come and live, or was it just 'form' again?) going to leave her home country and move to…Australia for goodness sake!

Listening to the radio with half an ear and sweeping up the sand she and Blue had brought in from the beach – despite the protective covers over the upholstery Stan would have insisted they remove every grain before getting into the car – it suddenly struck her how much she had, no, not compromised, that suggested give and take, over the years, but how much she had allowed Stan to impose his will, his fastidiousness, his obsession with utilitarian efficiency above all else. Looking around the kitchen with its dishwasher, double door fridge-freezer, garbage disposal unit, electronic toaster (bought 'for her' a fortnight before he died), all the appliances of this 'functional space', she wondered what had happened to 'the heart of the home.' And just as she was thinking this, she heard the word 'Yips' on the *BBC World Service* and turned up the volume. She didn't know much about it except that it was something Stan had complained of. The Yips, the presenter explained, was what happened to some golfers when they had to putt the ball into the hole with a putter. They would check the position of the ball, check the hole, check the ball, check the hole and when they finally made the shot, miss. By attaching electrodes to the brain it had now been shown that those most likely to suffer from the Yips were those who favoured the left, rational, side of the brain. Those who used the right, intuitive, side usually made a successful shot first time.

Meredith switched off the radio. She had made her decision. She knew what she was going to do.

Mark sent her regular clippings from the Australian press about crime in South Africa, about the impact of AIDS orphans on South African society, about continued racism in South Africa (*the cheek!*). A television commercial told her what an incredibly high chance she had of getting mugged, raped, shot. A leaflet dropped into her letterbox informed her basically that life was so terrifying it wasn't worth living. Another touted an 'affordable' funeral plan.

It came to her how much 'fear' was being used as a tool to manipulate people's minds. 'Fear' she decided was a highly contagious disease for which an antidote had to be found. Since it was certainly communicable by contact, she would avoid people who were infected. And if what most people feared was 'the unknown' then she would use a homeopathic approach: expose herself to new experiences, make the unknown known.

Charlie had been over the moon with her offer.

'Lock, stock and barrel?'

'If that's OK with you?' It would be easier she thought.

'Telling me it is! And you'll take care of Lassie?'

'Absolutely. It was all her doing in the first place!'

It was a long time since Meredith had felt so elated. She had it all worked out.

With the money from the sale of the 'lock-up and go' unit she could buy the little house cash, invest the balance and live off the interest. That was aside from Stan's investments and what his life insurance policy was paying out. She telephoned Mark. It had been a protracted conversation.

'What do you mean you're not coming to Australia?'

'I'm staying here.'

'But you've sold the unit?!'

'I know!'

'You can't just pull out of the sale now!'

'I'm not. That's part of the plan.'

'What plan?'

'I'm buying another house.'

'In South Africa!?'

'Yes!'

'You're mad, mom! Have you seen the crime statistics?'

'Yes, "white collar crime" is outstripping…'

'You know what I mean,' he clucked, 'Are you sure you're alright? You don't seem yourself.'

'Never been better.'

'What would Dad have said?'

'I don't know,' (Stan would have been appalled!) 'And I don't care.'

Mark was shocked: 'How can you say that?!'

'Because for once I'm doing exactly what *I* want to do.'

'And what exactly do you want to do, besides buying another house?'

'Don't you worry about that.'

'But we will worry!'

'Then you'll just have to. I can't let your worrying stop me.'

There had been a long silence.

'Whereabouts is this house?'

Mark had never heard of the area.

'You know what they always say mom: buy the worst house in the best area.'

'Yes, I know what *they* always say about lots of things but I'm not making an investment. I'm buying a home.'

She could relate to beautiful old homes with leaded windows and herbaceous borders and long sweeps of gravelled drive and cars with mahogany dash boards and abundant chrome, settling under the trees where doves burbled in the thick blue shade but, increasingly it seemed, with money had come crassness. People no longer bought a home they 'got onto the property ladder', made 'starter investments', 'traded up' until they found themselves in an 'upmarket area' where you never saw any people, only strange shimmery cars that undulated silent as fish over the swells of speed bumps and around the 'traffic pacifiers', and the residents had tight terrified faces and were always 'up in arms' about any threat to what they saw as their birthright and were never happy.

Mark phoned again, immediately after she'd replaced the receiver.

'What's the security like?'

'Same as most people's.'

Technically that was true. After all most people in the country – in the world! – didn't have any security at all. She didn't mention that there was a policeman living down the street. In Mark's book if a policeman could afford to live there, then it was definitely not a good area. And a *black* policeman? Unthinkable!

'You'd better get armed response.'

She managed to suppress the rising giggles. She'd already got that from Charlie who gave her a big bear hug when he had signed the Offer to Purchase form she had bought from the stationers.

'Well I hope you know what you're doing?!'

'You sound just like Dad – a chip off the old block.'

'I take that as a compliment!'

'And I *do* know what I'm doing. I'm buying a home where I'll be happy!'

Meredith wondered sometimes what would happen if the country did somehow manage to 'Stop Crime' as the slogan went. As though, seeing the poster, anyone with criminal intent would suddenly desist. The whole security industry would collapse. Millions of people would lose their jobs: those who made, sold or installed burglar guards, electric gates, fencing, barbed wire, razor wire, alarm systems, scanners, anti-hijacking devices, gorilla locks, gear locks, car alarms, guns, safes. There'd be less employment for security guards, policemen, helicopter pilots, detectives, lawyers, prosecutors, prison guards, paper pushers, cleaners and car guards. The insurance industry would shrivel, advertising would take a knock, media revenue would diminish and newspapers would go under. People wouldn't have to buy replacement cars, furniture, appliances, clothes and jewellery. The whole retail industry would implode. The more Meredith thought about it the more absurd it got. If crime stopped the economy would fall apart.

Meredith took Charlie with his army kitbag and his fishing rods to the airport and was strangely sad to see him go. There was plenty to keep her occupied. As Mark had said she had to find a garden service, a painting and decorating contractor, a removal company, and, firstly, a charity to which she could donate all Charlie's goods and chattels.

Mark phoned frequently, hoped she was being careful, using only 'reputable companies.'

'You mean as in Lloyds, Enron and so on?' she responded. Many of their acquaintances had lost thousands on the 'very reputable' Masterbond.

There were crowds of men and women in the Labour Bureau looking for work when Meredith got there just after eight one morning. She talked to one of the officials about the kind of skills she needed and in no time he had lined up a dozen men – some with certificates, some with references, some with nothing but the character of their faces to recommend them.

Within a few minutes, she was driving four black, able-bodied strangers to the little house. She could hear Mark: 'You must be mad, mom!' Maybe, but it felt remarkably good.

They scraped and repainted the roof and outside tin walls, cut back the bush and discovered a pond and brick paths. They removed the bath surround and revealed ball and claw feet. They restored the taps to their original brass. They removed the carpets, sanded and varnished the foot-wide floorboards which were in remarkably good condition. Meredith loved to look across their warm honeyed surfaces and see the light fan out, and, in the front room, as the sun leaned through the coloured panes of the door, see the shine overlaid with a wash of Vermillion and Cobalt blue. The dogs skittering over the bare floors would be part of the new soundscape of the little house.

Meredith had always lived in white rooms ('cost-effective, easy to touch up' Stan had said) so now she was going to have colour: the colours of blue delphiniums, of red hibiscus, of yellow sunflowers. Watching the men pouring the paint, gliding their loaded rollers up and down the much-painted tongue and groove wood panelling and then refilling their trays, she wanted to plunge into the bright pools of pure colour.

Those were happy weeks. Sometimes, hearing the burbling chat and frequent laughter of the men as they worked, she felt moved: how simple life could be.

Mark was horrified. 'Whatever you do, don't pay by the day – they'll stretch the work out!' But she had no qualms. They were doing a very thorough job for a lot less than she would have had to pay a contractor and were, themselves, earning a lot more than they would have working for one. She'd miss them when the work was done and they were gone, to stand once again in the queues of the unemployed. She wished she could find more work for them.

Climbing up into the loft Meredith found bentwood chairs, an oak towel rack and several carved picture frames. Under the house along with various ancient car parts, she discovered old enamel jugs and basins, buckets with wooden handles, a baby's bath and a small pink potty. Life had left them a little battered but the chipped surfaces were part of their appeal and rust had not set in. She found a collection of old blue medicine bottles, tobacco tins and a musical biscuit barrel. The knob had broken off but, gripping the stem with the corner of her blouse, she managed to turn the winder and, tinkling up from the years, came the sweet spell-bounding notes of 'Rockabye Baby'. Couched there in the earthy coolness underneath the house, her face filthy, her nails torn and dirty, her hair mussed, she went back many decades and was a little girl again caught with her hand in her grandmother's tattle-tale biscuit barrel.

Meredith went to antique auctions at Dales Brothers in town and bought a Victorian brass and iron double bed, an old yellowwood dresser, oregon bookshelves, an oak wardrobe and dressing table, and, a real treat! some Clarice Cliff. They would deliver her purchases when she had moved in. She pictured the old wooden furniture, with the patina of time wrought by many hands, against the bright walls, and their reflections overlaid on bare floors. She couldn't wait to see her gorgeous china on the dresser.

Several removal companies in the Yellow Pages used pictures of the Sydney opera house in their adverts. 'As though everyone wants to go to bloody Australia!' Meredith snorted and flung the directory aside. One of her new neighbours, the black police inspector, recommended a man who could do the job and one Sunday an old black man with a lorry, a young boy, a few blankets and several lengths of rope arrived at the unit to move her table, one or two other bits of furniture, trunks, suitcases and the boxes of books, to her new home. And when they were done she invited them to sit down at the table – which looked as though it had always been there – for tea and biscuits with Blue watching every mouthful.

'Tell him to smile,' Meredith said to the young boy.

'Smile!' Blue bared his teeth; the boy grinned.

'One biscuit for you!' he said.

'And another one for me!'

Then he turned to Lassie.

'One for you and another one for me!'

'*Hayi suka* !' the old man laughed 'You are getting double biscuits!'

Those first few nights were strange: no security gate to lock, no burglar alarm to set, no panic button to locate. With Blue and Lassie curled up like old lovers beside the bed, she slept beautifully.

Lassie had pined for her master for a while but with Meredith's attention and Blue's not always welcome interest in her, she soon adapted to the absence of Charlie, who sent a postcard of an Australian cork hat and said that things were 'Fair dinkum, mate!'

Meredith took Blue and Lassie for regular walks, always triggering a cacophony of barking from the neighbourhood's guard dogs. She had stuck a notice to her front door: 'Hullo, *Sawubona, Molo, Kunjani! Hoe gaan dit?* Sorry no CD's. Only LP's, no music centre, no play station, no microwave, no VCR, no DVD, no cell-phone, no Morkels, no Joshua Doore, only old books, old clothes, old bowls. Sorry.'

One day on one of their walks Meredith came across a disused wood and iron church and was wondering how she could clamber up to look through one of the ogival windows where several stained glass panes were missing when a neighbour came and offered to unlock for her. The church leaders were trying to get permission to demolish the building he said but it could take years. He held the dogs' leads while she went inside.

As she looks up into the simple pitched roof she is young again, standing in a wash of madder light pouring through the stained glass of the rosary window. Bach's Toccata and Fugue wells out from the organ loft, the occasional echo of knocked wood rings through the high hollow of the nave as her gaze soars up to the distant ribbing of the vault and she feels the pull, as if a large winged creature has come down to lift her up, up, up far beyond the small figure with its feet on the cool flagstones, lifting her to higher purpose.

That night she woke with a start. It felt as though a dozen ox-shouldered men were heaving the little house, trying to push it over. She heard ghostly bells and lay very still in the dark and then realised that the wind had risen and was rumbling up the garden, blowing furious air, whipping along and under the little tin house, turning the wind chimes into something supernatural. It seemed as though a hurricane was coming over the top of the ridge ready to wrench her small whimpering home from its mooring. The dogs stirred. Blue came trotting round to the side of her bed and lifted a paw. She held it warm and limp and friendly. She got out of bed and went to the kitchen. It was just after 2 a.m. She unlocked the back door and opened it tentatively but the bullying wind snatched it from her grasp. She propped it open and followed the dogs dashing out into the garden.

The wind had ripped off twigs and several small branches and came whipping around the house, turning her about, her night-dress swirling out like a big top tent so that she almost lost her footing and now the dogs were leaping up and now she was propelling herself with her right foot like a child, like a bright top, whirling round and round, spinning… spinning…spinning.

When the wind finally dropped she went inside, buoyed by lungfuls of fresh air, her muscles worked, her face aglow.

Sitting at her kitchen table with the door wide open, dunking biscuits taken from the repaired biscuit barrel and sipping tea, Meredith watched the dawn lighting up the sky and the strewn garden. She had gone outside in the middle of the night. She had sat with the door open. She was still alive. More alive than she could remember. It was as though fear had been a parasite which, finding that she was no longer a suitable host, had simply given up on her. She released the clockwork mechanism she had been idly winding and the biscuit barrel unspooled its little tune.

'Rock a bye baby on the tree top
When the wind blows the cradle will rock
When the bow breaks the cradle will fall
Down will come baby cradle and all.'

She could see it in her mind's eye: the nave divided into two floors, the older children upstairs, the little ones downstairs. Of course she would have to get onto the church and the heritage people but surely, when the state was inheriting more and more orphans whose parents had died of Aids and who had no one to care for them, surely she would get permission to make the alterations. She already had the names and addresses of several hard-working and reliable men who could help bring it all to pass.

The little tune was playing itself slowly out. The last long note died away. Silence. Blue put his chin on her thigh and looked up, scanning her face. She smiled. Mark needn't worry. She had found something to do.

The sun was just coming over the hill.

It was midday in Australia.

3

*H*earing a train screech to a halt at the small station beside the North Coast Road below the scrap metal man, pushing his trolley down the one-way street, thinks back to his long-ago journey. The trains are electric now but it was a steam train that many years before took him away from his family. Took him, in the tea-cosy hat his wife had knitted for him, with his knobkierrie and his bundle, to the gold mines of the Witwatersrand. Here he had spent much of his life, most of it three or four kilometres beneath the earth where every 100 metres the temperature rose one degree centigrade and the chances of dying increased.

But gold became harder to find and the few grams gleaned from a ton of rock less profitable. And so the scrap metal man, like hundreds of thousands of others, lost his job. The metal he works with now, though precious to him, is worth little, yet its price too is set internationally in dollars. Today copper fetches $2.00 a *kilogram, brass $1.50, aluminium $1.25, steel 10c. And those half portions of motor car that bring smiles to the people who watch them perched on trolleys or carried on the proud heads of a couple of men jogging through the traffic? Known as 'substandard' this metal earns just 3c a kilogram. For though the scrap metal man is no longer employed on the mines, the men and women who operate from the slick, air-conditioned offices of London and New York, of Tokyo and Johannesburg, hold even more power over him.*

The scrap metal man glances across to number 72 where the old Afrikaans man lived with his daughter. Though the Afrikaans language is disparaged by many English I liked its friendly warmth and found it often expressed what I felt more accurately than my mother tongue. Treurig feels *to me sadder than 'sad'.* Naar *more nauseous than 'nauseous'.*

Now the window where the old man sat always watching for the train, waving his stiff little-boy wave as it came, is shut, the curtains drawn. How could any of us know that at night when a soft rain smudged the tangerine lights of the station, the tracks could take the old man back to the tea-room bioscope and his lustful palm stroking a coy adjacent thigh and his mind speeding to lakes of wet light on foreign station platforms and to raincoated men in fedoras lighting cigarettes in cupped hands and to the sound of high heels faltering in the dark, and…on-and-on…on-and-on…on-and-on…to 'THE END' and always someone was dead or their heart broken.

#72

The Gaps In-between

If you positioned yourself correctly you could see the railway line from the window. The rails, rust-brown underneath, bright as blades on top, lay straight and long, bolted to the heavy wooden sleepers set at regular distances apart on the grey stone crusher. The rails were laid in lengths, not quite end to end, but with spaces between them so that when the sun beat down and the metal expanded the rails would not buckle but stretch across the gaps in-between.

Even though they are not steam, for there are electric cables overhead, and even though they are not the old red-brown carriages with their gold SAS & H and SAR & H lettering, for they have broad diagonal tie-like stripes of grey and yellow now, and even though they are not trans-provincial but serve the small regional towns, the old man is punctilious in the task he has set himself: to keep an alert ear out for the trains and so maintain a daily tally.

His thoughts speed ahead and shunt back on themselves and sometimes stop altogether leaving him stranded *daar doer in die bosveldt*, but the railway keeps him connected to his youth, when his arms were strong and his chest broad and his stomach hard as the coal he shovelled, when he had the power to make tons of rolling stock slide swift and smooth across the broad sweep of the veldt, the power to send a meringue-white cumulus billowing glorious into the high blue sky, when children waved and daughters had respect.

Jakobus sits in his striped pyjamas by the window. It is late afternoon and backlit by the flame-orange of the setting sun, his hewn profile encircled in a steam-cloud of white hair and beard, he bears, still, the markings of patriarchal good looks.

Baby has brought him his supper: a wooden bowl of savoury mince, peas from a can and instant mash potato. He eats with his favourite electro plated nickel silver spoon, worn now to yellow brass. For pudding there is jelly.

She has her meal – left-over lasagne heated in the microwave – on a tray in front of the television while she watches the soapie she has followed daily since its inception several years ago. She has told him that the programme would only upset him. And she is right for it shows black men and women kissing, white men kissing black women, black men kissing white women. And – *Ag nee, sies jong!* – men kissing men.

The truth however is that, no matter what the programme, she did not want him next to her, curdling the atmosphere. All she wants is for him to be dead. She wishes he would just get on with it like other people's parents. It is not that she has no feelings. Tears can well and spill over in a 30 second TV commercial. She smiles with moist eyes every time she sees footage of Nelson Mandela shining his face on that of a child. She wept when, because a manhole cover had been stolen to sell as scrap metal, a little black boy 'who loved to talk' his grieving mother said, was swept away in a sewerage pipe. But she finds it hard being in the same room as her father. It's not just that he eats with his mouth slack so that the mess of food slops around between stained teeth and thick mildewy tongue. It's not just the rancid smell that emanates from the sebaceous glands in his still abundant hair. Nor is it the nonenal odour that comes off his body. It is simply that *he is there*. With the constitution of an ox. *There* as if he has an unassailable right to impinge upon her. *There* full of self-importance, *bakgat* almost, oblivious of the pain he has caused her, of the shame that had snuffed the life out of her mother, of the disgust that had cracked the family apart. *There*, full of a depraved determination to sit it out, overstay what was never a welcome, even though, all those years ago, he had destroyed any hope she might have had of ever finding happiness.

There was a time when Baby wore pastel maids uniforms in XXXL and nylon sack dresses that came in a matching zippered bags; a time when, with a slab of Cadbury's chocolate or several Checkers' Chelsea buns or half a loaf of warm, white bread ripped off in urgent fistfuls and shoved into her craving mouth, she could assuage the hollow sensation for a while – though she hated herself more afterwards. But when, feeling obliged to do her duty as a daughter, she had given her father a home, even stuffing herself with food brought no comfort. Her father was still there, still cruelly alive. And so was the hollow sensation.

But this evening she is finishing the bottle of wine she'd so apprehensively brought out last night and has made a salad to go with the pasta and, sitting there with her plump bare feet – she'd even painted her toenails a shimmering shell pink yesterday evening – propped on the *riempie* stool watching the soapie, feels calmer than usual, and, hearing her father muttering to himself, feels a wry amusement and something even approaching pity.

She used to wonder sometimes whether perhaps he clung to the here and now because he knew what was coming to him in the hereafter, for he had heard it often enough from the pulpit of the *Nederduitse Gereformeerde Kerk*. Had wondered whether she herself, though less sinner than sinned against, might not too be eternally damned. But this evening she will not think of such things. She runs a slow finger down the dark, smooth shoulders of the green bottle, holds the glass of wine up to the last of the sun, sees how beautiful it is.

When her father first came to live with Baby – his *laat lammetjie*, the civil servant, the one who never married – he lived in the granny flat of the subsidised house which she told him afterwards she would never have bought had she known that they would chop down the large tree on the corner and so expose the railway line to view. The neighbours couldn't understand why she was so upset. Later she had had to move the old man into the spare room where she could keep an eye on him. She had caught him doing something dangerous. He chuckles now when he thinks about it. More than anything, more even than a box of Smarties, he enjoys a brand new box of *vuurhoutjies*, 'little fire woods', Lucifers. He likes to push the small crisp blue drawer slowly out from its yellow casing with the drawing of a lion on it and peer inside. For him it is, first, the back of a tiny blue lorry full of convicts, only their shaved brown heads showing. Shoved a little further it is the Black Watch regiment, tall busbies looming over pale white faces, that came out to the Union in the 50's. Pushed out some more, the little blue match box becomes a compartment full of young women with black beehive hairdos and bare white shoulders. But shove it out all the way and they're naked Jezebels sent by the devil to tempt him. He likes to take them, one by one, and swipe each across the flint strip and see her hair loosen and flare with such fire that it consumes her and, in the slow afterglow when her passion is spent, see her hair draped over her shoulders, black and dishevelled and done for. He likes to replace the used ones in the box, see how, though they all seemed so similar in the beginning, each one is different now that he has lit her up. Likes to see how the hair falls. Likes to see how the head droops. As sometimes, in the dimmed light of the corridor that ran between the train's compartments and the thick reflecting windows, he imagined he would see the nape of a white neck, his ivory fingers clamped like ornamental combs through a strange woman's hair, feel beneath his black lace-up shoes the world moving forward and back, forward and back, feel in the dark wet tunnel the steam building and – 'Who-ooooooowho who-ooooooowho!' he calls – feeling for the small black buttons of his trouser flies but finding only the placket of his pyjama pants.

He wants to pee. But Baby has thrown out his chamber pot. It's disgusting, she had said, that a grown man should use such a thing. *When* is he going to realise that we have inside flush toilets now, that the night cart doesn't come anymore to take the full bucket away and put an empty one in its place? Hadn't he noticed that for some time now there had not been a hooter for the 'natives' to be back in the location? Hadn't he realised that the 'natives' are running the country. And look! she'd said, clicking a light switch, we've still got electricity! And look! she'd said, turning on the kitchen tap, we've still got water!

She knew however that he would not accept that in the New South Africa (thanks to a Communist! Jo Slovo, the Minister of Housing) she, like all civil servants, police and army personnel who had served the Apartheid government, had *not* lost her job *or* the generous perks that went with it; that her boss was black.

And so now he has to get up, even in the middle of the night and go to the toilet and stand on the cold tiles in the narrow hour of the night guttering a withered penis in a shaky hand and with his testicles hanging in his scrotum, like small potatoes in a lisle knee-high, wait for the pee to come. And the pain.

Jakobus worked for the South African Railways all his life, first as a stoker and then, when that work became too heavy, as a conductor, long distance. He saw the Princesses, Elizabeth and Margaret, when The King and Queen of England toured South Africa on the Royal Train in 1947. Saw the following year Dr Danie Malan on the celebratory train when, supported by 20% of the English-speaking population who worried that Jannie Smuts wouldn't 'keep the black man in his place', the Afrikaner Nationalist Party had come into power, promising to ensure that God's Chosen People, the Afrikaner *volk* so long humiliated by the English, no longer had to be ashamed of who they were. The British Royal Family, themselves *uitlanders*, were different of course – Queen Victoria had invited Oom Paul to Buckingham Palace.

In Buckingham Palace you could have a chamber pot. In Buckingham Palace you sat on a golden throne. Here you have to sit on a plastic seat with your pyjama pants in a figure of eight around your ankles and the seat stealing the warmth from your *boude* and when you had pulled your *broek* up had to *sukkel* to tie a bow with the flat lattice chord. He looks down and sees that someone has put elastic in his pyjama pants. *Pap* elastic.

What have they done with his black trousers, the ones he was trying hurriedly to button, and where is his peaked cap? He must make haste, go and wake the ladies up with the clackety-clack of his ticket-punch rattling against the chrome door handles. He slides open a compartment door '*Tee? Koffie?*' and glimpses through a lace-trimmed armhole, the rounded flank of an outspanned breast and down the gaping neck of a night dress the wide kloof, the dark *vlei*. And he an ox craving the salt lick.

He was halfway through lighting the box of matches when she caught him. And she slapped his hand, hard. He sniffles now.

A railway job was a good job in those days. It came with a pension, a railway house, a free train pass – first class – and a complementary connecting bus for his wife and family to go on holiday every year. Hermanus, Mossel Bay, Buffalo Bay. Full of holiday homes now with names like 'Not now – later!' and '*Gatvol*'. One even was called 'Buckingham Palace.'

In Buckingham Palace they wouldn't make you get rid of things. In Buckingham Palace you could keep everything you wanted. Not like here, where people are always asking why you want to keep a thing.

'You don't need this!' Baby had said holding up the round leather box with three of his old detachable collars.

'I want it,' he had said, digging his fingernails into her forearm.

'What for?'

'Because.'

He had rescued the collar box and too the little leather one with the studs to fix the stiff collars to his shirt. Rescued the old boiled sweet tin full of pennies bigger than today's R5. And too: his safety razor, the coronation edition of *The London Illustrated News*, the maroon Bible bearing the South African Defence Force emblem and, inside, the printed message from the State President, P W Botha, to the soldiers: 'The Bible is an important part of your calling to duty. When you are overwhelmed with doubt, pain, or when you find yourself wavering, you must turn to this wonderful book for answers.' The Bible was spattered with the blood of his eldest grandson, killed fighting the Communists on the border. He has saved too *The Stoker's Manual*.

'What for?' she had shouted, her big soft face red with anger.

'What's anything for? What's the use of a watch that doesn't stop time?' he said. What he thought was: what's the use of having a daughter who doesn't love you.

She had felt sometimes like leaning suddenly over him, scooping up his chin and running a sharp knife across the plucked-chicken skin of his throat, or squeezing her hands around his oesophagus, anything to stop the incessant breathing, the rise and fall, rise and fall of his chest: *Sakke-pakke, Sakke-pakke*, never ending. Like those miserable train journeys, those unhappy holidays. Her mother sitting on the firm green leather bunk in the wood-panelled compartment with the *padkos* basket beside her, her father and she on the bunk opposite with the crocheted-squares blanket spread over their laps. The train going into the tunnel, and in the sooty darkness – it was only in later years that the lights came on in those tunnels – his hand on her leg pressing the pink satin of her new dress down between her thighs. And she turning to stone. And sudden daylight. And in the next tunnel pressing the heel of his hand down hard where the thick gusset seam skimmed the bone. And sudden daylight. And the next tunnel his hand under her dress, slipping his fingers up beneath the leg elastic of her *broekies*. And daylight. And the next and the next and the next. And daylight, daylight, daylight. And her mother asking had she then seen a ghost, she was so pale. And her father firing off rounds of hard laughter and staring through the bullet-proof overlay suddenly glazing his bulging blue eyes and pointing things out: non-existent kloofs and *vleis* no one could see through the thick train window with its little blind you could pull down. As her mother had done all her life.

And arriving at the holiday resort and seeing a sign for church services: '*Bring die kinders saam*. Bring the children. *Dienste duur nie lang nie*. Service doesn't last long.'

'We must go. We must pray for our sins,' her father had said.

'And what sins do you have?' her mother had laughed bitterly.

'Sins that only the Lord knows, isn't that right my girlie!' her father had said, reaching an arm around her shoulders to draw her close.

'*Los my!*' she had cried pulling away.

'That's no way to speak to your father!' her mother had said.

And so was her complaisance arranged.

And when she tried to damp down the anguish and hide the darkness and cover the gentle appeal of her sweet face and baby blue eyes deep under the folds of warm white flesh she'd set to rise like dough about her, she had kept repeating to herself: *Dienste duur nie lang nie. Dienste duur nie lang nie.*

And all through the long years of her ordeal, when she slept with the light on and felt the tight knot in her stomach whenever she heard her father's footfall in the night, the only place where she could find any peace was in the small backyard 'servant's quarters' with the white distempered walls and the red cement floor where Regina slept on the neatly-made divan bed that stood on bricks to prevent the *Tokoloshe* (the naughty little spirit with a penis that was so long he had to fling it over his shoulder) from hiding beneath it.

The 'girl's room' smelt of stoep polish and mottled blue soap. A mirror stood slanted on a shelf besides a jar of Vaseline. A candle had been fixed firm in a Sunbeam tin. It was here Regina – one leg folded beneath her, the other stretched out – sat on the bed and gently brushed the young girl's soft blonde curls. It was here Baby found solace for her troubled spirit.

And when, after finishing school, she had fought to leave home to study accounting, it was Regina who had said to her mother: 'When little birds learn to fly, the hen must let them go.'

She had sent Regina a postcard of a 'Rickshaw Boy' and 'Greetings from Durban' to which Regina had responded promptly on blue lined paper: 'In reply to yours of the last inst. Everything still goes well with us in life. We are still in what people call good condition. Here is naise and warm, everybody is oright. How is the weather to Dibin? How are you there? Please you shall salute your relationship. Thanks so much, yours in love. Regina.'

Baby had not written back.

When Regina's dropsy had made it harder and harder for her to get down on her knees to scrub the kitchen floor, harder to bend down and put the roast into the oven, to go to the 'coolie' shop on the corner for 'the Master', when, in other words, her parents had felt that she was no longer earning her small wage, they did as many people did, still do: They 'let her go.'

It was only fairly recently that Baby had started wondering about it. How could she have been so careless – for was that not what it was? – with the affections of the one person in all the world whose presence alone had so soothed her. She drew no comfort knowing that she was one of millions of white men and women who had 'forgotten' the black women who had fed and bathed them, played with them, carried them on their backs, mothered them in every way, while their own little ones had been so deprived.

She remembered the big creamy white pumpkins drying on the silver corrugated roof that snapped in the expanding heat, and how Regina would cut little orange-fleshed manikins from the peelings, or give her a bowl of sugared samp in a moat of cochinealed pink milk or teach her clapping games. And remembered how she would ask Regina over and over to sing the click song that began 'In my native village in Johannesburg, there is a song…' Remembered too how, pressing her pert white nose against Regina's broad brown one, she would reach up and pull off her *doek*, how she would tug her apron strings lose, hide her enamel bowl and spoon. How Regina had never shown her anything but a steady, warm love, reliable and strong as sun-baked rock. Since the new government had come into power some years ago, Baby had thought about these things a lot more, especially at work.

All over the world official buildings are intimidating places where the bang of a gavel or a rubber stamp applied, or not, can change lives forever. But Baby noticed that, now that there were no longer separate queues for different races, the few white people waiting were not so much intimidated as irritated and annoyed that they should have to stand in line. The black people who had stood, and still stood, in government queues sometimes for several days in a row, shook their heads and smiled, and wondered when *umlungu* would learn patience. Her black colleagues laughed at Baby's observations and invited her sometimes to join them in the park during the lunch hour. Just to slip off her shoes and walk barefoot on public grass, just to stretch out with her back to the earth and her face to the sky, just to sing out loud, as she occasionally felt like doing now, made Baby feel connected to life as she, brought up with the notion that white people must set a civilised example to black people, had not felt since the hours she had spent in Regina's cool backyard room.

She can hear him shuffling about now, her father – *Dienste duur nie lang nie! Dienste duur nie lang nie!* – still outrageously, unpardonably alive; his hands, those cruel, shameful instruments, powerless to hurt her now but his spirit still clinging to life as tenaciously as if he were connected to some high voltage power.

He had nearly torn the book, '*The Stoker's Manual*', trying to rescue it from the pile of things she was going to throw out.

'Here then!' she had yelled flinging it in his face, 'You'll need it in that place where you're going!' She had decided at the time that she would put the little book into the coffin so that it could be cremated along with his body. Then she would come home and flush the ashes down the toilet. Or better still find a bucket toilet. Preferably in one of the black townships. She had spoken to her colleague Sibongile about it. Sibongile had opened her eyes wide.

'You can't be serious! He's your father!'

'So what!?'

'You can't think of doing such a terrible thing!'

Baby had lowered her head 'You don't know the terrible things he has done to me. I could never forgive him.'

'It's hard but…'

'It's not hard, it's impossible!' Baby shook her head. 'If I *did* ever forgive him, I could never forgive *myself*!' When they'd stopped chuckling Sibongile told Baby of her brother. During 'the struggle' he had been taken to a police station and beaten until his blood ran; until he'd betrayed a friend. The friend was murdered. Her brother took his own life.

'At first I felt that he had betrayed us too,' said Sibongile 'not because of what he had done – it is given to very few of us to be saints – but because he didn't trust us enough to share his burden.'

Baby said nothing.

'Human beings have always suffered at the hands of others,' Sibongile continued, 'but how do we respond? Revenge? That's a one-way street that keeps changing direction, so nobody ever gets out of it!'

There was a long silence.

'I still wonder how I would have handled it if my brother *had* told me. Perhaps there should be gaps. Perhaps there are things we just cannot face.' Then she spoke of all those women whose sons and husbands had been murdered. And how the white men – the '*civilised*' men! – had drunk their brandies and Coke and grilled their T-bone steaks and *boerewors* on the very same fire where they were burning the bodies.

And the wives and mothers learning of these things at the Truth and Reconciliation Commission hearings had lifted their heads and keened to the heavens, had shuddered and slumped to the ground. And yet some, amazing even the angels, had found it in their hearts to forgive. And she spoke of how if someone, even someone thought of as 'evil', gives you a glimpse into the darkest part of their being, the things perhaps that made them what they are, they hand you enormous power, to give back – or not give back – their humanity and of how, in her culture, to deny someone his humanity was to deny your own. Those who were forgiven were those who had finally seen that their victims were human beings who feel pain and love just as they do.

'"Whites seem not to realise that black people have emotions, that they fall in love like white people do,"' Sibongile smiled. 'That's what Nelson Mandela said at the Rivonia Trial all those years ago.'

'I think maybe your people have warmer hearts,' said Baby.

She puts the glass down, studies the label on the bottle. She will buy more of it. Maybe half a dozen bottles. They had enjoyed it so much last night, she and her friend. She rolls the word 'lover' around in her mind, wonders whether it is too soon to use it.

Jakobus liked listening to the different sounds of the trains at different times of the day when the wheels engage with the rails: in the early morning when the air was cool and the world still, the clackety-clack seemed more pronounced; at midday in midsummer the sound smoother. But sometimes there was that other sound the train made – a long screeching squeal. Like a meat saw it seemed to him. Just like a meat saw.

And time and time again he hears it peak and fade. And time and again a memory approaches and recedes. It is as though his mind is struggling to get through to that thing, that deeply concealed thing, and it is as though the sound the train wheels make is sawing through whatever it is that is keeping the memory sealed. And now it starts to cut through the bone to the marrow of the experience.

A strapping blond boy of seven or eight stares into the butcher's window where the *boerewors* hangs thick as fire hose, his mouth watering with desire, for he is a poor boy from a large family. He sees the butcher's wife with a mass of wavy black hair and heavily made-up eyes. He has heard some of the men in the little *dorp* with its name written on the hillside in white-washed stones, describe her as a '*lekker stuk*'. She wears a long white coatdress, shiny black high heels and sheer black stockings with seams up the back which the men had said must surely lead to paradise. He sees the butcher, his blonde-lashed pig's eyes squinting through the layers of fat that upholster his red-veined face, watching him. Sees the butcher beckoning him. The door pings as Jakobus enters.

Now, sitting in his chair by the window, having his pudding some eighty years later he lowers his chin and sees where a poppy has suddenly bloomed red on one of the green stems that stripe his pyjama jacket and, just on the upper right-hand margin of his vision, sees the oscillating oval, sees that it is empty. He stares at where the spoon disappears into the curl of a fist he doesn't recognise. What happened to the cool, sweet jelly his groping mouth was so anticipating and where did this strange thumb, with its grimy concertina of knuckle flesh, its flat yellow spade of a nail threatening to tear his eye, come from?

'*Komm Komm*,' they smile at him and the butcher makes a big parcel of meat and manipulates the handing over so that the broad tip of his fat thumb rubs up and down the boy's smooth inner wrist. '*Ein Geschenk!*' he says.

The Baumanns were a middle-aged, childless couple, foreigners who lived at the back of the shop. There were rumours of some overseas scandal. Outside of business hours, they kept to themselves but every Sunday the smell of prime steaks being grilled on an open fire would waft along the wide dusty street into the open door of the *Nederduitse Gereformeerde Kerk* famously causing the new young *predikant*, mopping the sweat from his brow, to remind the congregation that they should not 'covet thy neighbour's wife – nor his *braaivleis*.'

One public holiday the butcher and his wife invited Jakobus to join them. They draped him in a butcher's apron which hung down to his bare, dusty toes and seated him in the polished oak carver brought outside for the occasion. There he sat, his feet barely reaching the ground, watching as the *wors* spat into the grey coals and the aroma of coriander seeds and sirloin steak made of his mouth a lake.

He manages now with the full force of his mind to bring his left thumb and fingers smartly around the imposter's wrist that protrudes from the sleeve of his pyjama jacket and arrest its movement. The spoon drops, clattering on the bare floorboards.

'*Ag nee wat, Pa!*' she shouts from elsewhere in the house. He cringes. Mommy is going to come and smack him again. But, he remembers, Mommy is dead. And he is a big boy now. He mustn't cry. But he does.

One Friday Jakobus had stood, forehead pressed against the window, at closing time. The Butcher had ushered him in, put up the CLOSED sign, and drawn the blinds. Jakobus could feel his knees knocking but told himself not to be a sissy. And then he had felt the butcher's huge arms around him, pulling him tight against his broad stomach. Squashed against the blood-stained apron, he felt the butcher's meaty hands on his bottom, lifting and squeezing, lifting and squeezing. And then he was being picked up and carried onto the counter, a pulpy, wet mouth suckling his earlobe, a tongue shoving into his ear canal, and a deep voice hoarse with emotion saying '*Komm mein Engel, meine Liebe, komm.*' Jakobus kept his eyes closed tight and uttered not a word.

The next Friday he went at exactly the same hour.

This time it was she who put up the closed sign. 'Is *sehr* hot *nicht so?*' she said taking off her white coat, taking off her black petticoat, standing there. 'You also hot *mein Engel?*' she asked, slowly unbuttoning his shirt. '*Ein* hot, hot boy…'

He visited the Baumanns often. Usually it was with only one of them while the other watched. Sometimes it was with both of them, sometimes in the bedroom and often in the coldroom amongst the hanging carcasses.

His mother took the meat with sad, thankful eyes and never asked a thing. His father, large and loud with disgust at his cursed wife's merciless fecundity, thanked the Lord for allowing him to provide so generously for his children.

It was surprising how easy in the end Baby had found it to talk to Sibongile. They had sat on the grass in the park eating their KFC takeaways and, for the first time in her life, Baby spoke of her girlhood struggles. Told of the shame and the self-loathing, told of the guilt and the fear, told of the desire she often had to end it all, lie down in the path of an oncoming train or do as the man who'd walked into a butchery and lain his neck in front of the meat saw had done, told of how her mother pretended not to know.

And as she talked, all the hurt and humiliation, all the anger and frustration she had borne all through the years, came welling up out of her and she cried old, bitter tears. Sibongile had stroked her hand as she talked and put a comforting arm around her and said she understood how hard it must have been for her.

Baby began to feel what she had always of course known, that she was not alone in her pain, and over the weeks began to feel less of an outsider among her colleagues. Began even to feel that her suffering had been some kind of qualification that allowed her to be part of the community held together by the old African belief passed down through the ages, 'We are who we are through other people: *Ubuntu*.'

And after that Baby had begun to mix more and take better care of herself and, though she still wanted her father dead, found life easier.

He hears her coming, runs a sleeved forearm across his face.

'Must we then feed you like a little child?' she asks, skilfully removing the red poppy from his jacket with the spoon retrieved from the floor.

He nods slowly. She shovels the jelly between his flaring lips and all the while he stares into her large pink face, wondering who she is. Then his cheeks pucker and he takes hold of her hand.

'Baby? My girlie?' he says scanning her face.

'No, not your girlie. Your grown-up daughter,' she says.

Most times when she has had to feed him she wants to ram the spoon down his gullet.

But not tonight.

'I'm…I'm…' he struggles.

Baby, alert to the moment, holds her tongue.

'Baby, I'm…' he tries again but cannot find a bigger word, so forms the little one so often and far too easily, used:

'Sorry.'

She takes a deep breath. This thing must not be hurried.

'Sorry for what? Sorry for spilling the jelly, sorry for dropping the spoon, what…?'

He is silent for a while. 'It is not easy…'

She says nothing. Waits. Not to hear him name the crime, for it is not words she wants. What she wants, needs, is to feel that he has absorbed her anguish, that he is inhabiting her suffering, knows in some part of himself what in some tiny way, it must have been like for her during all these long years – *Dienste duur nie lang nie. Dienste duur nie lang nie.*

She needs to feel that he has made himself vulnerable to her.

He swallows hard, looks at her with eyes that are filled at last with something of what she has so long wanted to see in him: evidence of fellow pain.

'I broke your heart; your mother's heart too. May God have mercy on me.'

She holds his long-ago eyes with her clear blue gaze. Then she bends down and wraps her arms around his shoulders, hugs him as if he were a small frightened boy. Kisses the top of his head.

It is a long moment and then when it passes, she says with a wobbly briskness 'Now I suppose we must read you a story.'

He turns up the lights in his eyes. '*The Stoker's Manual! The Stoker's Manual!*' He implores like a child with a favourite fairytale.

He gets into bed and hangs a wide, contented smile from the corners of his mouth.

She picks up the book with its cover illustration of a handsome bare-chested young man shovelling coal and the words 'London, Her Majesty's Stationery Office, Price 1s 3d Net.' It was the sweat and grime of his own hands that had stained the book he said; it was he who had dipped a nib-pen into proud ink to write his name on the title page.

'*Stoking means a great deal more than just putting coal on the fire…*' Baby reads. '*Strength is not the only prerequisite. The shovel should be used with a peculiar motion that only comes with practice.*'

He closes his eyes. Though he is not really listening to what she is reading, for he knows it almost by heart, he finds the cadence of her voice soothing, like the things in his mind coming in and going out, like the sound of a train approaching and receding, the long mournful whistle across the flat dry veldt that still could choke him with a strange longing.

'…*the coal is thrown first on the right-hand half of the fire and a short time is allowed to elapse before firing the left half.*'

While her lips and her tongue shape the words, her mind is somewhere else in last night's time: the feel of smooth shoulders, the pulsing of rapid blood and a soft wet mouth approaching the mound of a breast, the small touching of a tongue, the swift reeling back, the held moment as the room holds its breath.

'*The left-hand side should not receive its charge until all the gases have been driven off from the first charge placed on the right-hand side.*' Time held back for the rearing nipple.

'*In any particular plant a relationship can be found between the amount of steam made and the amount of draught required to make it.*'

And the exquisite response of barely brushed skin. '*At least once a shift, the gauge cocks should be blown through to ensure that the steam and water passages are clear. Opening the drain and then closing and opening the steam and water cocks alternately should do this. On closing the drain again, the water should return promptly to the true level.*'

A tiny shift…and it was as if all her nerves would buckle with the joy of it.

'*Coking method of Hand Firing. This method consists in placing the fresh coal on to the front part of the grate to a depth of about 10 inches, after allowing time for the gases to be driven off.*

'*Care should be taken in setting the dampers for banking so that the building temperature does not drop to such a point that it is necessary to force the boiler in the morning. On the other hand the dampers should not be left open to such an extent that the fire burns out causing a delay in starting next day.*'

She has been reading for nearly twenty minutes. She glances at the bed and sees a small sleeping boy.

She puts the book down and looks at him a long while. The tethers loosen in her eyes.

Then she gets up, places her lips on his ashen forehead and, with the softest of smiles, pulls up the sheet.

4

The day I died the man who lives in the converted garage at number 66 was taking his morning shower, lifting his face to the bright sharp needles and enjoying the water sluicing over his head and the sound of his own voice singing '…oooooo…oo-oo…ooo… ooo…ee mai… gin…'. Then he had heard the sudden screech of brakes, a high pitched whistle, a thud, a scream.

He is home again today sitting at his computer playing about with possible titles for the self-help book he hopes to write. 'If you're happy and you know it… thank your ex!' he sings. Types. There are books and papers strewn across the table, the ashtray (a monstrous thing his ex couldn't bear in the house) hasn't been emptied in months. A mosquito settles on his forearm. He stares at it in its sexy zebra-skin leggings calmly sucking his blood and thinks of her. Then he smacks his palm down hard, lifts his hand. Gotcha!

He is wearing the gift one of his daughters – no doubt at his ex-wife's suggestion – had coyly handed him one Christmas: a pair of Mickey Mouse underpants, baggy now and faded. Perhaps it's time he threw them out, along with a couple of the shirts and trousers he no longer wears. He'll put them by the gate. They'll be gone in seconds.

There was a time, he remembered, when white people complained about how ungrateful black people were. Probably still do. Like a chap in the pub he used to go to who kvetched *about how he'd given his old raincoat – he'd lost the belt – to his garden 'boy' and how 'the boy' had had the cheek to say 'No thank you, baas!'*

He types 'A legend in his own Y-fronts…' Chuckles. Funny how, instead of making people think about history – which is what flags are supposed to do – what most people thought about, seeing the New South African flag, was underpants. Brightly coloured ones as befitted 'The Rainbow Nation'. The Y shape at the hoist area was, according to the vexillologists, a symbol of the coming together of different elements, different people and their drive towards unity. Delighted at having found a new word, he rolled it around in his mouth, the way one might a chocolate, one from the Black Magic collection – a Caramel Caress perhaps; the tongue turning it about until the dark chocolate slowly dissolves and releases a delicious renascence of sublime flavour. Vexillology, with its potential for multiple interpretations, he realised could be a very vexing business. So could symbolism.

But enough already! He had found another public notice deserving of a bit of graffiti backchat. NO DOG FOULING. Good boys!

#66

GOD is LOUE

Richard's trouble started with a preposition; a little word to which the new reporter whose piece he was subbing, attached scant importance, and to which, Richard, according to his colleagues, attached too much. He was being pedantic they said. 'What's one little word? Let it pass.'

'Pass by, pass off, pass on – which?'

'Does it matter? Nobody likes being pissed on all the time.'

'Or pissed off!'

He had let it pass. The phrase with the dubious preposition had screamed from lampposts all over the city. Comedians raised their right arms and hissed 'Yes!' as they pulled imaginary lavatory chains. Journalists on rival publications sniggered as they scrolled down their columns. Citizens were outraged. The Leader of the Opposition beamed. Political commentators were wheeled out. Letters to the newspapers bayed for blood. A commission of inquiry was demanded. Resignations were called for. And no matter how much the Minister concerned protested, he could not shake off the rumour that he was involved in crime, concerned *with* rather than *about* crime.

Yeah, right! people said.

The chairman of the newspaper company in New York, one of the first to invest in 'The New South Africa', called the Editor. The matter would be raised at the next board meeting.

The Editor, newish, black, called Richard into his office and said that Richard had let him down, that he had expected more from Richard, was Richard perhaps trying to set his new boss up for failure?

Richard looked for job opportunities in New Zealand.

There weren't any.

'I *told* you. We should have moved years ago,' Madeleine said. She was an accounts executive in an advertising agency and earning more than him. 'But you wouldn't, would you? And now you're too old.'

'*Old!* I've still got most of my teeth and all my hair.'

'But not all your faculties.'

It was not unusual to be unhappy in one's job. Richard had read somewhere – he was always 'reading somewhere' – that 97% of people were unhappy in their jobs. But it wasn't only that he was unhappy, he was becoming unhinged, had developed mannerisms: smacking the right front lobe of his head with the heel of his hand three times in succession – smack, smack, smack. Running his fingers up the back of his neck and stretching his arms up towards the low polystyrene ceiling, or slumping down using his linked hands as a head support and popping imaginary ping pong balls from his mouth. He had also taken to spinning around in his office chair in slow 360 degree circles, his middle finger thrust pointedly into the air.

Not long after the preposition incident the Editor said that, since Richard seemed to have time on his hands, perhaps he might like to produce a few op-ed pieces. 'Something to cheer people up. Make them laugh a bit.'

'What's it about?' asked the Editor when Richard submitted his first effort.

'Black Empowerment, Affirmative Action, whatever…'

'Mmmm…'

'Change your company name, to Woza Inc. for example, do not change your attitude,' the Editor read. 'Tell clients that you fully intend employing a black executive – as soon as you find one intelligent enough. Shame, it's not their fault.' The Editor's eyes widened.

'*Ubuntu* is an excellent concept. Use it. When the guy washing your brand new company car asks for a raise, tell him you can't afford it. He must show more *ubuntu*. U booooooonto. Practise the pronunciation. Pepper your conversation with it. Give the scooter boy a new title, 'Schumacher', for instance, don't give him a new vehicle. If 'Schumacher' says his wife is ill, ask him which number wife that would be. If he says his father has died, say "Again!"'

'Get a new uniform for the "tea girl" – henceforth "Tea Lady." Something ethnic, with the type of headdress Winnie Madikizela-Mandela made famous. This will make her really feel part of the team and demonstrate to clients the full depth of your commitment to the new South Africa.

'If a black person doesn't pronounce your name, Labuschagne for instance, correctly, complain loudly. If you don't pronounce his name, Sipho for example, correctly, say *Bof* with a Gallic shrug.

'Despite what you may think, rugby is not the national game, soccer is. Pay no attention. Assume 'Shoes' is not a player's nickname just things that go with socks, as 'Fish', another player, goes with chips and that the correct response to Moroka Swallows is 'Swallows what?'

'Tell everyone that being white had absolutely nothing to do with your success, you had to *work* to get to where you are today. Use the K word frequently. The chaps in the pub will love you for it.'

The Editor put the piece aside, looked at Richard over the top of his glasses.

'I can't publish this.'

'Ja… I was kind of wondering.' If I'm going to go down, I'm going to go down whimpering, Richard said to himself as he left the Editor's office.

'You'd better give me your next piece to read first,' said his wife.

He did.

'If you call a meeting try not to have any women present,' she read. 'Women tend to have the idea that meetings are called to get things done. This is an erroneous notion. As any reasonably seasoned chap knows, the point of calling a meeting is to take as long as possible for everyone to arrive at the decision you have already come to.'

'You're right there!' she said.

'This has the added advantage of letting the outside world via your receptionist know how important you are: 'He is in a meeting'; 'He is still in a meeting' and so forth.

'If, despite all your efforts, one or two women do show up, put them down immediately. Though one can usually judge a magazine by its cover one can't always judge a book that way. Don't let ribbons and pussycat bows deceive you. Little Bo Peep may have been a push-over, Maggie Thatcher is not. Pearls and perfume are nothing more than a decoy. If her heels are very high she is probably very short. Beware! Very short people are deadly: Bonaparte, Bokassa, Bart Simpson.'

'I'm short!' Madeleine exclaimed.

Richard smiled.

'If her shoes are flat,' she continued 'there is probably a lot of the Girl Guide about her and like a Swiss Army Knife she'll keep popping up with ingenuous ways of cutting through red tape and easing bottlenecks. This is dangerous behaviour and could jeopardise your whole *raison d'être* i.e. attending meetings. There are several ways to deal with these upstarts:

1. When the tea is brought in, preferably by your PA wearing killer perfume, a mini that just skirts her shoulders, and an expression like a merino in heat, form a hook with your index finger and beckon any female in the meeting to come and play mum.

2. While tea is being served drum your fingers on the oak veneer, stare at the ceiling and make a joke about the menopause. For example: "How many menopausal women does it take to change a light bulb? Four. Why? Because it bloody well does."

3. If the women present still haven't left the room, push your chair back and put your feet on the table, scratch your armpits, massage your neck, clean your glasses. Blow your noses. Fiddle with your fly.'

   'Richard!'

4. 'Should you still not have got the desired result, stare pointedly at their pectorals while sucking your teeth and/or knuckles.

5. If they still haven't got the message push your chair even further back and scratch your crotch while staring into the middle distance, saying 'Um… where were we?' every now and again.

6. Conclude the meeting by arranging another. If she says she can't make it, ask 'Why? Time of the month?'

'Not funny,' said his wife 'Are you trying to dig a hole for yourself?'

'I'm not finished yet,' said Richard.

'Well I think you probably are!' said his wife adding that the world had moved on and she was thinking of doing the same.

Richard showed the Editor the article. 'You can smile-two-three, kick ass-two-three!' the Editor read aloud 'But remember, however you feel about women and some of us feel about them a great deal, behind every cock-up is a man.'

There was silence.

'Richard,' said the Editor, 'I'm seriously worried about you.'

'Tch!' said Richard, swatting the air and mincing out of the office, squeezing his glutei maximi. 'Hoist with my own leotard!'

Perhaps what his wife had said was right; perhaps he did have a death wish. Too scared to jump he had manoeuvred himself onto the window ledge of life waiting to be pushed.

'I won't be intimidated. Yet.' said Richard.

He shared his next piece with the blokes in the pub.

'The hardest part of living through a job slump is finding a job. The easy part is hanging on to it,' Richard began. 'The law has made it very hard for your boss to fire you. Take advantage. Note that desks have been replaced by 'work stations' thereby authorising work to make regular stops unhindered. However, the most important thing you can bring to your job, besides a hip flask, is attitude. Forget the bright eyes and bushy-tailed approach. You are not a squirrel. Attitude has been defined as "the posture in which a figure is represented in a painting or sculpture" to which you may safely add "office chair."

'Here's how to play your part in the job slump: Place your coccyx on the edge of the chair. Do your legs stretch forward? Excellent! You have assumed the correct posture. On either side of the office chair you will find two horizontal projections. These are known as arm rests. Use them. If you have positioned your arms correctly your hands should hang aimlessly from the wrists down. Should you wish to adopt the advanced position, locate the triangular declivity at the base of your neck – where the knot of the tie you once wore once sat. Tuck your chin into it. This will force your eyes downward and so prevent your seeing any work that may come your way. In extreme circumstances you may look up from under the eaves of your brow. This will give added nuance and insure that the work will slink off suitably chastised. You, however, will not lose your job. Go into any office at any time of the day and you will see many people in this position, all of them with jobs.'

'Third time lucky!' said Richard handing his latest effort to the editor and goose-stepping back to his desk. When the Editor had finished reading, he looked through the glass partition beyond which many of the editorial staff, all with jobs, were slumped at their work stations. He went to Richard's desk and flung the piece down.

'Please give me something I can use.'
Richard gave him a toilet roll.
It did not go down well.

It took Richard ten minutes to empty his drawers. Into the metal bin, stained with old cigarette burns (smoking was now done in desperate pulls in the passage) he threw the few things recently brought from the lovely old wood-panelled building, where the ancient heavy metal printing presses were housed in the basement, to the new 'specifically designed' press centre. (How the old gang had laughed when the floors – apparently not specifically designed to carry computers – had shown signs of stress.) Into the bin too went: a page of proofreader marks; a PRESS badge gained when that had meant something – when journalism was a vocation and hungry reporters, passionate about finding the truth concerning serious issues, had wanted desperately to go out on the job and get the story firsthand and could book a skilled photographer and a company car, with an eager driver, and work enthusiastically on their copy on the way back to meet the screaming deadline; a blue China marker for drawing greasy crop lines on thick glossy black and white prints. Into the bin too went the remains of a packet of Lemon Creams, two crisp bags, a condom with a 'Please Come' invitation, a plastic bowtie, a pot of glue with a slanted rubber teat that had leaked a permanent puddle into the base of the drawer in which three pink paper clips were forever trapped and a grubby pack of dog-eared yellow Post-its. Then he bent down and retrieved the China marker and put it in his pocket. Also a stale Lemon Cream. This he put in his mouth. He dumped all the copy from his computer onto discs and put them into a cardboard box along with his *Fowler's English Usage*, the company style guide, *Brewer's Dictionary of Phrase and Fable*, another of idioms and quotations, and a book called *How to Shit in the Woods* by Kathleen Meyer which he had found in a second-hand book shop squatting just leeward of *The Wind in the Willows* and *Much Ado About Nothing*.

The newspaper company encouraged resignations: heaps of money which could be used to increase shareholders' dividends was being wasted on journalists.

Richard turned to look back at the last decade of his life. He hadn't switched off his computer – why save the bastards money? – and stood watching the *Mystify your Mind* screen-saver perform its strange aquatic ballet. The pot plants, which had only recently been replaced, were dying again. They were always dying. It was the atmosphere staff said. His colleagues were hunched over, staring at their screens, like prisoners who had pulled their jackets over the heads, embarrassed to see or be seen. No one turned to say goodbye.

He walked down the stairs with his box, whistling. He felt remarkably good. He was free. Free of all the crap. Free of the fear of losing his job.

He met the Tea Lady on one landing, '*Hauw*,' she said, shaking her head in its elaborate *doek* when he told her. 'It's not good.'

By the time he got to the heart of the newspaper operation, the parts that really matter – the advertising and marketing department – he was singing: 'Pack up your troubles in a cardboard box and smile, smile, smile…' He shook hands in the traditional three stage way with the black security guards and the Indian man selling back issues from the front kiosk.

As he walked to the car park Richard spotted the beggar whom he had always resolutely ignored, went up to him and gave him a R20 note. 'God bless you!' said the beggar. 'God bless you! God bless you!' When Richard got to his car there was a lump in his throat.

He went home.

In the mail was a letter from the telephone company. He had written to them about his observation that the less time he and his family spent on the phone, the more they were being charged. Here was their reply: they'd seen the error of their ways. He smiled as he opened the letter.

According to the telephone company however, he, the customer was not only not right, that is to say he was wrong, he was also totally thick. He kept dialling the incorrect number. (Curious how he had only got thick when the telephone company had got their new technology, he mused.) Apparently he was also suffering from a contagious disease called 'Customer Misconception of the Tone System' of which the chief symptom was not being able to distinguish between 'the uninterrupted sharp teedil-tone', the 'long beep tone at half seconds' the 'beep tone of a quarter of a second repeated every quarter second' and the 'uninterrupted double ring' which remained uninterrupted until someone answered.

He would tackle this thing head on, Richard thought. When his wife came home he would tell her that he had managed to sort it all out. Then he would tell her his other news.

There was no mention of Telkom's 'Public Relations' in the telephone directory. So he called 'Media Relations.'

'You have reached Communications,' said an electronic voice. 'We can't take your call right now. Should you wish to blah, blah, blah, press one. Should you wish…press two.' 'Should' was beginning to sound like 'shit' – so was their service.

He called the 'Media Relations: after hours' number and got the double ring tone. The same person who wasn't answering before wasn't answering now. After 100 uninterrupted seconds he replaced the receiver.

He phoned the business hours number again but even the electronic voice had taken an early lunch. He redialled the after hours number. 'You have reached...' he knew what he had reached and his tether was beginning to snap.

He had previously noted 'The Telkom Hotline' in the suburban Post Office. He got into his car, drove there and found a vacant parking space. Thankfully there were no car guards around to wheedle a tip for making sure that his car would still be there when he returned.

Above the Hotline Telephone were instructions, thoughtfully marked 'Instructions' in eleven different languages. 'Lift the receiver,' he read, 'and a dial tone will be heard for five seconds after which your call will be answered.' He lifted the receiver. The dial tone was heard for 45 seconds after which it stopped. He replaced the receiver. He tried again and heard the 'long beep tone repeated at half seconds' – according to 'General Information' the line was now 'engaged.' On his third attempt he got the 'beep tone of a quarter of a second followed every quarter of a second.' According to 'General Information' the line was now fucked.

He went home. Life had taught him one profound lesson: When all else fails, call 'Sales'. He dialled their number; a voice answered: 'Faults.' Then he dialled 'Marketing Sales' which apparently was responsible for marketing the sales department. And yes, a real live human being answered! He asked for 'Public Relations.'

'One second' said the voice. He waited twenty. Another real human voice answered 'Sales.' At last he was getting somewhere. He asked for the 'Public Relations' department.

'Sorry' said the voice 'we can't put you through, they are on a different floor.'

He refrained from pointing out that he had once got a brochure from the company's internet services offering to take him 'around the world any time of the day…Imagine visiting the Great Pyramids of Giza…imagine seeing the Statue of Liberty…' Imagine having someone on the floor above take your call.

He had managed somewhere along the line to get the name of a woman who worked in the Public Relations department of the Main Offices which occupied several floors of a large city block. He drove into town, parked and succeeded once again in dodging the car guard, this one in a black and yellow vest making a bee-line for him.

A sign read 'Telkom SA – Public Relations: 13th Floor.' He took the lift to the thirteenth floor and asked for the woman by name. A blank stare.

'She works in Public Relations,' he offered helpfully.

'11th Floor.'

On Level 11 he was met by a sign: 'Entrance Strictly Prohibited: Telkom Employees Only.' There were none around.

On Level 10 two signs greeted him. The one said: 'Payroll/Salaries,' the other said, 'This is not Payroll/Salaries.'

On Level 9 he found 'Social Planning Offices' beneath which were several other notices: 'No facilities for storing guns', 'No vacancies/No forms.' And 'No firearms is allowed on this premises.'

On Level 8 he found the word so beloved of Di- REC- tory Enquiries: 'Welcome!' followed by 'Strictly No Visitors.'

On Level 7 he found 'Telkom Security and Investigation' along with a cartoon of Donald Duck taking an axe to a computer.

On Level 6 he found the word 'Stop' in large red letters. 'Please note the public are not allowed in this office without an appointment. Please proceed to the Telkom front office in West Street, by order of Management.'

On Level 5 he found 'Mental Health.'

On Level 4 'The Epilepsy Foundation.'

On Level 3 'Telkom: Human Resources.' The sun was streaming in. There were flowers on the workstation. The woman in the office chair behind it was stretched out reading a magazine. She did not look up.

It was lunch-time on the last day of the month. 'By order of management' he had now proceeded to the Telkom front office in West Street. There were 54 people standing in line to *pay* their bills. There were five tills each with a red rose in a twisted tubular vase that looked to Richard like the kind of turd a poodle on a diet of Chinese noodles might produce. Next to the rose on two of the tills was a CLOSED sign. In another queue 45 other people were waiting to *query* their accounts. Beneath a huge advertisement 'Telkom has a solution to help your small business be more efficient' were nine counters. Six were closed. A hefty 'small business man' suggested that Telkom's solution was that he close his business for the afternoon. Richard suggested a better solution – brandy and Coke – and walked out.

The pavements were full of rubbish – most of it imported from China and being sold at stalls all along the street. A man with a motor disability and a GOD IS GOOD sign pinned to his chest twisted his face in a contorted smile. Richard began to think he really was going nuts. Everything meant the opposite of what it said. Even the Central Business District was nothing like what the name suggested. In fact, Richard recalled, it was just as most businesses were moving out into the suburbs that the city centre had been renamed the CBD.

He wandered into the gardens in front of the classic neo-baroque style City Hall, a replica of the one in Belfast, Northern Ireland. Amongst the pigeons and the palm trees, several statuesque colonial gentleman stared stonily into the middle distance like stray guests at a cocktail party who don't know what to do with their hands now that the chaps have wolfed down all the *vol-au-vents* and there's no damn steward around to pour them another scotch. Richard remembered the telling crossroads sign that used to stand nearby informing the colonials how many homesick miles they were from London and civilisation.

A life-sized statue of a bloke lying down in uniform was commemorating the brave men of Durban killed in two world wars. Whites Only. In similar fashion other life-size, fully alive figures in uniform – those of delivery and dry-cleaning services – were stretched out commemorating their lunch hour. Blacks only. He wondered when the Square called 'Farewell' after a city father would be renamed '*Hamba kahle*' (Goodbye in Zulu) or *Voetsek!* (Piss off in Afrikaans).

He took a deep breath and phoned his home number on his cell phone and got 'the very long beep tone repeated at half second intervals'. A snide voice said, 'The number you have dialled no longer exists.'

Richard wandered into the City Hall where the morning function was drawing to a close. In the marble foyer a group of small boys in animal skins and burgundy Y-fronts were stuffing their faces with cream scones. Three large black ladies in yellow, green and black frocks sat, thighs spread, sipping tea, their pinkies sticking out from stout white cups. A pale male in a navy suit hurried by with a bundle of soiled damask and a furrowed brow urging someone to lift the red carpet NOW! Outside an Indian man was pacing up and down with a megaphone yelling, 'There is no change in the variableness of the Kingdom of God.' Someone else was selling wall hangings made of gold lettering stuck on to polystyrene. 'GOD is LOUE.' 'I'd like to meet this Louis,' said Richard. The puzzled trader studied the sign and then laughed along; he hadn't realised that there was a 'u' where a 'v' should be.

Richard wandered round the side of the building where the Natural History Museum was housed. Three down-and-out whiteys, who'd slept rough, were getting up from a bench next to a sign that said *Fossils*. He followed them into the lecture hall where people, with nothing else to do, were gathering to watch a young David Attenborough enthusiastically indicating dinosaur footprints in whirring black and white and falling over his coincidentally apposite words as he told them 'a succession of bitterly cold nights could have drained them of their heat and could eventually have led to their demise.' He glanced at the 'outies'. They were not, it seemed, taking it personally.

Richard went to the bottle store and bought a bottle of brandy and a litre of Coke. When he got home there was a message on the answering machine. Telkom was discontinuing his service:

'We have no record of your enquiry.' He poured himself a double brandy and turned on the television.

'Like sand through the hour-glass…' said the voice-over artiste of *Days of our Lives*. Richard settled back. 'Roman's gone,' said a woman in what looked to him like a black wetsuit but turned out to be her widow's weeds. 'Yes he's gone,' said someone else. 'I can't believe he's gone,' said a third. 'He's with God,' declared another. 'No he's not!' said Richard 'He's cowering behind the shower curtain preparing for the moment when in a few months' time he'll come popping out cupping his genitals and smelling of soap on a rope.'

Besides hiding in the shrubbery thinking aloud, the women were having the time of their lives staring into each other's peacock blue contact lenses and saying, 'I'm so sorry.' That's when they weren't pressing their Wonder Bras together and patting their silicone finger nails on each other's narrow couture backs saying, 'I'm so, *so* sorry.'

Then there was a guy called Jack who was in prison. 'Jack's still in prison,' said his wife playing with her diamond earrings. 'Still in prison!' exclaimed his most recent ex-wife. 'I'm still in Prison,' said Jack silhouetted against a bit of wobbly brick-patterned polystyrene. Two other ex-ex-ex-wives clattered across the studio grass. 'I sense something terrible, something evil…' said one sniffing the air as the camera sneaked up on another soon-to-be ex-wife eaves-dropping behind the plastic apple blossoms.

When his wife came home Richard's face was red.

'You've been drinking,' she said.

'No!' he protested, slurring his words, 'I'm just flush with failure!'

'Not funny.'

She got the house, the kids and the new Hyundai. He got the two cats (he didn't like cats but his elder daughter had apparently suddenly developed an allergy) and the old Passat. He found a half-furnished converted garage on the other side of town and loaded the Passat with cats, books, CD's, his laptop, an old black and white TV, an electric frying pan, worn sheets and towels and all the other items put aside for a jumble sale.

'Never mind, all good things come to those who get in the loop and push the envelope,' said Richard.

'Exactly,' said his soon-to-be ex-wife.

His elder daughter looked at him with disgust and said, 'I feel so sorry for you.' His younger daughter looked at him with compassion and said, 'I love you so much.'

'Don't worry lad,' Richard muttered to himself as the Passat back-fired down the street, 'One door closes and another slams in your face.'

He pushed a tape into the cassette machine and smiled as the thought struck him that being in *Dire Straits* wasn't always such a bad thing. Look what it did for Mark Knopfler.

He drove down through the suburbs with their leafy, razor-wired, high-walled gardens and electric gates, their patios and their pools, their signs: 'Neighbourhood Watch.' A Rolex no doubt, Richard mused.

With his pension fund and accumulated leave pay, Richard reckoned there was never a better time to write that self-help book he'd been planning. And if that didn't work out he could always find another job. A man of his experience and talent.

He'd always loved words.

'When I'm on *Desert Island Discs* and have to choose a book to take I'll take the biggest most comprehensive dictionary available!' he used to boast.

'Not very practical,' his mates had said.

Now, instead of having to worry about what subs, editors, board members and readers thought, he could spend all the time he wanted with words – talking to the TV and the print ads, writing on his laptop and reading the labels on various kinds of packaging.

'To Crush Empty Bottle: Remove lid. Do not cover bottle mouth. Compress as illustrated. Replace lid when compressed.'

'Bottled water: Amount of one serving. Calories: 0; Fat: 0; Total Carbohydrates: 0; Protein: 0.' To which he added: Intelligence: 0

He entered into conversation with posters, outdoor billboards, road signs.

The Lord is with you. Yes, but he's a bit short of cash.

The car that cares. But does it go?

We're on your side. No wonder we're losing.

He noticed that in Afrikaans 'Gents', '*Here*', also meant 'the Lord', that his baked beans can had 'BONE' on the Afrikaans side, that Italy's number one coffee, LAVAZZA, was giving an instruction: 'Wash your arse!'

The TV was full of programmes about cooking, eating, losing weight and shopping for things to cook, eat and gain weight. People were always going 'Mmmmm' and popping, whacking or tossing things into the oven. They had their way with words too, most of them, forcing them through a fine sieve so 'couscous' became 'coo's coo's' or chopping them up roughly with lots of 'there you go, mate!'

AM Shopping was a mine of information. One Einstein was selling 'exercise in a bottle', another creative genius wanted 'to reach inside and grab your spirit and make it take over the outside of your body.' 'He is so special,' said one of his groupies 'his spirit walks in front of him.' The pavements are going to get awfully crowded, thought Richard.

A woman in a one-piece told him how gross her bikini-line had been. A sixty-something fairy godmother waved a lavatory brush. A man who had 12 children said he had struggled to keep his family fed. Better you struggled to keep your family small, thought Richard and raised a glass to a Norwegian girl with a stud in her mouth and a take on life much the same as his: 'It pisses me sometimes off.'

What he spent of most of his time writing on his computer were emails. He saved them on disc and sent them all from an internet café.

Dear News Programme, Please can you get a new newsreader. Listening to your man telling us 'Psdt Thb Mbk n Dpty Psdnt Jcb Zm' is bad enough but it kills me watching to see whether popping his P's like popcorn, he will make it through 'Pretoria's piano-playing prodigies' without exploding onto the perfectly polished parquet.

Deer Seed Merchant, What a charming, olde worlde name for a bunch of bastards who would jack-roll Mother Nature herself to make money, take the food out of a starving child's mouth to increase profits. May you be everlastingly infertile, may your women be forever barren, and may your dicks wither and die.

Dear George Bush, How come you Americans go around the world chequeing (sic) on whether other countries have free and fair elections when in the United States of Arseholes the only thing that counts (other than those squint-eyed Florida chad-checking voting official morons) is money.

Richard had always hated 'all this fucking house-shit.' He had wanted to live in a hotel or in a room above a pub. He hadn't managed that but at least here in his hidey-hole he didn't have to feel guilty every moment of his waking life. It wasn't just that being a home-owner meant there were always things to do – grass to be cut, the pool to be cleaned, gutters to be cleared, skirting boards to be repainted – it was that one was living in a perpetual state of pending catastrophe: if shit wasn't already happening it was on its way, big sackfuls of the stuff. Even if there was nothing that needed doing, his wife had had a way of making him feel guilty from the moment he woke up. His first thought of the day, when he'd become aware of the rise and fall of the obtuse shape beside him in the double bed, had been 'Bugger, she's still alive!' Then he'd quickly start taking long slow breaths until he felt her shifting, the mattress changing slope and heard soft footfalls on the carpet, the bedroom door opening and closing, and he'd lie there for a few golden minutes letting the tension ebb from his body until he felt able to gather his energies, gird his loins and get up to face 'Wife'.

If left to themselves men were such simple creatures. On his own he could cut bread directly on the work surface, knife tomato sauce into his mouth, spoon baked beans straight from the can and wash it all down with as many oblivion-inducing, guilt-free beers as he wished. He could leave crumbs on the surfaces, dishes in the sink, clothes on the floor and books all over the unmade sleeper sofa. It amazed him how all the tiny peripheral issues became the centre of people's lives.

Perhaps, he thought one day as he stood in his little kitchenette whacking a dish cloth around the surfaces, perhaps, like the colour of one's eyes, the state of one's kitchen was handed down with the genes. But even here, he did sometimes feel he was being taken advantage of. There were creatures living in his pad. Creatures he hadn't known about, bumming off him. There were cockroaches in their tail-coated uniforms like self-important doormen taking regular meals in his kitchen. There were ants gorging themselves in the sugar bowl. Fruit flies picnicking on a half-eaten apple. The gecko on the ceiling had taken a new wife. It was the ex-wife, or so he imagined, who was now a transparent corpse squashed in the jamb of the kitchen door. The new couple would scurry under the old rust-freckled fridge every time Richard came into the kitchen. There were borers devouring the window sills. In the neglected garden, worms were eating the guavas, *muisvoels* munching the paw paws, paradise flycatchers wolfing the mulberries and weavers scoffing the bananas – fruit the landlady said he could help himself to. Outside, the female cat was poised to pounce on a bird. The male lay in the sun fast asleep. Richard pictured how the female would react if the old chap told her he could no longer support her. Not with sympathy or pity, but with disdain. As if she had known all along that of course a shit like him would let her down. He could imagine her packing her belongings and sweeping off, tail high (her anus always looked to him like a cross-section of a banana) taking her favours elsewhere. The male would probably weep, useless bugger that he was. He had grown quite fond of the dribbly old chap who came home in the early hours of the morning with congealed blood and bits of fur missing. And no food.

With the dish cloth still in his hand he suddenly felt the vault of his throat collapse. Memories of small happinesses when his daughters were little and he their hero overwhelmed him. He loved them achingly. But seeing them now was painful. His elder daughter had taken to keeping her arms limp by her side when he hugged her. His younger daughter had taken to slipping her hand in his and leaning her head into him whenever she could.

Since his mojo was still eluding him he decided that before trying to write that book, he'd look for some work. He applied for a job teaching journalism in a small college that had been going for 70 years. He didn't get it. They appointed a twenty-two year old with a four-year journalism degree and no experience.

He thought he might be able to earn a bit marking exam papers at another 'school of journalism' but found he didn't understand the questions. The Head of Department looked at him askance. How could he call himself a journalist and not know that feature articles came in shapes like egg timers, champagne glasses, Martini glasses – some even with an olive in the middle!

'I think I'll give a new twist (lemon) to *mens sana in corpore sano*, a healthy mind in a healthy body,' said Richard.

'Yes?'

'*Mens* insane in corporation insane.'

'And what does that mean?' asked the HoD.

'In a fucked world you're fucked,' said Richard, 'Well, something like that.'

'I see,' said the HoD.

Maybe one day a job would find him but for the moment Richard decided that looking for one would kill him. He got rid of the TV. He sold the car. He started having informative conversations on future prospects with car guards. He roared with laughter when petrol and other car-related prices went up, he grinned when drivers cursed breathalysers, he waved cheerily at traffic cops.

On the busy road below the one-way street there were minibus taxis and frequent brightly decorated privately owned 'Indian' buses. One day he caught one and found that, for the price of a local stamp, he could go all the way into town.

A notice behind the driver said 'Please move to the back of the bus. It's going the same place as the front.' That was the way with the world too, thought Richard, the only white person on board. All the windows were open. The red brushed velvet curtains, knotted at the ends, banged against the frames. Above the driver's head bobbed red satin hearts embroidered with I LOVE YOU and I'LL LOVE YOU ALWAYS and even I'LL LOVE YOU ALWAYS *AND* FOREVER. There were stuffed toys hanging from the cassette player and a buoyancy amongst the passengers. One or two smiled quietly through the shrill melody that came from the singer's private emergency 'Jolene, Jolene, Joleeeene, please don't take him just because you can.'

Looking out of the window he glimpsed, on the rear window ledge of a Hyundai, two white school hats exactly like his daughters' and managed, just in time, to stop his face from crumbling. His wife, his *ex*-wife, would die if she could see him now. One of her corporate clients was a bank specialising in car finance and Richard's paper had carried their advert headlined 'Just because you have lost your job doesn't mean you have to catch the bus.' He wondered if he might attempt another article.

'Never use public transport. Catching anything – AIDS, gonorrhea, syphilis – is more acceptable than catching a bus. Getting into debt for life is much better than getting into a bus for half an hour. Disdain people in old (usually paid-for) cars. Make employees, who drive unacceptably dated cars, park where they can't be seen. When a white person, particularly one who lives in the posh suburbs, gets hi-jacked, organise a protest march. When a black person gets hi-jacked pay no attention. You bought your car (on terms of course) for its power. Use it. Flaunt your borrowed/exploitative wealth. If someone relieves you of some of it, emigrate. Aside from taking your children to school don't carry passengers in the back seat; it's infra-dig. Don't you yourself ever get caught sitting in the back seat of a car. Neither your image nor your marriage will ever recover.'

Catching the bus became an adventure for Richard. Each bus was different. Some, with names like 'Lovers Paradise', 'Free Willy' and 'Bad Boys' throbbed with ferocious rap – long chains of rude words at 110 decibels. 'Some aunties like it,' said one driver in wrap-around sunglasses, 'They go to the back and sit on top of the speakers to feel the doef doef go into them.' He caught one bus with airline seats and a TV that was showing the kind of movie that made middle-aged women get off sooner than they should and school boys miss their stop.

Conductors were constantly busy, directing the drivers, helping the elderly, hoisting crates of beer, bags of maize meal and small children up and down the stairs. They also happily loaded the stock that helped some people make a living: bundles of freshly shaved broom handles, two metre long sheaves of newly cut sugar cane, branches of litchis. A single street trader could sometimes bring as many as seven or eight boxes of fruit, cool drinks, beer, chips and even ice, aboard – without anyone batting an eyelid or the trader having to pay a single extra cent.

One of the drivers told Richard that there was a cow on his bus once. It stood in the aisle and shat. No extra charge. 'In this business when you can gross R4 500 for ferrying the main course and 75 wedding guests from Durban to Umtata and (minus the cow) back you don't get dainty about such things,' he said.

He caught the municipal buses too which, in the evenings, went via the North Coast Road to the townships, and occasionally someone would start singing and then all the passengers would join in. 'What are you singing?' he asked the lady next to him once. 'We are thanking God for being with us through today's working and asking him to look after us through the night.'

Richard started wearing vests and sarongs made from cotton which he bought by the metre from the fabric shops in the Indian quarter. At the Hospice Shop he bought an ancient rucksack labelled 'Canvas Workers. (Pty.) Ltd. 107, Plein Street Cape Town' with a metal frame and leather straps and harness 'Made in Oslo, Norway' and decorated it with African designs.

He began exploring parts of the city different from the usual shopping malls and recommended restaurants his wife had dragged him to. He walked briskly, held himself well and developed the clear eyes and taut skin of a man in glowing health. Local people cautioned him against going to certain areas. He went.

'Where you from?' they asked.

'Durban.'

'Oh, I thought you overseas.'

He took it as a compliment. And nothing bad ever happened to him.

He saw how everywhere the entrepreneurial spirit was scraping the barrel for scraps on which to survive and how sellers were themselves buyers. Even the women who slept under plastic shelters on the street outside the station, where they wove and sold baskets, presented a potential market in the city's precarious food chain.

An elderly woman was selling white powder in small plastic bags with a photocopied drawing of a rat: R2.50. Chatting to her he found that she bought the rat poison in bulk, repackaged it, and made a profit of R150 a week.

A young man had bought a 100 litre plastic drum of paraffin which he was decanting into containers customers brought from home.

Two girls wearing white dresses and maroon jerseys to resemble nurses were giving free blood pressure tests to promote their *muti*: R25 a bottle.

Another young man was selling 'value added' plastic bottles to which he had attached long tubes and syringes. They looked to Richard like some kind of terminally unhygienic intravenous drip.

'I don't get it,' said Richard, 'do you stick the tube in your arm?

'No, sir!' the young entrepreneur laughed, 'up your bum!'

Outside the government offices a photographer was taking passport photos, his clients posing with their heads beneath an open-ended apple carton strapped to a palm tree.

Two young men were selling ball point pens for filling in forms.

Outside an undertakers a milliner was selling hats, black mostly, using the silver-backed windows, behind which the bereaved wept, as a mirror.

That same afternoon he met a man in a pub who said he was struggling to come out on R35 000 a month. 'This bloody country!' Richard gave up going to these pubs where all people seemed to do was whinge.

He remembered that lunch hour in the dying days of 'the old' South Africa when he had gone to the march protesting the murder of Chris Hani, the black leader of the Communist Party, killed by a white immigrant. It was at one of the most crucial times in the country's history. A huge crowd with only a handful of whites toyi-toyied down the main street. Two or three windows were smashed, a car was overturned and things thrown – it's what people do when they're angry. Later he heard a white radio announcer calling the marchers 'savages'. His own paper had compared the scene to a battle zone: 'like Beirut.' It was nothing of the sort and he had felt ashamed. It was thanks to responsible people on all sides that the country had not plunged into chaos. And in London's Trafalgar Square, the then still current orange, white and blue flag had flown at half-mast on the South African embassy to mourn the death of the leader of the Communist Party! Nelson Mandela praised the white Afrikaans lady who'd helped track down the far-right Polish killer.

He remembered with shame too when (despite his wife's loud protests), a few years later, he had taken his daughters to a Freedom Day celebration. Except for some officials and a group of children from an Afrikaans school, they were the only white people there. The children sang '*Bobbejaan Klim die Berg*' – which struck him as a bit iffy until he heard that the baboon was climbing the mountain to annoy the *boere*. The children's choir was warmly applauded and, though to start with, the black people next to them were wary, after a while Richard and his daughters were included in the pleasantries and the biscuits being offered around. They left after three hours, before the main entertainment. His paper carried the headline 'Riot at Freedom Day Celebrations.'

One day Richard's ex-wife told him she was remarrying.

'One out of two divorces ends in marriage,' he said. 'Congratulations!

'And you, don't you want to get married again?' she asked.

'No,' said Richard. 'No offence!'

He longed occasionally for the warm potential of a woman's body in his bed but his mind was not ready for a new relationship. He was beginning to mellow and enjoy the effortless pleasure of his own undemanding company.

'Well don't you at least want to make money?'

'What for?'

'So you can do what you really want to!'

The new husband took Madeleine and the two girls to Sun City for the Easter weekend. Richard went down to the Golden Mile beachfront, a time and a place rife with crime according to the media. He had gone very early and by 6 a.m. had already seen a crash-helmeted poodle on a motor-bike, an outie (they weren't called tramps anymore; they no longer tramped) up a tree and six wet *sangomas*. The poodle, relieved of his helmet, was achieving the same end for his bladder among the table legs at the all-night XL restaurant where the owner wore a peaked cap, bottle-thick glasses and the pale energised look of a man who has had no sleep but has made an awful lot of money. Several dozen people were breakfasting on beer. One placed a sandy flip flop upside down on the table with a *maitre d'* flourish, 'Beer and crumbed sole,' he beamed. Flushed with alcohol and happiness he yelled, 'I love you! I love everybody!' Two white female power walkers in pink peaks, arms pumping like pistons, determinedly paid no attention.

The *sangomas* had travelled down from Ixopo on the back of a truck and having placed their cow-tailed *amashoba* on the sand as nonchalantly as if they were beach towels waded into the ocean in buckskin anklets, cross-over chest beads and black and white beaded head-dresses. They were collecting sea water to use as an emetic or as *muti* to protect their crops. They'd bought the plastic containers from a man who, with several dozen 2 litre plastic milk bottles bulging weightlessly on his back transmitting a white translucent light, looked like a large moth.

Already the sea was crowded with bathers, the women hiding erogenous thighs in Lycra tights. Like the Vaalies – or Gauties as the people from the Transvaal (now Gauteng) were currently called – who had frequented this beach RESERVED FOR MEMBERS OF THE WHITE RACE ONLY in years gone by, many of the women were bulky with buttocks the young men classified, as they did large twin speakers, 6x5's.

Aside from Richard, there was only one white person in the water: a middle-aged, big-bellied Gautie who had come down with his wife on a second honeymoon. He smiled when Richard told him he was pretty unique. 'I know. People was telling me we was mad – all the crime! But it's been *wonderlik*!'

Although the beaches were no longer segregated, people still kept to their own groups. In one area Indian men sat on chairs on the grass while the women served food from plastic fold-up tables stacked with Tupperware and large silver saucepans.

The whites, confining themselves to an area where they could drive their 4x4's on to the beach and launch their jet skis, turned their backs on Richard as he walked past along the water's edge.

The mini-bus taxi parking area resembled a tightly packed township of reverberating mobile discos with narrow 'streets' filled with people dancing. '*Yebo Baba!*' they called to Richard. TKZee, Trompies and Mdu thudded from a battery-operated Sony. The young men and women danced *pantsula* style. It looked curiously like the hokey-pokey – only faster, looser, hipper. The older people lay on grass mats and rugs keeping an eye on the sizzling *braais* that filled the air with rich meaty aromas.

Almost every lamppost bore an over-burdened bin and a sign '*Lahlala udoti lapha*' with a brave little arrow. The walkways were congested. Shoals of people going in opposite directions glided past each other with supple ease. Their smiles were wide. A little too wide, some of them, with pupils large and unfocused. They were happy, very happy.

Richard spoke to a policeman. A quarter of a million people visited the seven kilometre stretch of beach that day. The only violent crime occurred when a man attacked another with a broken bottle. The next day the headline in the paper, *his* paper was 'Beachfront Chaos'; the report quoted 'terrified mother of three'. A British newspaper reported that the Durban beachfront was overrun by 'hordes of Zulus.' Fuck! It's their own bloody country! That's why it's called kwa Z U L U! he screamed.

It was only after he had promised to take them shopping as well as lunch that, with some reluctance, Richard's daughters, back from their 'Five Star' holiday, agreed to spend the day with him in town. It was with even more reluctance that his ex-wife, horrified at his idea of 'fun', had been persuaded to allow them to go into the Grey Street area. 'The girls went there on a school excursion once to look at old buildings – Art Deco apparently! – and they were all so terrified they walked around with their fists to their chest, brandishing sharpened pencils!' She had insisted on dropping them off. 'You can't expect them to catch a bus!'

They walked down the little arcade that formed part of the golden domed Mosque – the biggest in the southern hemisphere. The small inter-leading shops in the double storey arcade, named for the school, the *madressa*, established along with the Mosque more than a century ago spilled out onto the pavement under the overhanging balconies. The Indian shop-keepers sat on plastic chairs chatting amongst themselves while their black assistants yelled enticements to passers-by. The stock reflected the needs of people living simple lives: Primus stoves, charcoal irons, tin baths and bulbous rubber syringes in assorted sizes. There were cell-phone shops too now.

At a tiny store that specialises in beads, imported from Slovakia, up-country women doing their month-end business in the city queue to barter the flat circular hats, necklaces and belts they've made for more tiny coloured beads in various grades. Four generations of Muslim men, the oldest with a long white beard and ivory *khurta*, the youngest cool in jeans and T-shirt, serve the women. At midday, verses from the Koran, intoned through the mosque's public address system, are dissolved in the passing swell of *kwaito* music as people alight from minibus taxis besides the red-brick revival style Catholic cathedral.

'How come the Emmanuel Cathedral was built in this part of town, and St Mary's Church in the centre?' asked his elder daughter.

'Because the English colonialists were Protestant and didn't want the Catholics on top of them.'

'Weird!' said his younger daughter looking through the frame she'd made of her fingers. 'If you stand right here you can see the Hindu temple, the Mosque and the Catholic cathedral right on top of each other.'

It was time for lunch. There was much coming and going at *Little Gujarat* but they found space on a bench at one of the long tables. The menu was scrawled on a blackboard. There was no cutlery, just a sink in the corner where you washed your hands after your meal. The food, all vegetarian, was delicious and cheap. The girls tried to copy their neighbours eating vegetable *breyani* with their hands and scooping bean curry up with their *rotis*. They stole *puri patha* and potato *bajees* from Richard's plate and laughed when people asked

'Where you from?'

'From here.'

'No, which country you coming from?'

'South Africa!'

It was only when they spoke some Afrikaans that they were believed. Other than tour guides and tourists white South Africans were seldom seen in this part of the city.

After the meal they bought a recipe book and then went shopping for ingredients: lentils from a shop where all sorts of grains were scooped from rolled down sacks, spices from a stall where the different reds and yellows and ochres stood in soft pyramids, vegetables they'd never seen before – leaves that were rolled or still on the vine, marrows with spikes and twists, green beans long as their forearms.

They went into sari boutiques and felt the silks between their fingers and in a fabric shops bought lengths of bright African print. And they each bought a sun hat crocheted from colourful plastic bags.

A man was selling tatting needles on the pavement and they bargained with him over one of his runners with citrus yellow letters edged in shocking pink for their mother's kitsch collection. But once they had bought it, it seemed that the runner, imbued with the spirit in which it had been made, wasn't quite as tacky as it had at first seemed: *Be kind to all mankind and make the world more beautiful.*

'You know Dad, you know when Mommy told you about those sharp pencils…' his elder daughter said.

'Yes.'

'I didn't do that…Well I did, but then after I dropped a pencil I put them both away.'

'Why?'

'Because a man picked it up and gave it back to me like this,' and holding her right hand in the crook of her left elbow, her palm open, she made the customary Zulu gesture. 'But it wasn't just that. It's what he said, when I dropped it.'

'And what was that?'

'"Sorry!" He said sorry, but I didn't drop it because he bumped me or anything.'

Richard smiled. 'Yes, in Zulu culture it doesn't matter whether or not one is the cause of someone's misfortune, it is that the misfortune has happened and you are expressing sympathy for them.'

When they parted the girls hugged him and said they couldn't remember when last they'd had such a good time.

It was afterwards when he was sitting on the Indian bus next to a woman with two small children, one of whom he took on his lap, and was enjoying the sprung surprise of his hand on the puffy hair of the spell-bound toddler looking up at him, and was feeling vitally connected to the whole flux and whirl of life and experiencing an emotion that felt a lot like love, that he realised that he had never been happier.

He *was*, in that moment, doing exactly what he liked.

Perhaps after all God was Loue.

5

Ants glide up the trunk of the tree that grows on the verge. The bark is lime-coloured, luminescent in the fibrous light that passes through the green organza of leaves.

The scrap metal man drags his trolley to one side to make way for the blue and white police vehicle coming up the incline. He has an in-built fear of authority, but the black policeman recognising him from the day I died, greets him warmly. In some ways the policeman envies people like him. Envies them their poverty to which no mortgage, no car payments, no lights and water bills are attached. Envies them the rich camaraderie of the townships.

The only time the people on our suburban street came together was when there was an accident or, because of the road works on the main road below, the water is occasionally turned off. Hearing the cheery recorded apology and encouragement to 'take as much as you need' the neighbours come out to the water truck with buckets and basins and, united by common human need, shyly smile and maybe say a few small words and there is a brief fragile neighbourliness that makes the policeman, and particularly his wife, sick with longing for the robust liveliness of the township they left for 'a better life.'

Under Apartheid this area was designated 'WHITES ONLY' and few dared break the law but from the early 1990's people of other races moved in and, though the whites complained that the value of their properties would fall, the demand for houses actually pushed prices up.

Under Apartheid, I broke the law. I, an old maid living in isolation on the dry broad plains of the Karoo – where the setting sun limned the backs of the Angora goats and the sound of their bleating carried in the fast cooling air as the sun followed its bloody path to sink behind the long, quiet range of purple mountains as darkness fell – I broke the law of the land. And broke it in the most scandalous manner possible.

The man who lives here at number 59 has had his troubles too and the house itself seems to have withdrawn from the world. It is hardly visible behind the unkempt hedges and shrubs and the tenacious creepers festooned like extravagant streamers. He used to be a teacher, an Art teacher, I'm told, and there was often music coming from the house. He played the piano beautifully. Sometimes he played the same piece over and over. As though his heart were breaking. Something I recognised.

People saw him on the news one night; none of us have seen him since.

#59

It was always the Light

His earliest memory came to him quite late in life. He was standing in the Louvre in front of a Bonnard and the fall of yellow light in the room in the painting, and the yellowed light suffused about him in the gallery, took him back to the yellowy light permeating her perfumed bedroom. He remembered how, through the smoothed-out wrappers of the sweeties which were his reward, his eye had tinted the world gold and purple and rose-madder. Remembered how he had split the rainbow and made taut stripes of colour lean from the bevelled edge of the big round mirror of her dressing table. Remembered how he made the cut glass powder bowl with its deeply tapered incisions, incandesce in a criss-crossing of bright blades which he could, by simply inclining his head, retract. And how, once, the silver-backed hand mirror had thrown back the crushed damson of his mouth. And how his mother had laughed.

But it was not the light in the painting that had retrieved the memory, it was the floriferous décor. It was now as vivid to him as if it were that very morning that she had called him, as she did every morning, 'David darling!', to the floral-papered bedroom with its woollen carpet strewn with woven flowers, and the richly flowered curtains and pelmet, and the flowery valence and counterpane, and the efflorescence of cushions on the queen sized bed. He felt again how the blood drained from his head, how the air leaked from his lungs, how his stomach rebelled as he crouched there in the half light that filtered through the gathered abundance of her floral frock, his face pressed against the soft, warm dough of her bare flesh slightly moist from the bath, his nostrils locating a faint brininess lurking beneath the extravagant dredging of talcum powder, one small rounded hand pressed to her thigh clutching the thick pink band of finely ribbed elastic as his fledgling left arm muscles pull downwards and his right arm muscles tug the fawn stocking top upwards, his fingers struggling to hoist a lip of it over the hard rubber nipple to engage the metal clasp. Until fashion changed the four rear suspenders of his mother's corset were always his responsibility. So was her happiness.

David's mother, whose talent had never matched her early ambition to be a world-class opera-singer, had had four miscarriages before his conception and so his gestation, through all its phases, was sprung with tension that came from a rock-solid determination to keep him clutching on at all costs and abundant transfusions of love. Music, she believed, ahead of her time, would encourage the foetus to develop and so, as he remained cubbied in the shifting light and warmth of the womb, opera and other classical music had reverberated through his developing form as frequently and simply as nourishment had filtered in from the placenta. His need for music was always just as natural to him as his need for food.

Before even he could read music, long before he understood key signatures and *Legato* or *Allegretto* or grasped that 'Every Good Boy Deserves Food' had actually nothing to do with eating, David would stand beside his mother's flowery abundance, and, in the intersecting circles of light thrown by the candles ensconced in the two brass arms that projected from the polished rosewood piano, would watch the shadows shift among the black and white keys as her plump fingers nestled softly or flew falcon-swift up and down the keys while she leaned her generous body into the music and opened her crimsoned cupid's-bow mouth voluminously wide and he would know exactly when to reach up to the score holder and turn the page.

At least one critic commented in later years that it was David's early exposure to the tonal aspects of music that had informed the qualities of light and shade in his painting.

Clothed in *broderie anglaise*, his hair wound into soft locks, forbidden to mix with other children who were deemed to be little more than sources of infection and injury, David grew amongst grown-ups. He was precocious in speech and kept himself entertained for long hours modelling figures from plasticine that came in ribbed pastel strips wrapped in thin white paper or wielding his treasured Crayola crayons in their Springbok livery to make skilful pictures in which his mother invariably appeared with a very long, hefty arm sheltering a very small David. His father seldom featured.

Knowing how much the carrying of the child to full term had meant to her, David's father, a travelling salesman who had gone 'up North' in the war, would have done anything to please his wife. He lay great store too by 'peace and quiet on the home front.' And so, though he did not agree with some aspects of her child-rearing, he did not get involved. When he set off on one of his frequent trips with his sturdy leather suitcase in the boot of the Austin A40, his last words to David were always 'Look after your mother.' And every time he returned, along with the chocolates nesting in luxurious layers in a generously padded, beribboned box for his wife, he brought David a tin of Sharps toffees with a picture of a puppy or a kitten on the rounded lid 'for being a good boy, looking after your mother.'

To celebrate his fourth birthday David's mother invited the Ladies Choir for morning tea and 'a spread' which stayed veiled beneath a flower-embroidered net until, to a chorus of oohs and aahs, she whipped it off and revealed Victoria Sponges, *melkterts*, cheese straws, brandy snaps and *koeksusters* displayed on paper-doilied plates and three-tiered cake stands. His mother, pinky stretched out, index finger pressed to the knob on the lid of the floral Prince Albert bone china teapot, poured long streams of amber liquid into the pretty matching cups and into the new *Royal Doulton Bunnykins* mug David had been presented with on his very recent weaning. The birthday cake had 'Happy Birthday David' piped in pink icing and bore four pink plastic ballerinas in silver tutus, their heads crowned with candy-striped candles. The choir ladies sang Happy Birthday in four-part harmony.

'Make a wish David!' they called.

The day after his birthday his mother enrolled David in ballet classes as she had determined to do when first she'd felt the foetus move. Elated by that unmistakable assumption of life kicking in her womb, she had visualised *entrechats* and *grand jetés* on sprung stage floors, had smelt the resin, heard the long-stemmed pink roses thud, for there was no doubt that the child she was so preciously coddling would one day be taking curtain calls at the Sadler's Wells.

While his musicality was undoubted, David's thighs rubbed together when he walked; he had flat feet and no elevation and, in first position, had to keep his heels apart to accommodate his knees. The girls (he was the only boy in the class) sniggered and called him 'baby elephant' not just because he was tubby and clumsy but because of the way his low-slung grey-shortsed bottom seemed to simply subside into his solid little legs.

But twice a week the dutiful boy pulled on his black leather pumps with the elastic over the instep, while his well-padded, green-eyed mother watched the little girls criss-crossing pink ribbons around their pretty ankles. When this scene repeated itself over the weeks, David became impatient. When was his birthday wish going to come true? He knew what he wanted more than anything else in the world: a sister. Every night when his mother tucked him into bed in his room with the Dolly Varden dressing table and gave him a wet sloppy kiss, he asked Jesus – and the stork – to deliver a baby girl to his house. And he would lie awake sometimes listening for the flap of wings, praying that they would hurry up and bring his sister wrapped in a pink blanket tied with pink ribbon just to be sure. But David remained an only child.

People smiled at the mother and child pair: the large women, who wore her hair in a treble-like loop; the bespectacled boy with the brass buttons of his blazer straining over his tummy, rounded like a bass clef. They seemed not to accompany each other in the normal way, but to be integral to the very essence of one another.

In ordinary school-work David was well above average; in music he was excellent; in every aspect of art he was truly gifted and while the other children were making paper mache puppets with tennis balls or Christmas decorations with pegs and pine cones, he was allowed to draw and paint whatever he wanted.

It was David who, after school one day when his father was away, found his mother slumped on the bloodied floral carpet of the bedroom, her frock bundled up between her legs, soaked and streaked with dark spindled blood. He had run to a neighbour to call an ambulance.

His mother had been trying to give him a little sister he was told. He didn't know how all this blood fitted in with the white, immaculate stork but he did know that it was all his fault. That if he hadn't prayed for a sister this would never have happened.

It was from this time his revulsion began. He found blood, any blood, repulsive, and so too women's bodies and a glimpse of feminine hygiene products – the very phrase 'sanitary towels' repelled him – on a chemist's shelf made him feel sick to his stomach and in later years even the tell-tale scraps of cellophane paper in pristine bathrooms could trigger an attack of nausea. He loathed the smell of Dettol with which his mother sometimes washed leaving her flannel floating like a turtle in the milky morning water, and associated all antiseptics like Jeyes fluid and so too open drains, the vegetal slime of used vases, the smell and ooze of estuarine low-tides and all things bloody with the messiness of the female sex and, while he got on well with women in ordinary life, any hint of physical intimacy repelled him.

His mother had stayed in hospital for a fortnight and when she came back with her 'insides' removed she seldom smiled and the scant music she played was always in minor key.

He blamed himself entirely.

And did all he could to atone.

Transmuting every drop of tenderness he could draw from his being into sound, he sat at the piano and tried, several times a day, to pour the poignant rising and descending melody of Mozart's Piano Concerto No. 21, in C Major K467, the *andante* movement, her favourite, like a balm into her soul. To no effect. He could not ease her pain. Despite all his efforts: the pictures he painted for her, the flowers he picked (never too short as his father did) and arranged for her, even the breakfast muffins he baked for her following the oil- stained recipe in *Mrs Slade's South African Cookery*, his mother's spirits did not lift.

One day after she had sat at the piano accompanying herself for a long slow hour singing 'Happy Days are here again', *lentando* with closed eyes and wet cheeks, his father locked the piano.

She no longer wept but sat on the chintz-covered arm of the Queen Ann chair staring out of the bay window, intermittently and needlessly, clearing her throat. And the glaucous eyes, imbued with unrestrained sorrow she turned on David, broke his heart. 'Happy Days' was always and forever the saddest song he knew.

When she became 'a danger to herself' the specialist recommended 'a place' in a small town a few hours away. She was going to leave home, leave her husband, leave him. It was all his fault. He had failed to make her happy. Often when his father was away he sat on the floor where she lay slumped and cradled her as though she were the child, he the parent, and rocking back and forth, mothered her as best he could.

It was David who helped her pack. David who, from the edge of the back seat leaned forward and through the gap between the front seats reached for her soft warm hand and held it tight, as she sat staring straight ahead while his father, as had become his habit, assumed a desperate cheerfulness and endlessly belted out 'She'll be wearing silk pyjamas when she comes, when she comes, she'll be wearing silk pyjamas when she comes, she'll be wearing silk pyjamas, she'll be…' as the road unspooled before them.

It was only when he read the sign in the parking lot of the spacious hospital grounds and saw the wild-eyed women, with stocking tops for hair bands, rush up and slap her on the back and say, 'You're one of us!' that David realised what was happening. She was being committed to a mental asylum, a madhouse, a 'loony bin'!

Matron showed them around. There were no locks on the inside of the dormitories and, they were told, the toilet doors were made so that, in case of emergency, an orderly could crawl underneath. There were no dressing gown cords allowed, no high hooks, no sharp instruments; the inmates ate with plastic spoons. But there were books in the lounge – Georgette Heyer, Daphne du Maurier, Howard Spring – and a piano. 'You'll give us a tune, won't you girls?' Matron said turning to two elderly women in candlewick dressing gowns. They shuffled coyly to the double stool and thudded out *Chopsticks*. The piano needed tuning. Badly.

Since David would soon be starting high school and since his father would have to get back on the road some time and since there was a good boarding school in the town adjacent to the asylum, it was decided to send David to school there; he would be able to visit his mother regularly. This was where, in later years people said his father had compounded his earlier mistake, had abrogated his responsibilities to care for his wife. And so David, overweight, solitary, short sighted, sensitive, found himself thrust into the boisterous ruck and maul of an all-boys boarding school where sporting prowess was of supreme importance and initiation and fagging part of the hallowed tradition.

David's academic ability was well above average; his athletic prowess non-existent. He chose not to participate in the school's music programme but in Art, which was taken seriously, he blossomed. His Art teachers were impressed by his particularly sensitive rendering of light and shade to give shape and form. And the more perceptive and intelligent of his History and English teachers appreciated the understanding he had, that few ever attain, that it is too the light in which we look at things that makes us perceive them, as we do, in entirely different ways.

Though his Art teachers were impressed with his talent, they were concerned about the subject matter: a broken tube of lipstick on the damson-smeared tiles of a urinal floor, a kitchen with an electric chair at the foot of which lay a smashed child's mug (the perspective of the angled Royal Doulton potter's mark was perfect), a dressing table with a cut glass vase (his rendering of the fall of light here was particularly skilful) of snowdrops that dripped vermilion droplets on a lace-trimmed cotton runner. When pressed for an explanation he shrugged his sloped shoulders. The school contacted his father who said he had no idea where this subject matter had come from. Probably just a passing phase.

David's visits to his mother were not a success. He sat on the edge of a Morris chair in the lounge with its worn autumn leaf carpets and thin bull-rush patterned curtains, licking fig rolls and attempting to make conversation about the darkly framed Theunis de Jongh prints leaning down from the picture rail or the school play his year was putting on or the inedible boarding school meals. She made no response.

And just when he thought that the divide between them could not have been wider, it broadened out even more and he despaired of ever reaching her again. David, in his smart striped school blazer and cap, could find no trace of the beautiful mother he so adored in this vulgar-mouthed coarsened creature who came into the public lounge with a clown's lipsticked mouth, laddered stockings that sagged around her ankles and a head full of purple plastic curlers speared so tightly that her scalp seemed covered in painful welts. 'The bastards can't give me shock treatment now, can they sweetie?' she said. It seemed to him that a total stranger was speaking through her once lovely mouth, looking through her once loving eyes.

Back in his narrow boarding school bed, he put a pillow over his head and, as quietly as he could, sobbed himself to sleep.

And so his long, lonely school years continued, lifted only by the occasional art prize and much enthusiastic praise from an ever-growing number of people of influence.

When David was 18, having been exempted from military service on the grounds of short-sightedness and flat feet, and just about to start his training as an Art teacher, his mother died. He maintained his composure to such a degree that relatives suspected that he was repressing his grief. The truth was that he had been several years in mourning and what he felt now was something like relief: the alien who had occupied her body after they had so systematically cauterised her spirit, had at last been evicted and his dear mother could finally rest in peace.

During his college years, a particularly conservative time in South African society when, in certain cities, replicas of Michelangelo's *David* and displays of bathing costumes and underwear were banned from shop windows, he produced work that caused controversy and question marks over his suitability for the teaching profession.

His sculpture *Jumping Child* gave the mundane (or so familiarity had rendered it) act an almost ethereal quality, the tensing of the gluteal muscles and those of the thighs and calves were frozen in that infinitesimal fraction of time when the feet are just about to peel off the earth. The energy that it exuded was infinitely refined, less a physical vigour than a spiritual frisson, giving a sensation, a concentrated essence, a distillation of what it was to be sprung with life. The child, naturally, was naked.

Through awards and the sale of his work David managed several times over the years to go to Europe, where he envied the easy integration of art and life and thrilled to the varying quality of light in different skies.

It may have been the angle at which the sun was coming through the glass roof but he had fallen in love once with a face in the window of a moving train at the Gare Saint-Lazare in Paris. His train was pulling out as the boy's train was pulling in. Through two thick layers of *Societe nationale des chemins de fer francais* glass and several metres of steam-filled air, though he had never seen the boy before, he recognised his inamorato. And he spent ten foolish days in Paris looking for that exquisite tilt of neck, that flop of hair, those long lovely *Blue Guitar* hands.

He thought he saw the boy again in Italy. He was staying in a fourth floor room in a Florence *pensione*. The curtain blew into the late Italian light as he stood at the window looking out at the flagged square below. He stood a long time watching.

A nun in a black habit and white wimple crossed diagonally through the *piazza* and a plump, angry mother shooed three small children into a tenement building. And then there *he* was at the grand piano that had been wheeled into the square for a concert, playing a Corelli sonata. David recognised him from the fleeting moment in the Paris station. He ran down the several flights of stairs and into the square. But there was no one there though the stones still seemed to echo *pianissimo* and the clock, six hours out, struck midday. Or midnight.

In Venice it was a fleeting glimpse of fingers stretching from a shuttered-back window over a canal in the early evening to hang a dripping singlet, but though he searched the neighbourhood, he could not locate the owner of those exquisite hands.

In Villefranche, where he had spent two companionable weeks, he had seen, beyond an open door in his host's villa, the cage of hinged young bones pale and precise against the wide dawn window, the linked chain of the spine, bending pliant as a bicycle's in such easy beauty, the sculptural perfection of those pale palpable buttocks, textured as the paper upon which already he is brushing the wash of colour… And parental voices raised, bags packed, cabs called. And so were friendships forever ended.

A school trip. A water shortage: SHOWER WITH A FRIEND. The needles of steaming water and the diffused light in the mist of the small enclosed space, wet slippery bodies, the fresh bar of soap like alabaster sliding across the glazed planes, down the gleaming flanks, into the gullies, and with the aperitif of small resistances, around the dear tenderness. In smoothing gentle hands over this sublime young body he found a brief exit from the mundanity of his own.

And so were jobs lost and harder to find.

Conscientiously stretching the length of his resistance to that exquisite concomitantly imagined point where postponement is no longer bearable and he feels again his blood quickened by the prospect of what he has so long yearned for, he struggled to accommodate the harsh rectitudes of a skewed morality where touching a beautiful skin was a sin, and breaking it open with weapons was not, where you could with impunity fill shelves and walls with vulgar things but could be charged for being in possession of loveliness; for, he thought, it was not beauty alone that was in the eye of the beholder, sin resided there too and the tongue of a snake receives particles from the nest where the baby chick hides for its own survival.

It was through art and the sculptural power of light that David reached for the sublime. His chiaroscuro series of paintings won acclaim: doorways leading off from doorways, rooms from rooms, some flooded with daylight, some lit from an unspecified glow that fell oblique across the canvas. And always just a single solitary form, if form at all.

David's father remarried shortly after his wife's death. And some years later David's maternal grandparents left him a small house in Durban. Until recently he had kept it tenanted and when eventually he decided to make it his home, did his best to avoid his neighbours.

* * * * *

A plump, dampish figure in a white bath sheet, he comes from the front door out into the moonlight that casts a faintly mauve tint on the pallid slope of his shoulders and the smooth convexity of his upper body which fits into the towelled receptacle of his pelvis like a pale egg in an egg cup. Thickets of twisted bougainvillea encrusted with cerise and magenta blooms send out long thorny shoots, a florescence of fragrant purple, mauve and white quatrefoils glut the Yesterday, Today and Tomorrow, overrun the slope. The air is replete with their cloying perfume. David steadies himself against the Jacaranda which spreads its skirts in voluptuous violet bloom about him. And suddenly down through the years comes the name of his mother's perfume: TABU.

The way light leans in the ends and beginnings of days, the geometry of old bicycles, the neat silhouettes of lean cats, young ankle bones, long bleak landscapes, small bare trees, eyelids lightly veined with the blue of thin milk, smooth white limbs in emerald velvet water, young toes gripping rock, a creamy complexion with a sprinkling of cinnamon, the sound of sea sucking shale, lean music. In these he found beauty.

In the muddied confines of his mind thoughts dart fish-like too slippery to grab, hard to make head or tail of. But a sudden gleam of silver leapt through the murkiness, and lay dashed on the shore. Tomorrow, today! they will come for him. They will come and with cameras rolling will capture him, eyes glittering beneath the paperweights of his lenses, and, in a 20 second slot on the evening news, end it all.

They will come and, with rapacious eyes and brutal hands, abuse the dear lovely things that gave him succour in the long lonelinesses of his life: the postcards from Florence where he had become besotted with his namesake (not the Michelangelo but the Donatello with the cant of hips that gave a contrapuntal air of impertinence and coiled energy, bravado almost, to his exquisitely modelled sex); the signed photograph of Nureyev, with the muscled undulations of his parabola'd body suspended in space; the folio copy of Leonardo's anatomical drawings; his own half finished life drawings and soft pastel sketches. Exhibit A, B and C if it pleases the court.

Their rough, rude hands would paw through his treasured collection of old photographs, painstakingly gathered over many lean years, which, in the matt slightly textured surfaces of thick creamy paper, held the delicate images, as beautiful as any flower, filled still with the concentrated sap, with the immanence of the bud, which, the tips of his fingers barely making contact as they stroked, gave him such exquisite pleasure.

They would take too the series of egg tempura he had done one blissful week in a hayloft in Tuscany, covering the bales with calico which he rendered with almost as much joy as the *contre jour* figures.

He wondered what they would allow him to bring. A toothbrush? Soap? He kept a wrapped cake of soap on his work table, lifting the opened end to breathe in its pure clean sweetness and remember.

They would tear him apart.

The Barbarians would come and with twisted eyes take crude flashlight photographs of the forms he so lovingly, so worshipfully, sculpted, the ones he could not bear to part with, to be parted from. He remembered how the light fell into the Paris street; how it sliced down behind the Crillon into the *demi* on the small, circular café table as the boy passed.

Bach's concerto in C minor for oboe and violin floats out into the night. Moments into the Second, the *Adagio* movement, with the oboe sustaining the long pure notes of liquid sound, it comes to him that the most sublime music emanates from the vibrating guts of slaughtered cats, that the ivory notes the pianist depresses with infinitely nuanced touch are cut from the tusks of butchered elephants, that the gland of the civet cat makes the sweetest perfume. Beauty is Pain and Pain Beauty.

His eyes are luminous. For him there is no beauty without pathos and no beauty that does not draw something from him, does not make some ineffable demand of him. Since this behest is always impossible to fulfil, beauty has gone on forever being beautiful and he, in his most intensely happy moments, has been unutterably sad.

Small birds shear the silence. A wild goose honks with the same sound his wooden stool makes when he turns the core to adjust the height. The light comes.

Its pale transparent flesh stretched between the tender stripes, the banana tree unfolds its bannered beauty and stands in ribbed translucence facing the day.

The sun comes over the hill to bring the rapid shift and slant of early morning light. But the day will not be fine. He takes off his glasses to polish the lenses. The light swells and oozes towards him. When he puts them on again, the light is clean edged between the leaves and in his mind he splits the air like mica into thin tightly packed layers, cross sections, each a fresh composition where leaves, gold-lit in tiny currents of air, spin, and birds dart and fall. He looks into the wedging light, along its broadening beams where the air is busy with life, abundant as soft winnowing sawdust. Sunlit ants glide in wide loops like glitter on glue.

Dogs bark. His flung-over-the-fence daily newspaper thuds.

A verboten suburban cock, brazen, crows.

The train sashaying on scoured tracks screeches to a halt.

A siren wails.

6

Coming down the incline, the scrap metal man wonders briefly what it is that makes this particular part of the street look different today. Then he sees that another non-indigenous tree has been chopped down. He has heard this talk of getting rid of aliens. It upsets him. He feels kinship with these non-native species. Though he is not illegal and considers himself largely accepted, the fact remains: the scrap metal man was not born in this country and the cruel comments he sometimes hears made of black – but seldom of white – foreigners makes him feel uncomfortable.

There, in his country, the earth did not produce the things that made men grow rich, the things the white man wanted: diamonds, gold, copper, and so, when the white colonialists sent men demanding tax money which he did not have and sent other men offering jobs so the men could earn the money to pay the tax, he made his decision.

It was with a sore heart that he left his wife and little ones and the country of his birth where, as a small boy, he would wake up in the hut by the side of the lake where the water was thick with fish, the trees lumpy with ripening fruit, and the rich, sweet soil abundant with vegetables. It was many years before he saw his family again and saw that his children hardly knew him and that his wife was wife only in name. He had taken a new wife in South Africa and he'd made more babies. And so had many men secure in the idea that their children would look after them in their old age but now, though old age had come, that assurance had gone. Because of AIDS that killed many in the prime of life, grandparents were now caring for their deceased children's children on the government pension.

A breeze shapes itself to the curve of the hedge, snags in the wounded fractions of sliced leaves and the stumps of clipped twigs where the green wetness pumps.

The day I died had been stifling. The American student who shares number 48 was not home then. Today she is sitting barefoot on the red stoep steps smiling into her cell phone. Hoping to deepen her tan, she is wearing a short skirt and no top. Her hair is plaited tight to her head like rows of mealies and she is wearing African beads. She hears the familiar whistle and catches a glimpse of the scrap metal man's hat above the high hedge as he passes and smiles to herself. It is the sort of hat her mother wore at her sister's wedding.

#48

Mary Anne Peeps

Hey!

This is Mary Anne Beauregarde from South Carolina with some REAL EXCITING NEWS! I'm doing my 'junior year abroad' out in Africa! Here at the University (College to you and me!) of kwaZulu-Natal, in Durban, South Africa! Sweet!

I'm an English Lit major. I aim to be an editor on a travel magazine. For my Creative Writing Project I'm keeping a blog ☺ ☺ ☺! I've titled my CWP 'Mary Anne Peeps' after this guy called Samuel who, my Prof told me, lived in London, England, and published a journal about stuff around him way back in B.C. I think. DEFINITELY B.B.G. – before Bill Gates! Go online? Forget it! Sam DIDN'T EVEN HAVE A TYPEWRITER! He had to like physically *write* it all out? Must've gone through a ton of pens! I also heard of this German girl called Anne Frank who kept a journal during the War. Now what I don't get is WHAT WAS A GERMAN GIRL DOING IN NAM?

Which I guess means I should tell you about me. I'm 19, my star sign is Gemini, and I have peacock blue eyes (well peacock blue contact lenses actually) and blonde (OK bleached blonde...I hope I can get my roots done soon!) hair. My skin is white, well pinkish, I suppose but I'm planning on getting a tan, as ALL-OVER AS I CAN! I'm a size ... no, let's not go there! My ancestors came to the good ole U S of A, 'the land of the free and the brave' from France about a million years ago. The Beauregardes had this kinda mansion! outside Charlestown which is really neat. Guess they must have been rolling in it. Don't ask me what happened – WE ARE LIKE DIRT POOR. My dad's SUV is nearly three years old; we EAT IN (TV dinners) about three times a week. ☹

Why did I come out to Africa? Reckon I always wanted to. First of all to help the poor black people, second of all to see lions and tigers in the jungle and third to meet Nelson Mandela. He is like MY NUMBER ONE ROLE MODEL.

Later!

Hey!

For those of you who don't know who Nelson Mandela is, he is like this ICON, also known as MADIBA, an old-timer dude, who wears cool shirts and was wrongfully imprisoned for 27 years and when he came out he just forgave everybody. I thought it was to do with robbing Ireland, but it seems his *prison* was on THIS ISLAND CALLED ROBBEN ISLAND! You can visit his cell on Robben (Dutch for seals by the way) Island, just off the coast of Cape Town. And where exactly is that? Well, Africa is this big piece of land that runs from Florida down to BA (Buenos Aries for you outta-spacers) only of course it's like a hundred miles out in the Atlantic Ocean. South Africa – A DUMB NAME FOR A COUNTRY IF EVER THERE WAS ONE! – sits at the ass-end of Africa. Cape Town's on the western side and Durban is on the eastern side, on the Indian Ocean! It's called the Indian Ocean because it's full of Indians.

Later!

Hey!

First things first. Thanks for your email Frank. (Is that your real name?) 'Forget about your roots, babe, you're blonde down to the bone,' you said. Gee gosh, that's so kind of you! Also Frank says it's called the Indian Ocean because it's across the way from India – maybe one day I'll stand on tippy toes and get to see the Taj Mahal!

I'm sharing a house in the suburbs in a street where whites, Indians, Coloureds (a racist word back home but not here) and even blacks (i.e. African Americans) live. Everyone has walls or fences in back AND in front but all the houses are different. The nearest mall is about 20 minutes away – THE GATEWAY THEATRE OF SHOPPING – and it's got me really hyped! IT HAS AIRCON so guess where I'll be spending EVERY FREE MOMENT! Because this house, like most houses in Africa – the hottest part of the world! – has no air-conditioning and I mean like NO AIRCON! ZIP! I think I'm going to, like, die.

Another thing that's going to kill me is NO ICED WATER. You can go into a restaurant and, forget about ice, they don't bring your glass of water, period. I mean you could be dying of thirst! People suffer out here. There's a FOOD SHORTAGE. It must have got worse since McDonalds closed down. Can you believe it? It used to be on campus but one day they just banged the doors shut and took down the golden arches. Don't know where they expect poor starving people to eat now!

Later!

Hey!

Not sure if you're kidding but thanks anyway Thelma for sending me the recipe for iced water!

I'm sharing the house with two South African students. Elise who is Afrikaans speaks this weird language. It sounds like someone struggling with a throat full of gravel and a mouthful of cotton candy. Her Dutch ancestors came out to the Cape about 360 years ago when there was no one else living there. About 170 years ago they packed their covered wagons and crossed these mountains with their servants and their BIBLES to get away from the British. Funny that. I think the British are kinda neat (love their cute accents!) but as my grandma says, 'There's no accounting for tastes.' (Telling me! Can you imagine eating HOT MUSH for *dinner!* That's what the African Americans – maybe I should just say Africans now! – eat. They call it *phuthu.* I call it 'poor you!')

Anyway the *voortrekkers* which means something like 'forward movers' ('That's a joke!' says Andy the other housemate [cute butt☺!]) set off to start a new life. They were very religious and very brave. E.g. There was this Battle – of the Bleeding River, I think –WHEN 500 INNOCENT WHITES WERE ATTACKED BY LIKE ABOUT TEN THOUSAND SAVAGES!!! Three thousand of them passed away but not a single Boer was murdered. Doesn't that just show you the power of prayer!

Later!

Hey!

It's kinda scary getting all these emails from you guys out there! My seminar leader says I can make my CWP – Creative Wring Project (in case you didn't know) – interactive and include your stuff (with initials for ID) IF THAT'S LIKE OK WITH YOU GUYS? Hope this means I'll get a really good grade and maybe get to publish this!!! And you'll see your name, OK, your initials! In print! Cool!

So here goes!

L W L

The power of prayer!? It shows you the power of the gun! The Boer women, good Christians that they were, stood behind their men on the ox wagons in a D-shaped lager – the river was on the one side – reloading the guns so that their men could kill as many as possible! *Innocent!* you say, the whites had been moving in and just taking over the land, much of it grazing land, for themselves. *Savages!* you say, the Zulus were highly organised and very disciplined and had nothing but spears and shields and their bare bodies. Or did you think they were issued with bullet-proof vests and goody-bags with Big Macs and Coke. What's more, and this is NB, they were defending *their own territory*! Instituting what you misty-eyed dumbfucks would call Homeland Defence.

Under Apartheid the anniversary of this day, 16th December, was a religious holiday – Dingaan's Day – even in Zululand!!!

J v d M

On the holy day of 16 December 1961 your Mr Nelson Mandela launched *uMkhonto we Sizwe*, the Spear of the Nation, MK, to commit acts of sabotage. Their leaflet said: 'the time comes in the life of any nation when there remain only two choices: submit or fight. That time has now come to South Africa. We shall not submit and we have no choice but to hit back by all means within our power in defence of our people, our future and our freedom.' Yes, your Mr Nelson Mandela were a terrorist and it was only just before he went to New York that the gentleman was taken off the 'Most Wanted' list.

Listen lady, don't believe everything what peoples is telling you!

B M

Viva Nelson Mandela Viva!
Viva MK Viva!

F T

One man's terrorist is another man's freedom fighter. It's the victors who write history.

Christians always have God on their side when they win. Where is God when they lose? Bob Dylan said it all in *With God on Their Side*.

Hey!
First of all: Let's like lighten up!

Second of all: There must be some mistake. Oprah had Nelson Mandela on her show. She wouldn't have dreamt of it if he was a terrorist.
Third of all: Who is Bob Dylan?
NB Your stuff is coming through in ANY OLD ORDER so you guys will just have to figure it out for yourselves.

Here's a message from my other housemate Andy, 22, pre MBA. (Like I said: cute butt☺!)

'Elise is talking crap. The Boers only left because the British, who took over the Cape and made it a British possession in 1806, were trying to stop them having slaves. We English-speakers don't celebrate 16th December because it's the *Boere*, the Afrikaners, who fucked up the country with job reservations, the immorality act, kicking people out of their homes etc. There's nothing for me to reconcile about. Being "a pale male" I don't even know if I'll get a job when I graduate.'

☹ That's so sad!
Later!

P du T
What about the rest of Africa where there were no Afrikaners?

Couple of facts:

1. Zambia (Northern Rhodesia): the British grabbed it AND all the copper for themselves but in 1960 when they 'left' there was NOT ONE GOVERNMENT HIGH SCHOOL because they needed 'the munts' to work on the mines not get educated and challenge them!

2. Mozambique and Angola: after the War (the Second World War, NOTHING TO DO WITH VIETNAM!) the Portuguese started a cotton industry forcing people (complainants were 'pacified') to grow cotton instead of food, turned it into textiles in Portugal and sold it back at high prices. Because the fertile land was all used for cotton, not food, people starved. COTTON WAS CALLED 'THE MOTHER OF POVERTY'.

3. The Congo: Cruellest of all. King Leopold of Belgium treated it like his personal estate.

4. Namibia: the Herero and Namaqua genocide by the Germans between 1904 and 1908 killed up to 100,000 Hereros and 10,000 Namaqua and is seldom talked about.

The list goes on!

X D

'No one living in the Cape' is bullshit! What about the San (called Bushmen – no nothing to do with George W[anker] Bush! Or his dad George H W Bush – a previous Head of the

CIA by the way! Stick that in your pipe and smoke it. Wake Up guys!) and the Khoi. Some 'Bushmen' did survive but the Apartheid Government said they were not part of the 'fauna'!!! of South Africa.

S N

Hullo Mary-Anne! Hope you are enjoying your stay with us. Here's a little (true!) story for you:

There had been a very long drought and the Khomani San people of the Kalahari, who had been evicted from their land 50 years before, believed that only when it was returned to them would the rain come. One day some years ago when the sky was blue and not a cloud in sight, the then deputy president Thabo Mbeki stood at the edge of the bone-dry Kalahari and said, 'This is your land. Take it, care for it, thrive on it,' and signed the documents returning it to the people. Their leader, a very small man was moved to tears and reached up to kiss Mr Mbeki on the cheek. And, I don't tell a lie, the clouds gathered straightaway, the rain began to fall AND THE DROUGHT WAS BROKEN. It was reported in the newspapers.

N F

Love your blog, Mary Anne! About your coloured lenses – don't they like make you see the whole world peacock blue?

P du T

Oh yes, and by the way, the Immorality Act which forbade miscegenation i.e. black and white being physically intimate with each other, goes back to 1927 – long before the Apartheid government and the sexual offences act!

Hey!
A law enforcing immortality! How cool is that!

Hi Mary-Anne
This is Moses, you know, the black guy (the one with the big holes in his ear lobes) in your CW class doing poetry.
This poem of mine needs a bit of an intro so here goes…
Under the Apartheid government blacks (about 80% of the population) had only 13% of the land. Also there's a lot of car hi-jacking specially BMW's (Beemers) and 4x4's or Tonyengenis.
    So here's the poem:

AN INDIGENOUS PEDESTRAIN HAS A PASSING THOUGHT

You stole our land sir
or did you buy it for a bead?
it was just lying there you said
not doing anything

so do you mind sir
if you borrow me your Beemer?
it's just standing there you see
not doing anything.

Later!

G M

Is that's what they do at university these days! Incite crime and call it poetry! It's absolutely, bloody shocking! My friend's 19 year-old daughter had her Rava stolen the other day and she was so traumatised she had to cancel her overseas trip. Our number one priority in this country should be STOP CRIME!

J v d M

Listen lady, bet you don't know why a SUV is called a Tony Yengeni. It's after this black big-shot who used his position in the ANC to get a discount on his 4x4. I ask you what kind of a person are that?

F T

If people didn't want this type of car to show off in there would be no market for the stolen cars. It's big business. Syndicates are only fulfilling orders! Robbing from the Rich and Greedy to *sell* to the Rich and Greedy. It's a funny, ole world!

B M

Address Greed and you address Poverty.

F T

Hullo Greed! (Get it? Ha-ha-ha!)
Greedy people *are* punished: imprisoned 24/7 behind their own high electric-wired walls, tinted car windows, Ray-Bans.

L W L

It might interest you to know that one of the most memorable moments of the Truth and Reconciliation Commission hearings occurred when a former Apartheid security officer, Jeffrey Benzien, explained how he used the wet bag method to torture his captives. Lots of people remember seeing on television the moment when the victim asked his torturer 'What kind of a man are you?' Most wouldn't remember the name of the tortured man: Tony Yengeni.

V O

That's no excuse! Lots of whites also suffered. My son died on the border defending this country.

K Z

I am indeed very sorry that V O lost his son. I feel his pain, for I too lost a son in action.

But painful as it is I think it's time to speak the truth. What those young white boys were fighting for was not 'this country' (which may I gently remind you was also my people's country) but for what they saw as a threat to the continuation of their own way of life.

B N

I'm looking for a Mercedes 3 series, full house, mags, cheap. Good commission paid. Reply soonest. All communication strictly confidential.

S N

The land claims being settled are mainly in the urban areas and you can only claim land that was taken away from you since 1913 – so Black people will still be without land. Also many are settling for cash. But cash goes! Land is forever!

Z M

The 13% was inherited from the English-speaking United Party's Natives Land Act of 1936. Before that, under the Brits, the Natives Land Act allocated only 7% to the African population! This was in 1913 – barely ten years after the British (with the help of many blacks who also fought on the other side) won the Boer War which they said they had partly been fighting to *protect the rights of black people!!!* South Africa was now part of the British Empire and a group of South Africans *of all races* went to London to plead for votes for everybody. They were totally ignored. What's new?!

S N

The land issue is huge and has to be sorted out properly all over Africa. In Zimbabwe it was only when the farms of whites (currently 1% of the population) were seized that the international media started to take notice!

K M

'We are the finest race in the world and the more of the world we inhabit the better it is for the human race'!!! That's what Englishman Cecil John Rhodes said.

It all started when Lobengulu, King of the Ndebele people, had the misfortune to get a visit from a certain Mr. Rhodes who openly said he had two ambitions:

1) to get filthy rich
2) to make Africa – if not the world! – British.

He made a fortune out of diamonds in Kimberley and then set up 'The British South Africa Company.' He gave it this name to pull the wool over people's eyes so they wouldn't realise all his shenanigans in Matabeleland which lay beyond the borders of South Africa. Then he entered into private 'treaties' with African kings which allowed him *with no further consultation* to open mines, make laws and enforce them with his own police etc. Any objection was called a rebellion and put down! Rhodes invaded the Shona territory with 500 British policeman and 200 men. Promised each of them gold-prospecting claims AND A 3 000 ACRE FARM! They raised the British flag at Fort Salisbury and took possession of the whole of Mashonaland. Lobengulu died of a broken heart! The whole country passed into white hands! Imagine if the opposite happened. It's time whites pinched themselves and woke up to their good fortune.

Hey Guys!
Know something? I'm not that interested in politics! Nor are my parents. Actually they were back there for a while. When Bill Clinton was in the White House, well in the Oval Office with you know who! I think he should have been impeached. You can't have the leader of the free world telling lies!

Another person in my seminar group is writing poetry. Marike says she wrote this one 'when I overheard two born-again white women in the library asking for the Miracles section.' The song she refers to is the Afrikaans national anthem which Nelson Mandela insisted be part of the new anthem in the new South Africa.

On OVERHEARING a REQUEST for 'MIRACLES' in the LIBRARY

the miracle is
how wondrously the sun leapt from
its high mundane place to
light up the face of the black librarian

the miracle is
that wet honey bloomed in those salty island cells
that the 'hordes' that soared over
those morning glory hills that red-circled day
thrummed shields of forgiveness
that from their throwing arms white doves flew
that hope bellied their banners

that green shoots still poke from our pencilled crosses
that the cotton that burst from the boll
still speaks such wisdom
that ten years in we still sing *Uit die Blou*

the mystery is
how patience can be so patient unwinding

the long bandages from our minds
breaking open our eyes

Later!

B M
Viva Nelson Mandela! Viva!
Viva Desmond Tutu!

L W L
Christian missionaries taught Africans to think everything white/
British was good and everything black/African was bad. They
filled them with self-loathing so they could 'save' them. Africa
has never recovered!

K M
Africans are regaining confidence and the West doesn't know
what to do about it. Just like the Apartheid Government in the
70's when Steve Biko and Black Consciousness made people
proud of being black. What did those who came to Africa to
civilise us do to Steve Biko? They chained him up naked to a grid
in a jail cell for 18 day and beat him to death.

B M
Viva Black Consciousness! Viva!
Viva the African Renaissance! Viva!

T G

'The African Renaissance' is a joke! In the 14th century Europeans looked back to Greek and Latin poets and artists and philosophers for inspiration. What can Africa look back on? Leaping about in animal skins, banging their tom-toms and droning on about the oral tradition which most of us are already heartily sick of!

J U

I am doing research for my PhD titled 'The Cultural Significance of Linda Lovelace and The Deep Throat Phenomenon: its Role in the Commodification of Fellatio in Middle America from 1972 –1979.' I would be grateful for more information on the oral tradition in Africa.

Z M

T G is typical of a certain breed of white: nothing good can come out of Africa! In Zimbabwe, which T G no doubt still calls Rhodesia (<u>Rhodes</u>-ia), Cecil Rhodes still rests in peace in the Matoba hills with amazing vistas of the land he plundered. Btw, the name Zimbabwe comes from a word meaning a royal palace. Around the time of the Boer War an Englishman called R N Hall (in case you think I'm making this up), throwing aside what he called 'all the filth and decadence of the Kaffir occupation' tried to prove that the Phoenicians built the royal palace but archaeologist have since shown conclusively that the Zimbabwes (there were about 200 of them!) were built by the Shona people around 1100 AD NOT the Phoenicians!

G H

When the Aswan dam was being built archaeologists found proof that the advanced Egyptian civilisation had actually begun in black Africa. The University of Chicago's Oriental Institute will have more. Sorry I don't have their web address but I'm sure you'll find it if you Google.

D M

'Do they not travel through the land, so that their hearts (and minds) may thus learn wisdom, and their ears may thus learn to hear? Truly it is not their eyes that are blind but their hearts which are in their breasts.' The Holy Koran S XX11 46. J G.

J K

Yebo! You are welcome in our land *inkosazana*.

Ponder this: people who by various way and means brought civilisation did not bring humanity. In central and southern Africa we speak many different languages all founded on the one common root 'ntu' meaning humanness.

You Americans you say 'Think Positive!' but, and I hope you will forgive me for saying this, your optimism seems only to be a means to a better *material* end. You are not a happy people. It seem to me that where the world has gone wrong is that it follows America where what you *have* is more important than what you *are*.

I salute you and all your family members. May God bless you. *Sala Kahle*!

B M
Yebo! Hamba Khale!

J K
America is constantly and aggressively selling its way of life, creating desires and therefore a market for its products so that its citizens can go on being fat and unhappy and go on consulting therapists, buying slimming drugs and devouring all the self-help books they keep churning out! I know BMW is not American but I worked on their account. Their advertising platform was something along the lines of 'BMW – for people who like to get their own way.' And what concept did they use to sell their aspirational product. *Ubuntu* of course!

K L
How true it is that man's value cannot be measured in material things. Allow me to misquote Dr Martin Luther King: 'people are being judged not by the colour of their skin but by the contents of their *wardrobes*.' (And if you are going to use that please do me the courtesy of acknowledging me as the source. Details available on request.)
The world is dying of consumption! Pun definitely intended. Especially apt since the dictionary calls it 'a wasting disease.' Waste and DIS-ease! And if anyone plans on using *that* please do me the courtesy etc. (see brackets above)

G H
Hi Mary-Anne!

Please can you tell me where's the best place to get some genuine American Levis? And how to get a Green Card. Africa is a mess!

T H

Who made the mess? Europe divided Africa like schoolboys dividing trading cards with no thought for what people living there wanted. And after 'independence' the Europeans said these false countries should buy weapons to protect their false borders. Who from? Us of course. How do we pay for them? We'll give you a loan. How do we pay the interest you'll charge? By producing the things we need and want. We'll pay you. (At a fixed price that suits us of course.)

'Kleptocracies' simply copy their kleptocratic example. Like white big shots, some of these black big shots take the money that should go to their own people, back to Europe to shop. Mainly for properties and – laugh out loud! – GOLD and DIAMONDS!!! In pre-colonial times communities had grown organically and run themselves according to the needs of the people.

J H

What a nerve the Western powers have preaching democracy to Africa! Were the governments they imposed on this continent democratic? Of course not or the people would have voted them out! Every colonial power ruled by decree, bureaucracy, intimidation. There wasn't a whiff of democracy! Yes, in pre-colonial times societies lived in balance with Nature and in balance with each other. They sorted their problems out by discussion and compromise.

T D

I agree. Democracy! What is democracy? Democracy is where 51 people say 'this is the way it should be done' and 49 (often understandably resentful if not angry!) people who may think entirely differently are told to shut up!

Democracy is where a couple of years before the next election, tough but necessary things are not done and other things that shouldn't be done, are. Anything to win votes. Democracy is where, if you don't toe the party line, you are kicked out of the party! Democracy is where the man with the smallest conscience, and the most money, wins! Nothing to do with how to make society and the world function better for the good of everybody.

Hey Guys!

Whoa! I'm not actually that mad about history. I mean that's all IN THE PAST. And the past is over. OK?! So, I say, let's just get on with today!

I'm still really hoping I'll get to meet Nelson Rolihlahla Mandela. Rolihlahla – what a funny name! It sounds like rolly-haha but Sipho in my creative writing groups says it means 'Trouble-maker'. That's kinda crazy! What trouble did Nelson Mandela ever make?!

Andy has borrowed his mother's SUV and he's taking me into the jungle to see some lions and tigers and alligators and things. Can't wait! And I've invited him back to Disneyland. Fingers crossed!☺

Reckon I've gotten enough on my blog so I'm good to go. My seminar leader hopes it 'will strongly demonstrate the power of

the internet for people to communicate with each other.'
Fingers crossed and crossed again for a good grade!!!
Love you guys!
STAY COOL!

Mary Anne.
PS:
Jabu in my seminar asked me to post this little story he wrote:

Umveli and the Meaning of Life

When Umveli was little and wore nothing but a cotton vest to cover his small round belly, he would sit on the old man's lap and, silently gazing into the ancient face scribbled with the joy and the anguish of many years, would listen to the legends and the stories he told of his people. And though he did not understand all the words, he loved the sound of them and the way the sentences rose and fell with the old man's breath as he spoke.

Through many summers and winters, through the long short pants he so proudly wore when he was starting classes and the short long pant he so shamefully wore when he was finishing school, Umveli would stop and talk to the old man and would feel in his heart a longing for the contentment that seemed to sit about him like the mists on the morning hills.

It was only natural then that when the envelope came Umveli should run and take it to the old man.

'Tatamkhulu I have completed my education,' said Umveli and great was the excitement in his voice.

The old man's smile was slow.

'Look Tata I have the certificate!' And from the envelope he took the thick sheet of paper with the gold printing and his name written in black ink.

'It is a fine thing, this paper,' said the old man. 'It means that you know some things from some books that some people think you should know. But,' he said tapping his forehead, 'it doesn't mean that you are finished with learning.'

'What do you mean, Tata?' asked Umveli, his heart heavy with disappointment.

'Can you tell me the meaning of life?' asked the old man.

Umveli thought for a long time. If I say one thing, the old man will say another. And if I say another thing, the old man will come up with a third.

'No' he said finally.

'That is a wise answer,' said the old man, 'Knowing that you don't know is the beginning of wisdom.'

'So what is the meaning of life?' asked Umveli well pleased with himself.

'That you will have to find out for yourself!' said Tatamkhulu.

'But how Tata?' asked the boy.

'You must go on a journey and the people you meet and the things you see, the animals in the bush and the birds in the sky, the fish in the rivers and the rivers too, they will tell you. And when you know the answer you must come back and tell it to me.'

So Umveli went home and told his mother what the old man had said.

'The meaning of life?!' his mother laughed, 'The meaning of life is to get a job!'

But because she loved him and knew that he wanted to follow the old man's advice, she gave him her blessing and the money she had saved over many months for a smart outfit for his first day of work. And so Umveli set off on his journey which took him through many thoughts in many places.

'What is the meaning of life?' he asked the mountains and the mountains replied majestically, 'Life … Life … Life', which might have been an answer or simply the echo of his words.

He asked a man sitting cross legged on the grass. 'Aum,' said the man.

He asked the stream but the stream just babbled incoherently and went to join the river.

He asked the river who, rushing by, said 'Life is flow. Or flux.'

Which is what Heraclitus had said two and a half thousand years before.

Then the river bank, hearing the question answered: 'Life is having things pass you by.'

But, like many banks, the bank was known to be slippery.

Don't listen to him, said a woman weaving a basket from the reeds that grew by the river. 'Life is what you make it.'

Sometimes as he went along these untrodden paths Umveli carried a longing in his heart for his mother and for his brothers and sisters and for the father he had hardly known.

But the sky consoled him with a sunny smile saying, 'It is only when you know what it is to be blue that you can really know what happiness is.'

'Yes,' said the beggar who had the answer in the palm of his hand, 'life is a coin with two faces.'

'But it's what's in the middle that really counts,' proffered the sandwich seller.

'Life is humbug!' said an old professor taking the wrapper off a black and white sweet and popping it into his mouth.

Then a scientist told him 'Life is an atom,' which was what Democritus had said around 300BC. But that idea too was bombed.

He asked a nun who said, 'Life is a habit.'

But a beggar going through the garbage said, 'Life is rubbish.'

'And a mess,' said an army officer sitting down to a meal.

'And a muddle,' said the woman sorting out the washing.

Umveli had been travelling for many days and many nights and though he had travelled many miles he did not think he had got very far. He did not seem any closer to answering the question the old man had set him.

So he put it to the lake and the lake calmly replied, 'The meaning of life is to live to the full.' But the stone Umveli flung into the water said, 'Life is creating ripples' and disappeared.

'Life is a breeze,' said a small wind coming through the trees.

Then he asked a cave and the cave just yawned and said, 'I'm in the dark.'

But the woman who drew the pictures on the cave wall said, 'Life is something you draw from inside you.'

And the children sliding down the hillside on bits of cardboard giggled, 'Life is a game.'

'Nonsense,' said the rock, 'Life is hard.'

Though a feather floating by disagreed.

So he asked the woman with a bucket on her head. 'Life!' she laughed as the water sloshed and slapped the metal sides. 'Life is a container. What you put in is what you get out.' Which is something that the Duke of Edinburgh who lived in Buckingham Palace with his wife the Queen had once said. 'But then too,' the woman stumbled on 'life can be wasted.'

The *donga* said, 'Life is a rut.'

'But you can get out of it,' said the gravedigger climbing out of a hole in the ground with his shovel.

'Life is too short,' said the Tokoloshe which is also what the Sophists believed a long time ago.

'And too busy,' said the bee.

'Life is just the same old shit day after day,' said the dung beetle with his nose in the air.

A little disconcerted by that Umveli looked up at a tree and asked the crow who said he would show him directly and then flew off in a straight line.

So he asked the owl, known for his wit, what the meaning of life was. 'To woo!' said the owl hooting for Umveli to get out of the way or he'd be late for his date.

'Life is about adapting to change,' said a chameleon turning scarlet with embarrassment.

'Life is a bitch,' said the dog. And then he died.

And sometimes when Umveli looked at the horizon which he never seemed to reach he wondered whether the meaning of life was something that was always there but that you could never get to.

And one day when he was sitting in the rondavel of an old Xhosa man he heard the high-pitched whispers whistling from the mud walls of the small round hut. He had heard that sound before.

And the old Xhosa man said, 'That is the sound of the *Nomatotlo* – the small spirits that go all around the world to gather knowledge and bring it to you.'

Then Umveli remembered that he'd heard the sound before in the computer room at school. 'But you have to know how to get them to give you that knowledge,' the old man continued.

'Just like the internet,' said the boy very excited but the Xhosa man did not know what he was talking about.

So Umveli went to a cyber café and the internet said, 'Search me!'

And Umveli began to wonder if indeed that was what he should do but then he thought about the old man. If the answer could be found sitting in one place then why did the old man send him on a journey. He was sure that IT was not the answer.

And then one evening when the sun was setting and he and a Khoi Khoi man were walking side by side in the long leaning of the light, the Khoi Khoi saw that Umveli was always in his shadow. And the Khoi Khoi halted and told the boy to take several paces and stop. And he did. 'Now you are free,' said the Khoi Khoi. 'No man must walk in the shadow of another. Like all things that are born and all things that die, like all things that blossom and all things that fade, you have a right to be on this earth and to be who you are – which is unlike anyone else.' And he bade him goodbye and a safe journey home.

His mother was overjoyed to see the son who was so dear to her heart and set about preparing a feast to celebrate. But first Umveli had to go and see the old man.

With the passing of the days his hair had turned the colour of the thorns on the acacia tree, and with the passing of the nights his eyes had become half moons on the wane.

'I have been expecting you my son,' he said. 'Now, tell me: what is the meaning of life?'

And Umveli waited a moment and then he took a deep breath and began. 'I saw many things, Tata, and met the creatures of the earth and the birds of the sky, the women who worked in the country and the men who lived in the cities but each one had a different answer.' And he told him all that he had experienced.

And when he had finished the old man asked, 'And all this time while you were listening to all these men and women and all these creatures and the mountains and the rivers what were you doing?'

'Nothing, Tata. I was just being myself.'

'Ah,' said the old man nodding his head sagely, 'So you do know the meaning of life.'

And he gave a deep contented sigh for his days left on this earth were not many.

7

A cat asleep on a carport is startled awake by the rushing clatter of sudden crusher being delivered on North Coast Road. The road does not in fact run along the coast; one can however catch a glimpse of the Indian Ocean from Connaught Bridge which crosses the Umgeni – 'place of the sweet thorn trees' – as it flows past Springfield. Several generations ago Indian women would sit here in the soft green shade, watching over their mules and donkeys at water troughs while the men caught the tram to take their freshly harvested garden produce to market.

Now no trams run and Springfield is an industrial estate and the only people who spend time on the riverside are the cardboard collectors: women who carry babies on their backs and unwieldy piles of flattened cartons on their heads that will earn them a few tiny mustard-colour coins – 8c per kilogram.

The women and their little ones sleep there among the bushes and wash in the river. How do they manage when the blood comes? Such pain it bore me every month after they sedated me and took me from the farm to the hospital in Port Elizabeth. It became for many long years, almost unbearable, the pain. And to no purpose.

The street starts to dip more steeply here but today the scrap metal man has no trouble keeping his trolley steady. If the weight is excessive or unbalanced he could buckle a wheel or drag to one side. It can be hard going uphill. Harder still coming down as gravity's forcefulness pulls faster than is safe. A man needs strong muscles to keep control.

On the day I died he had struggled with his load trying to achieve the equilibrium needed to advance safely. The items of scrap he had collected were awkwardly shaped, too wide, too long, too heavy. One of them, an iron rod with a sharp point, stuck out dangerously and had wounded him in the temple. The wound now has healed and left a scar that looks like the underside of a roughly stitched button on an army greatcoat.

Florence, the domestic worker – once known simply as 'the girl' – at number 46, is putting Madam's son's soiled clothes – rugby gear, Nike track suits, several pairs of Calvin Klein boxer shorts and endless dark socks – into the Miele washing machine. She hears the bright quartet of notes above the shrieking wheels of the scrap metal man's trolley and recalls that sultry day when she had heard, above the noise of the Kankane birds nesting in the wild fig tree, a sudden running, the screech of brakes, the echo of a scream, the high cry of the child.

#46

The Kankane Birds

There are many hills in kwaZulu Natal and they roll, more or less green and ever more thickly populated, to the very edge of the city of Durban. Spilling down the closest of these is a settlement of over 50 000 people. This agglomeration of cobbled-together homes has developed because, like their white neighbours, the residents want to live close to jobs and schools and opportunities rather than in the distant townships and the costly transport Apartheid had assigned them.

There are a surprising number of trees left among theses higgledy-piggledy dwellings, some called Toyotas because of the stencilled name on the packing case walls, others are skilfully crafted of mud and saligna. There are birds and the sound of cocks crowing throughout the day. Washing flaps dry in the warmth and the breezes, and sometimes at night when the moon hangs yellow between the clumps of tall bamboo and the hillside is lambent with the amber light of oil lamps and candles, one can catch one's breath at the beauty of it.

To Florence, though the wind may blow through and the rain fall in, her tiny dwelling is not a shack, a hovel, an *umjondolo;* it is a cocoon, lined with the undemanding presence of small familiar things, infused with the subtle scent of her children's warm bodies and a slight smell of paraffin oil and of cooking. It is home.

Florence comes back from work early on a Friday and is resting on the bed she shares with her two young daughters. Her son, her first born, Philemon, sleeps with his uncle and boy cousins in another place further down the path.

Tautly pulled and running above her bed from end to end of the room is a length of nylon rope. This is the family wardrobe. Clothes, washed and ironed, are draped neatly over it. A tin bath leans against a wall, a black iron stands on its heel on the thin floral plastic cloth which covers an arrangement of boxes that serves as a chest of drawers. There is a small Primus stove on which the iron is heated and some of the cooking done.

Next to the bed on the fifties-style dresser, cream with black handles, stands an empty Nugget shoe polish tin which acts as a candleholder. In a glass jar various coloured toothbrushes, their bristles flared from use, lean like scant bright flowers. An old wind-up clock ticks.

On one of the dresser drawers is a faded promotional sticker for a popular deodorant: 'I love my Mum.' Florence remembers the day Philemon brought it home, keeping it flat between the pages of a schoolbook.

'Close your eyes!' he'd said.

He had struggled a little trying to peel off the protective paper, pushing away any help from the more dextrous fingers of his sisters.

'No peeping!'

And then he had stuck it, slightly askew, onto the chipped cream paint.

'Open!'

'*Hau!*' she had called, clapping her hands and holding them pressed together.

'*Hau*! That is very nice! Me, I am a lucky woman!'

And Philemon, whose name means 'one who is affectionate', had glowed.

It is a mild afternoon; the sun has worked its way across the ridge and long fingers of buttery yellow light fall through the gaps in the walls. Florence glances at the clock. It is a little before three. Her daughters have been back from school for two hours already and she can hear them playing hopscotch a little way down the path.

Now the high school learners are coming home. She listens amongst their chatter and laughter for Philemon. And there he is. Her heart warms. How different he sounds from just a few months ago. Already his voice is rich and lovely, like his father's.

It was the voice that seduced Florence. She wonders where he is now, how many children, other than her three, he has fathered. Does he even remember that he shares a birthday with his son who will be sixteen soon? She is saving up to buy a football shirt for his birthday. He is good at football. He practices a lot. One day he will be a star, he says.

And there Philemon is coming through the door. He is so tall now he has to stoop.

'*S'bona* Ma!'

'*Yebo, kunjani?*'

'Ma, can I take the key for Uncle's room?'

'What do you want to do in that room?'

'Homework Ma!'

'Homework on Friday? You think I am stupid,' she laughs, 'I know you. You want to play the radio.'

'*Hau*! Ma!' he laughs taking the key. 'The homework is too much!'

'Tch!' she clicks her tongue. 'And when the batteries are finished?'

'*Haibo!*' he says, 'stay and rest now Ma.'

She smiles. She knows her son, he is a man, he doesn't think ahead.

Outside, a little way down the path, a 14-year old girl is waiting with two school bags. Her face is lovely: wide smooth forehead, high cheekbones, dimples when she smiles. Her hips are broad, her thighs plump, the buttons of her gingham school dress strain across her chest. She faces across the path but her eyes look sideways, towards where Philemon is coming out of the door, holding up the key, triumphant. He puts a finger to his lips, shhh. Pretty turns towards him rounding her shoulders and hunching shyly forward with her arms twisted around each other and her fingers locked together. She looks down briefly, slides her eyes towards him. A slow smile lights her face. Philemon draws her to him for a moment. Then he shoulders the school bags and takes her warm damp hand in his and they walk down the path, past the cotton nappies flapping on the wash line, past the house with the door with MUSGR… sign-written up its length, past the three-room dwelling where Philemon's aunties and some of their neighbours sit doing beadwork, making Aids brooches in bright colours for the tourists.

Philemon unlocks the door and the two go inside. The mud walls have been lined with flattened blue and green Long Life milk cartons to insulate and decorate the room. Behind the door is a poster of Orlando Pirates football team. There is a chair, a table with a basin and jug, candles stuck in Black Label beer bottles, soap, matches, a comb and a mirror. A shelf holds neat piles of folded blankets. A narrow bed with a sponge mattress is covered with a leopard print bedspread. Under the bed is a tin trunk.

Philemon takes off his school blazer, hangs it over the back of the chair, hooks a finger under the band of his tie and pulls it, still knotted, over his head. He takes off his shoes and socks and undoes the top few buttons of his school shirt. Then he pulls the trunk from under the bed, lifts out the radio and turns it on. 'P Four,' the announcer says in a smooth seductive voice 'The heaaaaaaaart and soooooooooul of KZN.' Pretty, propped up on one elbow, stretches out a little on the Uncle's bed. She can't believe that she is really here. Alone with Philemon. She used to dream about him. Then two months ago he started walking her home from school. Now her friends tease her about her *sthandwa sami*, her sweetheart.

Philemon puts the radio next to the bed and sits down beside her. Then, quietly, confidently, he takes off her shoes and socks and places them neatly next to his. Pretty smiles; it makes her feel married. Philemon strokes her hair and smiles into her eyes. The song on the radio tells her 'You are the one, baby…you are my first, my only loving baby.' Pretty eases down onto the mattress and looks up at him with luminous eyes. Philemon lifts her chin and presses his mouth to hers; he puts his other hand on her chest and slides it down the front of her dress, the buttons pop open and there is his hand under the white vest with the little pink bow on it and he is holding the warmth and rippling weight of her young breast in his cupped hand, bringing his mouth towards it, breathing in the perfume of her body. Pretty closes her eyes, and raises herself up closer into him, feeling her whole being loosen and when he asks her softly 'OK?' her body has already reached beyond where her mind had ever thought to go. 'OK,' she whispers.

When they left the room – Philemon being careful to lock the door and put the key in his pocket – they picked their way down the steep gulched track towards the *Spaza* shop.

He has put his tie on inside out. She has lost the second button of her dress. But what did those things matter when Philemon's head can touch the sun, when he can cross valleys in a single stride, swim oceans with a dozen strokes; when Pretty can hear the finch in the banana tree sing so joyously, can see the eye markings in the velvet blue of the looping butterfly, can feel her feet in their flat black school shoes floating above the shiny protrusion on the rocky path.

At the *Spaza* shop they say a lingering goodbye, their fingers hooked, their foreheads pressed together as though a drawbridge were meeting and feelings were flowing freely across. Then, breaking the link of their fingers at the last possible moment, they turned to go their separate ways, she to the house of her grandmother, her guardian, he back to his family.

His sisters and cousins run to greet him. He picks up the smallest one, twirls her around.

'Me! Me!' the others cry, their little heads bouncing up and down as they jump.

'Wait!' he says catching his mother's proud eye.

There is *phuthu* porridge and cabbage for supper and Philemon's appetite is keen.

'*Yo!*' his auntie says watching him eat.

'*Hau mamkhulu!* I am hungry.'

'Let him eat, he is a growing boy,' says Florence.

'*Haibo* Ma!' he says, 'I am a man.'

The women smile. They notice that he whistles while cleaning the pots, his wrist turning with electric speed as the steel wool scours round and round, skimming the surfaces to silver.

'You'll rub holes into the pots!' they tease, shaking their heads.

As Pretty turned to go home to her grandmother's house a boy who had followed them to the *Spaza* shop fell in step with her and offered to carry her schoolbag. She refused his help. But he persisted, tugging at the strap.

'No!' she said, flinging her fingers at him, 'Go away!'

'Why? Don't you like me anymore?'

'I never liked you!'

'Oh! So now you only have eyes for your *sthandwa sami*, your sweetheart!'

'*Hamba!* Go away! Don't come near me.'

'How near did he come to you then, eh? Tell me that?'

'Go away!'

'*Senikenaya ocasini?*' and he made a circle with his left thumb and index finger; pumped his right index finger in and out. 'Have you?'

'It has nothing to do with you!'

'So you have then!'

'Get out of my sight!'

'*Hau! Isifebe! Isifebe.*'

'*Isifebe! Isifebe!*'

Pretty was distraught; she pushed him away, shouted at him. People were staring, gathering around, talking loudly, what was going on?

'*Isifebe! Isifebe!*'

'Why are they calling you this terrible thing?' the grandmother shouts, eyes ablaze, running out to Pretty stumbling down the path amidst the taunts.

'From what fire is this smoke coming?' the grandmother tugged at Pretty's school bag.

'What have you done?' the grandmother snatched Pretty's arm and twisted it hard.

'Talk!' she cried grabbing her by the shoulders and shaking her. But Pretty would not talk.

'Talk!' the old woman dug iron fingernails into Pretty's forearm.

But though Pretty screamed in pain she spoke not a word.

Anger flamed in every fold of the old woman's face. She lifted her hand and whipped her fingers at the girl's head. Pretty raised her arms to shield herself but the old woman's hand struck her with a burning sting. 'Talk!' the old woman, shouted. But though she screamed Pretty said nothing. The old woman hit the young girl again and again. The air resounded with slapping and screaming and the shouts of those who had gathered around. It was only when her wrath had finally consumed itself that the old woman stopped and, howling like an injured dog, dropped to the ground and began to rock back and forth on her haunches. Pretty, sobbing with pain, ran into the house, pulled a blanket around herself and tossed about on the hard mud floor until finally she turned her face to the wall and the sobbing subsided.

The women of the neighbourhood gathered around the old lady, talking and gossiping into the night, about this thing and about men, and how they took advantage of women, and how they abandoned them and left them with a child, maybe three or four even, and no money.

One old *inkosikazi* said it had all started when the British were in charge and told every man he had to pay poll tax. On the farms the men had had no money and little need of it. Now they had to leave the women and children and go and work on the mines and in the cities. Far away from their wives, far away from their children, far away from their cattle and their kraals, they were lonely and full of longing. And the longing for the warmth of a woman's body was stronger than the pull of their traditions and they took new women to their beds and at Christmas came home to their wives who bore them yet another child nine months later. Others said no, that was an excuse, it was just the way men were. Not taking any responsibility.

Pretty lay with the blanket pulled over her head, making believe that Philemon was there with her, wrapping his body around her, stroking her head, soothing away this hurt, this misery. She made a clearing in her thoughts, a space where it was just the two of them folded in together and, finally, she fell asleep.

When the others had gone the old woman, her *gogo*, overwrought, stayed outside wrapped in a *kaross*, listening amongst the crowded shacks to the clink of bottles, and the burst of big male laughter as the last of the men's Friday night parties died down and her thoughts began to stray and slowly, softly she started to sing. Sad sweet songs of longing and of home. Of the farm among the green kwaZulu hills where the little ones ran in the sunshine and breathed fresh clean air. Of the young women, with the big rectangular tins on their heads, chattering up the path in the twilight and the slap, slap of the water against the silvery sides. Of stories murmured around the flap and fall of the fire, of drifting off to sleep with the sweet smell of wood smoke, of waking to the warm fragrance of sunlight trapped in straw. She held onto the long buzzing notes of her songs, drawing them, from the deep places within her, out into the cool night air.

If this thing happened there in the country, the girl would tell her mother how the boy had seduced her and if the mother saw that it was true she would send a messenger to the boy's kraal and arrangements would be made for the *ukuhlawula*, the compensatory cow. And if the agreement was broken the matter was taken further, even to the chief. The young ones were respectful of their traditions and the ancestors. But here! Here they just roamed around doing nothing while the transistor pumped them full of sex talk and rude words. And here the only higher authority was the police and they wouldn't be interested. Unless…

Most people lie in on Saturday but Philemon wakes early, so full of energy that he feels he would explode if he had to remain in the fuggy room with his uncle snoring on the bed – *Pretty and his bed!* – and his cousins curled up in blankets sleeping on the floor. The sun has not yet come over the ridge. He dresses quickly and leaps like a goat down the rough path to the sports field. The *Kankane*, their long beaks sharp as assegais, leave dark green tracks in the dew-silvered grass. Philemon runs onto the field. The *Kankane* lift their grey bodies, big as cats, and with loud vulgar squawks, fly towards the houses on the hill. He is feeling on top of the world and, scanning the AIDS awareness billboard 'I have had sex. Will I die?' laughs out loud. 'Eh *mamparra*!' he feels like shouting to the whole wide world, 'Of course you won't die! You will live forever!'

The *gogo* too rises early, shouting to Pretty to get up.

'You have one last chance! Talk!'

Pretty says nothing.

'*Lungile*, alright,' says the *gogo* 'you won't talk. We will do the test.'

Pretty draws her breath in sharply. This, the virginity test, with a neighbour as witness, is what she has been dreading. Unless a miracle happens she is finished.

Wearing only her vest, she lies propped up on her elbows, her pelvic floor lifted. Her grandmother spoons the water into her and watches as though she were gauging the level in a cup. Pretty tenses every muscle in her body. Perhaps if she concentrated hard enough she could be saved. Oh God, please let the water stay, she prays. The grandmother peers. She can see no water. The seconds pass.

The grandmother stares down at the sinful girl. The girl stares up at the roof. Please God! Please God!

The waiting time is past. The water has not appeared; it has entered into her, just as the boy had. '*Hau!*' the grandmother cries. 'So it is true!'

'This girl has lost her most precious possession!' screams the neighbour. 'He must pay!'

'How did it happen?' the *gogo* yells 'Did he force you with a gun?'

Pretty opens her eyes wide 'Of course not!' she whimpers.

'With a knife then?'

Pretty stares at them in disbelief. And then appalled that they could think such things, astounded that the transcending joy that had filled her body, the happiness that filled her heart could have drawn forth such anger and ugliness, exasperated by their blindness, she bursts into tears.

Philemon sprints across the field, throws a somersault, sprints again, throws another. His blood is pulsing: Pretty…Pretty… Pretty. And now he races around the field, overwhelming jubilation streaming from his body. He runs faster. Now he is running around the edge of the field, around the edge of the world. Faster and faster. He'll get really, really fit. He'll practice every day. The Buccaneers, Orlando Pirates, will see how good he is. Bucs will sign him. Bucs will give him lots of money. Big bucks! He will pay *lobola*. He will marry Pretty. He will buy his mother a beautiful house! He will buy his sisters cell phones that take photographs!

The Grandmother marches Pretty to the Police Station on the main road just beyond the settlement. The police doctor examines Pretty and confirms the results of the *gogo*'s test. The officer on duty writes down the name of the accused and the charge. When they get home the grandmother, with the help of a neighbour, writes a list. When it is done she wraps an elaborate *doek* around her head, throws her shoulders back and turns to Pretty.

'While I am out you must pack your things.'

Philemon 'Fast Medicine' Khumalo is in stunning form! Sporting his snappy new corn-rows hairstyle in front of a packed FNB Stadium, Orlando Pirates' brand new signing is hot! Within 30 seconds of the kick-off he left-foots the ball straight past the keeper and into the goal… the crossbar strains, the posts lurch, the ball bulges the back of the net, sweet and true, the capacity crowd roars approval. 'Fast Medicine' indeed! But there is no letting up for the *wunderkind*! And here he is again taking the cross, and this time he heads it right over the keeper! Goooooooooooal! the Super Sports commentator screams. Philemon turns to show his number to the cameras: the famous No 17 shirt has been reinstated. And who better than 'Fast Medicine'! But this is no flash in the pan; today the most talented striker in the country goes through the defence like a dose of salts! Can he do it? Can he get another goal? Yes, indeed… Man of the Match, Philemon Khumalo, has scored a hat-trick! The crowd cannot contain themselves, the stadium, cross-stitched with X'ed forearms, throbs with the stamping feet and the vuvuzelas of the Buccaneers' supporters! The skull and crossbones is tops. But this is no ordinary match, this is the Cup Final and Pirates have won, under their new Captain, Philemon 'Fast Medicine' Khumalo! He rips off his shirt, and with arms raised, index fingers pointing heavenwards, does a victory lap in front of his adoring fans, and here is Bafana Bafana's hot new cap…*Haibo!*…Here is Bafana

Bafana's internationally renowned Captain! holding the golden trophy aloft. And South Africa has won the World Cup! The President catches his eye, nods his smiling approval, the crowd rush towards him. Jostling bodyguards, they lift him, and carry him aloft to the VIP parking where his brand new silver *waBenzi* convertible waits. Philemon 'Fast Medicine' Khumalo who will go down as one of the greatest sporting legends of all-time, turns to his passenger, his *sithandwa sami*, his sweetheart, his inspiration, the beautiful, the one and only Pretty!

The *gogo* strides up the hill, her long shiny shins snapping like scissors beneath her blue *tshwetshwe* skirt, her elaborately tied headscarf awry, her eyes aflame, shouting, shouting, shouting. Florence, bewildered, comes out of her room, people gather.

'Your son, your son!' shouts the old lady. 'You must pay!'

There must be compensation for this thing that has befallen her charge, the *gogo* cries. The boy's family must pay the damages that she has listed. They must uphold the traditions. She will see to it, or else. The old lady is shouting so loudly that eventually, just to keep her quiet, just to make her go away, Florence agrees to pay. The old lady stops shouting, goes home muttering.

Philemon 'Fast Medicine' Khumalo is walking home. As he nears his mother's room he sees the whole extended family sitting outside talking loudly to each other. His mother is in tears.

'Where will I get the money for the things she wants?' she cries. 'Where will I get the R52 for the *Umfundisi*? Where will I get the R70 for the travel expenses?'

The aunties cluck their tongues '*Haai Suka!* Travel expenses? From where? From the *Spaza* shop?' and they fall about with laughter. But Florence finds no comfort in their mirth. 'Where will I get a cow? Where will I get two goats?'

'*Woza* Philemon!' someone calls. And now he begins to understand something of what it is all about.

'Did you do this thing?' she asks.

'It's not like that, Ma!' Philemon says, 'I love her!'

'They are demanding compensation,' Florence cries.

'But how can that be?' Philemon asks, 'She loves me!'

'I have no money!' Florence cries.

'But she loves me!' Philemon insists, 'You will see! She loves me!'

'*Asanimali!*' Florence wails, 'I have no money!'

What Florence and Philemon did not know was that a docket had already been opened. Name of the accused: PHILEMON KHUMALO. Charge: RAPE.

Although there was still a week before the long school holidays, the *gogo* has decided that there were more important lessons to be learnt and it was with a heavy heart that Pretty sat in the minibus taxi winding its way over the hills to the family kraal.

She gets out with the few gifts she has brought and greets the members of her extended family. The little ones shy away and hide in their mothers' skirts; the older girls stare in awe at this city girl with the slidy eyes who has been so disgraced.

Through the days and weeks she spent on the farm Pretty watched from the sidelines as the girls prepared for the annual reed dance, the *Umkhosi womhlanga*, when, bare-breasted young girls in bright beads and short skirts from all over Zululand would present a reed to the King at the Royal Palace. But only those who pass the virginity test.

Every night when Pretty lay down in her sleeping place she went to the clearing in her mind and felt Philemon's comforting arms firm about her, the press of his body. And every morning when the *Kankane* birds woke her, felt his absence, and felt a deep hollowness there just beneath her ribs.

And when Philemon went to sleep, his mind too was filled with Pretty as he crossed off the passing of another day that shortened the time till school started and he would see her again.

It was with just one day to go before the deadline the old lady has set, that the *gogo*'s messenger was sent to Florence to demand the damages. Florence was distraught; she could not keep her promise. When the *gogo* was informed she went straight to the police station. It was time to take action.

And that very night when Philemon's waiting had dwindled to mere hours and Florence was lying awake with worry, the police arrived. With flashlights tunnelling the dark and barking dogs straining to be let loose, they banged on the uncle's door, 'Philemon Khumalo we have a warrant for your arrest!'

Amidst the masculine commotion and the high keen of a woman in pain, he feels the cold steel of the handcuffs click around his wrists, sees his mother's wide wet mouth, the hurt in her wide wet eyes and he cries out 'But she loves me!'

'Shurrup!' Their boots kick at his legs, their rough hands push his head down, bundle him into the police van. From the back of the van that bumps over the rough track Philemon sees, through the caged window, the AIDS awareness billboard lit from the highway. They tell you you can die, he thinks. They don't tell you you will go to jail!

There was a time when a worried woman might wait up all night for a husband to return, when a son would never arrive for a ruined family occasion, when little ones would cry for a mother who never came home. Then distraught relatives would go from place to place looking until the missing one would be found. In prison. Or in the morgue. Or would not be found at all. In those times when so many were jailed for not having with them 'the pass' – the documentation that allowed them to be in this area – the arrest of an employee could provoke sympathy and sometimes outrage amongst the white population. But this no longer applied. People are 'up in arms' about the crime rate and 'innocent until proved guilty' holds little sway. 'Lock 'em up and throw away the key!' 'Bring back the death penalty!' And rape is the most abhorred crime of all. So Florence does not share her burden with her employer. It is with a heavy heart that she tidies the Madam's son's bedroom; hangs up the clothes he leaves strewn on the floor; stacks the books and papers cluttering his desk. He is the same age as Philemon. She keeps a photograph of her precious boy in her wallet, glances at it during snatched moments of the day and the small sleepless hours of the night so that his fresh eager face can keep her going and give her the courage to squeeze a few hours off here, a day there, 'to sort some papers.'

Florence climbs out of the minibus taxi opposite the Regional Court and walks past the vendors selling sweets, loose cigarettes, single bananas and enters the building. 'DANGER:' says a sign in the foyer 'SLIPPERY FLOORS.' The security people doing body checks ask 'Any fire arms? Gas bombs? Any car mirrors?'

'Car mirrors?' asks a white lady.

'For to take photographs.'

Florence walks the long corridors full of smart men and women with voluminous briefcases clip-clopping, smiling, chatting. Outside the courtroom where the bail application is to be heard three beefy white men are passing papers around among themselves. On the wall above them is an advertising poster: 'You haven't won till you've sunk the Black: Black Label Beer.' Florence enters the court and sits as close to the front as she can. A female Indian lawyer with a gold nose ring is talking on her cell phone. 'Ok my darling!' Gold bracelets jangle on her other arm as she hands out her business card from a brass card case. A policeman sits in a swivel chair polishing his teeth with the lid of his ball-point pen. The prosecutor is searching through the pink-ribboned manila files she keeps in a carton covered in Christmas wrapping. The defence lawyer, provided by the Legal Aid Board, is paging through a dilapidated law book. On the wall is a calendar donated by 'Wheel and Steel.' Someone has changed 'Steel' to 'Steal.'

The magistrate enters. The court rises. There is movement on the stairs that lead up from the police holding cells. Florence leans forward and there he is! Philemon in his blue trainers and a clean striped shirt. Florence feels her heart expand, her eyes fill. He looks well. But now he is no longer Philemon, her son, her first-born, he is The Accused. The interpreter, an older man in a dark suit and white shirt, frayed at the cuffs, stands next to him to translate the proceedings into Zulu.

'Are you aware of the seriousness of the crime?'

The interpreter puts the question to Philemon.

Philemon replies and a chuckle ripples through the crowd.

The magistrate bangs the gavel.

'Order!'

'What is his reply?'

'She loves me,' says the interpreter, baring a half-moon of yellow teeth.

'Order!'

Philemon scans the gallery for his mother.

'Does he have any assets? A house?'

'No.'

'A car?'

'No.'

'A few cows, goats?'

'No.'

'Maybe a chicken?' The gallery titters. Philemon smiles at his mother.

The defence lawyer knows that bail is very rarely given in cases of rape and is only granted under 'exceptional circumstances' and submits that his client wants to be given bail so that he can continue with his studies.

The Prosecutor says he can go to school in prison, is he aware of that?

No, he isn't.

The gavel comes down. Bail refused.

Florence sits, hands clenched. Not having the money to pay any sort of bail, she has been spared the shame of failing her son. All she can do is pray that her boy will be strong and come through this thing. 'Don't worry. I'm fine,' he mouths as he passes in front of her, back down the stairs into the holding cells of C R Swart. The very name chills her blood; she has heard terrible things about what can happen to a man in this and other prisons.

Inspector Ntuli from the Child Protection Unit drives the police truck up the rough road into the informal settlement and parks where he can. He is not happy about this case, State v Philemon Khumalo. His female colleagues in the prosecutor's office have interviewed the girl but got nothing out of her. Now he must go and see her. He used to have to treat the accuser's evidence with caution but now with more and more rape charges and few convictions it is very different. The pressure is on. The women are marching! The women are crying out! The government must do something! He must get a conviction; he must get the girl to talk.

People greet him with curiosity as he picks his way down to the dwelling.

The girl is not there. 'You must wait,' says the *gogo*, and she sits there calmly chatting about the farm where she grew up and how there was space to keep a milk cow and grow cabbages and pumpkins and beans. And mealies that bore three cobs apiece. And how a woman could get strong just stamping mealies. And how the *phuthu* was yellow and rich and full of goodness. Not like this white shop-bought maize meal you had now. He feels like yelling at her to go back there then! Grow her mealies! Make her *phuthu*! But he has to humour her. 'Don't they add vitamins and minerals?' he asks.

'*Hayi suka*!' she says 'Add! What is this add! This maize meal is empty, even the cockroaches don't bother with it. The children's hair is rusting; their skin is turning grey. The food is no good.'

She keeps talking but the girl does not come.

A week later when Inspector Ntuli arrives for another appointment again the girl is not there. This time the neighbour, a social worker, chats to him and tells him the girl has been traumatised and must go for counselling. He hears giggling from inside the house. He knows that many people, Indian as well as black, use the 'traditional damages' to try to get money but, if there is a formal charge, the case has to work its way through the legal system. The giggling gets louder. Inspector Ntuli shakes his head. The law says a male who has sex with a girl under 16, even if she is compliant, can be charged with statutory rape. And people like him have to drive these cases.

Back in the city the inspector pops into the government clinic on the ground floor of the building where he works, to chat to the woman dispensing contraceptive pills and condoms free of charge.

'When I was young,' she says, smoothing her blouse. 'There was no sex before marriage.'

'And after marriage?' he teases.

'Tch!' she shakes her head, smiling. 'But now! The girls too they want it. And young! They must be 14 years before they can get contraception. But what can I do? If a girl is 13 or even 12 and wants it, I can't turn her away! I can't be responsible for a baby having a baby!'

'I don't know!' says the inspector 'There's Customary Law, there's Statutory Law and then there is you!'

'What you mean – *mina*?' she laughs

'Why are you giving these things to little girls? So they can have sex, ne? And then the boys get arrested! And everyone shouts RAPE!'

'Well what can *I* do about that? The government must sort it out!'

In the foyer of the Child Protection Unit is a sepia poster of a little boy standing on a suitcase reaching up to kiss a little girl. The caption says 'First Love.' Inspector Ntuli shakes his head, 'This little *intombazane* will be going to the clinic for contraception too one of these days. And then this little *umfana* will be arrested!'

It is early morning and the streets around Warwick Avenue are bustling with trucks being unloaded and men with barrows taking the crates and boxes into the Sunshine Market where the stall holders are stacking pyramids of red tomatoes, soft piles of fresh lettuces, loose heaps of green beans. There's the drumming sound of potatoes rolling onto drawer-like tables, the clang of tipping scales, the drone of voices with here and there a cry 'Fresh coriander!' 'Two cauliflowers, five Rand!' Florence selects four firm oranges, three Granny Smith apples and a small hand of bananas. Then she makes her way out and across the street where buses wheeze and minibus taxis roar and enters a small shop with a wooden counter in front of which stand slope-lidded bins of grain. There are long bars of mottled blue soap, boxes of Reckitts Blue, rolls of chew tobacco and there! The Boxer tobacco she has come to buy.

Today is Philemon's birthday. Florence has taken the day off work to visit him. She has no money for the football shirt now but, through telephone messages, he has begged his mother to bring Boxer tobacco. Philemon does not smoke; it will win him friends. In the next-door shop Florence buys orange squash, Rama margarine and a loaf of white bread. From an open stall outside she buys 250 grams of mixed sweets.

The minibus taxi fills quickly with women going to visit their men and then speeds up the freeway to Westville Prison, pulsing with rap music 'motherfucker … motherfucker.' The women turn a deaf ear.

There are four visitors' booths. Florence sits on a bench waiting her turn. Three times now Philemon has stood in the dock. Three times now the case has been postponed. But all the time he keeps telling himself over and over again: 'She loves me! She loves me!'

When he sees his mother Philemon waves exuberantly through the thick glass pane. She smiles at him; he is looking well. They talk through the intercom. He is delighted with what she has brought.

'I am very lucky,' he says, 'to have you for a mommy!'

Florence bites her lip.

He is fine he says. He is going to school but it is not as nice as his other school.

He talks about Pretty.

'When I see her in court,' he says, 'I will say "Hullo darling" and she will smile at me. She loves me. They will see.'

Going home Florence sits with her face pressed against the taxi window. She once loved a man. Today is his birthday too.

There are 40 officers in the Child Protection Unit, four of them responsible for the central area of the city. At the moment one of them is boarded, one is on leave and one is off sick. Inspector Ntuli is getting cross. This case is wasting his time. He will speak to the headmaster at the school and arrange to interview the girl there.

The days are lengthening now, light seeps earlier into the crowded room where the youngsters awaiting trial sleep, night falls later. Outside the cluster of face-brick prison buildings that spread among wide lawns amidst high fences, the coral trees are beginning to bloom, gaudy against an improbably blue sky. The days have widened out, the weeks have turned into months and spring is here. Philemon hears the loud squawking of the *Kankane* overhead. Pretty…Pretty…Where are you? Where are you? It is spring and inside Westville prison his heart is breaking.

'She loves me!' Philemon fits the words to the cries of the *Kankane* sitting on the prison roof. How much longer will he have wait? He wills the birds to take a message to Pretty. 'I love you!' he shouts, 'I love you! I love you!' He listens to the cries of the *Kankane* moving across the sky. 'I love you! I love you!'

Pretty has been told to stay sitting at her desk when the bell rings for the end of the school day. Inspector Ntuli wants to talk to her.

She hears the *Kankane* overhead and turns to the window. The birds are landing on the sports field. She gathers her things and works her way up to the front of the class. When the bell rings she rushes out of the door and she is running, she is running, she is running, like the wind she is running, her blood pulsing: Philemon!…Philemon!…Philemon! And now, her face alight with purpose, she is racing across the sports field. She is running faster, faster. Now she is sprinting to the edge of the field, to the edge of the world. Faster and faster. She loves him! She will show them. She loves him!

Philemon hears someone calling his name.

'Philemon Khumalo?'

'Yes!'

He goes down to the office.

'Charges withdrawn!'

8

The day I died the ice cream van, playing its poignant little tune over and over, piped a promise of cold sweet creaminess in the mouth, a sliding coolness in the throat, as it came to the bottom of our one-way street.

The scrap metal man had been wearing an old khaki bush hat that day. Torn, splattered with blue paint, the ventilation eyelets rusted, the stitching unravelling in places, the hat had disorientated me but how grateful I was for his large labourer's hand that gave me the comfort and the human warmth I had not known in years

Utopia Scrap *has been told that the rate payers are again 'up in arms' as they always are. This time because 'their' money is being spent on replacing snipped copper wire, sliced off brass taps, truncated street poles, absent guards on road bends, missing manhole covers. The criminals, they say, must be 'brought to book'.*

That day the scrap metal man, pushing his trolley down the decline, had planned to turn off onto the verge a little further down to redistribute his load before the street dipped more sharply. And then he saw, coming from the large dilapidated house into the street a little ahead of him, the child on his toy motorbike.

With small body bent forward, legs kicking backward, bare yellow soles to the sky, thighs braced, gripping the handles hard in small tight fists, down the street he went, the rough grey tar streaking relentless beneath the whooshing of the wheels as gravity seized him in its relentless grip. Feeling a hard wind skimming back across his cheeks, the sky pressing down, flattening his soft dark curls, his eyes huge with elation, down he went, down the middle of the street, down towards the dip, down towards the bend, his eyes huge now with terror.

The house at number 42, where they used to have those wild parties, is empty, and on the garden wall where the grey-limbed frangipani still drops its fragrant cream and yellow flowers, the two signs remain securely fixed: 'These premises protected by Chubb' and 'Make my day!' – an invitation to potential criminals from a snarling Rottweiler. There'd never been a dog.

A window has been boarded up; a crack has wedged open the brickwork of the braai stand where charred logs, shining with a silky quilted blackness, still lie. Bottles glint among the weeds growing up into the patio. Mosquitoes breed in the dark sludge in the bottom of the swimming pool where slim boys, their bodies folded like paper clips, once dive-bombed in a spattering clatter of shimmering blue water.

And the young family that used to live there?

#42

Blood Cries

The rain is coming down again, fine and in wide sheets, blowing in from the Atlantic. He stands at the small cottage window looking out into the bruised Irish sky. Then he turns and goes to the fireplace, nearly as tall as he, and, from the dark cubby-hole recess in whose baked dryness previous generation had stored socks and tobacco and tea, takes the caddy and measures the fragrant leaves into the chipped brown teapot he has set to warm. He wraps his hand in a fire-blackened towel and lifts the old iron kettle off the hook that hangs in the fireplace and angles the swan-necked spout so that a silver rope of water frays into the leaves to begin the gentle infusion of flavour. When the tea has brewed he pours a thin stream into the mug, spoons in sugar from the white SUICRA bag and settles into the old beech rocking chair to suck up the sweet comforting liquid with a pleasure all the deeper for not having been as easily achieved as with a tea bag and an electric kettle.

Slowly sipping, listening to the percussive rhythm of the drips that drop and ping and plop into the tins and bowls and buckets he has placed to collect the leaks, and watching the concentric circles eddy out from the centres, Patrick remembers how his mother had scolded him for boyhood misdemeanours, the consequences of which, she had said, could ripple out far beyond what he might imagine. It was only recently that he had realised that the conviction with which she had spoken came not from principle but from experience.

It was knowing that in kwaZulu when a man's soul is troubled, he goes to the place of his birth to seek the advice of his ancestors, that had decided him to come to this remote most westerly part of Europe on the edge of the Atlantic where tall breakers built up their watery height across long wide acres of ocean to crash against rock and begin to eat into the small damp land that seemed stitched to the sky with constant rain.

* * * * *

She stands in her mother's Durban kitchen in a sports bra and a leopard print sarong, slicing onions. Though it is early evening the heat is relentless. Her hair, retaining the scant residue of an old perm, is sun bleached and tied back in the hot hollow of her neck. She pushes away a lock fallen over her tanned cheek with the back of her hand. There is a thin white seam of healed tissue running diagonally down her jaw-bone and, on the inside of her wrist, the red reminder of a burn. Her mother (her parents had divorced when she was seven) is out with friends and she and the boys have just come in from the beach, happy to have the house at ease about them. Declan, nine, has flung himself onto the couch in front of the TV. Daemon, 11, is slinging the damp beach towels over the line outside the kitchen window – without the pegs his grandmother always insisted upon. She allows herself a wry smile. Though she is nearly forty, Lynne still feels the power of her mother's disapproving eye. She wonders whether it was out of some sort of retribution, some idea that since her mother was going to disapprove of whatever she did that she would give her something she could really, and with justification, discountenance.

Although when she first met him, Lynne herself was in some way intuitively aware of the incipient risk Patrick seemed to present, she had cast her fears aside and with what had become habitual bravado, allowed herself to fall crazily, madly in love with him. Utterly besotted, she had simply and unhesitatingly stepped off the edge and dropped down down down, exulting in the fall not attempting to stop herself, her silent screams elating her.

Daemon comes into the open-plan kitchen.

'You're crying, Ma!'

'No darling,' she smiles 'Onions!'

'Dur!' yells Declan.

Blonde and lithe-limbed, the boys are doing fine, she tells her colleagues, anyone who asks. And they are – on the surface of things. She draws Daemon towards her, presses her lips to the top of his head and tastes the salt in his damp sticky hair. He has his father's build and soon will grow too tall for her to kiss in that way – perhaps in any way – for he will no doubt pull away from her, as is the way of growing boys. She feels a surging warmth in her belly. She loves them so much, her boys, her two beautiful babies. Will she ever be able to make it up to them?

* * * * *

'Connemara,' Patrick's mother had said. 'Connemara's where your roots lie.'

That was all. She refused any further information. He had flown to Dublin, hired a car and asked for directions. 'Connemara? Follow the signs for the West, it's very well signposted,' people had said and they were right. There were signs all along the road that later twisted through the bleak, rocky, unbearably beautiful landscape.

After several hours he stopped at a garage. 'How much further to Connemara?'

'You're in Connemara!' the man laughed with a sweep of arm that seemed to take in the entire universe. It was then that he bought a map and discovered that Connemara was not a town but an entire region and that trying to trace family by his mother's maiden name was like looking for a Naidoo in Natal, a Jones in Wales. Alone, eyes closed, in the small hired car, his fist like a gavel punching his right thigh, he felt more lost than he'd ever felt in any of the dreams that had so disturbed his nights. He didn't know what to do.

When he had gathered himself together he drove further until he saw a signboard: *The Shebeen*. Shebeen? That's what illicit drinking dens were called in South Africa. He felt the sign was signalling him to stop. He parked the car and went inside. It smelt of peat softly burning, of wet wool drying.

The pub was full, the welcome warm. And after a few jokes and yarns and several jars and shared rounds, he met a man who offered him the use of an old stone cottage standing empty on his land. 'You can keep it warm for me,' he had said. Patrick gratefully accepted.

He recalled W.B. Yeats and his small cabin and hoped that he too might find that peace that comes dropping slow. He had thought that here he might be able to forget it all but, caught between the sodden skies and the sodden earth, he felt his pain intensifying and finding remembrance of sorrow all around became saturated with it.

In the hard places where the ribs of rock protruded through the lean land and the ruins of small stone cottages, their gable ends like gravestones commemorating the famine, still stood, he felt the deep pain of it all and, too, the intensity of love that people down through the generations and in faraway places all over the world still felt for the dear country that had succoured their roots.

In the mornings he strode stout-booted across damp fields disturbing the wood pigeons that flew in low arcs across the sky. And in the evening stood leaning against the low lintel watching the slow fading of the light. And the only thing he forgot was the reason for which he'd come.

* * * * *

Meticulously recorded and set on continuous play, the volume turned right down, it, all of it, would, Lynne feared, stay in some more or less accessible place within her boys all their lives, and could in twenty years – in twenty seconds! – time without warning come blasting up, out of nowhere, out of everywhere, out of deep inside them.

Girlfriends and wives (she was assuming some normalcy) coming from a different rearing might, through a long painful process, gain some knowledge of what could trigger the brooding sulks, the derisive laughter, the sudden deafening outbursts that she foresaw: certain phrases, a critical observation, a phone call. But who would know the potency of the sound of bottles being smashed, male voices chanting *a capella* on the hi-fi, whimpering behind a closed bedroom door.

Lynne had not wanted children. Wary of Mother Nature's cunning push towards procreation and the mundanity that seemed to go with it, she had shied away from 'suitable' men, been attracted to strangers passing through, to other women's husbands; had taken to men who offered excitement and urgent sex that carried a dangerous edge and no commitment. Like bungee-jumping with the seduction of rocks. Like free-styling into the allure of a storm at sea.

She had only recently come to realise that it was not mundanity she had wanted to avoid all those years, but the intimacy that a more lasting relationship would eventually demand. By trying to keep her 'love affairs' on a purely physical level she would never again suffer the deep pain of emotional rejection as she had when her father had left.

She sensed in Patrick something of the same kind of fear, the fear of getting too close to someone, the fear of failure, of being found out, though in relation to what neither quite knew.

It was when he told her that what drove him was the pursuit of unfettered ecstasy and its ultimate realisation, whatever the price; when, listening to him where he sat across the restaurant table looking solemnly into her eyes, not touching her at all; when she felt her body turn to liquid, her nerve ends sprung and alert with ferocious anticipation; when the words he was meticulously saying affirmed that he, surely, could monumentally fulfil the singular and overwhelming need in her, that she found herself smitten.

When that first time he had laid her out, constrained her movements, blind-folded her, rendered her powerless, did what he did, what she had not even known to desire, she was awe-filled that the barriers could, by this infliction and endurance, be so dissolved, and, by the white hot processes of some strange alchemy, be transformed into something on a high, almost sacred plane. It was for her a coupling undreamed of, elemental and addictive. Tunnelling through the blind terror of it, emerging into a brilliant transcendent light, she both welcomed and feared where this intensity might lead.

* * * * *

A picture of a previous Pope stuck to the inside of the door with thick yellow sellotape, a tract on the Sacred Heart wedged into the frame of a darkened mirror, a small missal in an ink-stained drawer, these, the remembrances of those who had lived here before, evoked in Patrick a bitter-sweet nostalgia.

He opens the roman missal, its thin pages edged in gold, and reads the message written on the inside of the cover in a slender slanting hand, the black inked letters dissolving into a fuzz of yellow: 'Lord teach me to accept and have patience over me in my intolerable loneliness.' He feels a sudden rushing bond with the no-doubt deceased who had written those words, who had held this very little book in their hands. Grief rushes over him and he sits in the lamplight murmuring as he turns the small, foxed pages.

'Holy Mary Mother of God, pray for us now and in the hour of our death.'

Before the mass on the day of the funeral Patrick's mother had sat there in her cultured pearls and professional coiffure drinking gin and tonic from a Waterford crystal glass and had told him matter-of-factly (now that she had been released from the pact she and her husband had made) that, actually, the deceased was not his real father who, by the way, she had not seen or heard of since the terrible mistake she had made one night after a *ceilidh*.

His mass-insisting, novena-saying mother had had a deeply regretted one-night stand the sin of which had resulted in new life – *him!* – and he was supposed to be OK with that!

She had sat there in full couture mourning, her silk-stockinged legs at beauty queen angle, and, twisting her diamond rings and making extravagant signs of the cross, had told him that a novice nun at the home for unmarried mothers had foolishly handed her the newborn, the '*wee dote*', destined for adoption, and that much to her subsequent regret, she had, on a whim, taken the infant, conceived in sin, and run away; that she had sacrificed all her independence for him; that he should be hugely and eternally grateful that 'Dad', who had met her while on a trip to Ireland looking for his ancestors (the irony would hit later) had found and fallen in love with her and had so adored her that, though she came with an overdraft (him!), he had taken on the burden, had had her illegitimate son's birth certificate somehow revised, and had brought them both to South Africa and given her (and him, lest he forget) a life free of financial worries.

Patrick could not bring himself to accompany Lynne and the boys in the chief mourners' car his mother had reserved for them but friends seeing him afterwards – his pale anguished face, his stumbling gait, his disjointed speech – remarked how very deeply the death of his father seemed to have affected Patrick.

And then things began to fall into place. Little niggly things that had never seemed quite right yet not wrong enough to pursue. Like why there was such a gap between his birth and that of his sisters, to whom he had always felt so different, like why his 'father' (he had started making the inverted-comma gesture in his mind) had taken only a perfunctory interest in his achievements, like why he had always felt uncomfortable around him.

This man, to whom he was supposed to be so grateful, had been nothing but an impostor; it wasn't fair.

'Fair! You should count your lucky stars,' his mother had said 'You grew up in big houses with swimming pools, servants…you don't understand what Ireland was like in those days!'

And so he, the ingrate, was made to feel guilty for not being able to 'forget about it', for wanting to know his own blood. He had hardly spoken to his mother or his half (he used the word with bitter relish) sisters since.

*****

It was on a whim and with some sense of daring and defiance that, shortly after they met, Patrick and Lynne took their wedding vows in a registry office, not telling family and friends until afterwards.

For a while all was well. And then, at the pinnacle of the good times it seemed, things changed and there was a brittleness between them; it was as if a bird singing its delight out on the topmost branch of a tree had suddenly stopped. And the joyful creature had fallen stiff and cold to the ground.

And then slowly things got better again. And when they were happy, which eventually they were for a while once more, were incredulous that fate had brought them together. But, always, when the good times were at their height he seemed to pull back, ask himself what he, a miserable sinner, thought he was doing in the Garden of Eden. And then, having decided that he was trespassing, precipitated the fall.

In time the instances of happiness became briefer, were spaced further apart and each of them wondered when that time would come, which surely it must, when they would no longer be able to revive the bird, feel the push of air beneath taut wings, the buoyancy of the small warm body, the song in the throat.

And then the children came. And things were forever changed. To her surprise Lynne found a deep pleasure in being a mother. Despite small moments of incredulity that he was actually a father, Patrick, feeling ousted, remained largely indifferent. The enemy, mundanity, invaded their lives, and sex became perfunctory and unsatisfactory. Yet still she remained drawn to him, to what she felt emanated from him: the intimation of an enthralling mystery.

He started drinking more. To help assuage his guilt she joined him, but soon found she could not keep pace. And then he started hiding bottles of spirits and drinking alone. And, coming from behind as she stood by the splattering grill turning the burgers, or when she leaned over the ironing board wielding a hot spitting iron, he would wrap his arms around her waist, draw an after-shaved cheek across her hair, nuzzle the back of her ears, and then suddenly, taking his cue from some tension emanating from her (a reflex to the pressure of things to be done, an aversion to the oppressive power of his embrace, the alcohol on his breath) would draw away and start the performance:

'So I'm not good enough for you then!'

'You know that's not true!'

'You've never trusted me.'

And then, much as a guard on duty suspended between boredom and fear which makes for a dangerous carelessness, she said:

'I wonder why?'

Plates broke. The boys hid. Arguments grew more frequent. Violence increased. And the boys, awakened in their beds, drew their bodies into tense kidney bean shapes, pretending the sounds they heard were just the hadedas squabbling on the garage roof.

And then the parties began and the boys were sent to their grandmother's on weekends. And, when the last of the guests had gone, she would hide under the duvet in the darkness behind the closed bedroom door (experience had taught her that to turn the key was to pull the pin on his hand-held grenade) in the hopeless pretence of sleep, willing time to keep the threatened moment at bay beyond the peak of his rage when he would no longer be capable of directing his loud feet down the passage, wrapping his hard hand around the door handle, pressing a firm finger on the central light switch, and, as though opening the lid on a long suspected cache of treacherous love letters, snatch the covers off her knotted form, and, grabbing her slender resistant shoulders, shove the searchlight of his contorted face into the smooth, assumed blankness of hers and shake her for making him feel this way.

And later, when exhaustion meant she could resist no more, she learnt how to untether her mind and, powerless within her noisy receiving skin, became compliant to his will, colluding with the slamming of his knuckles beneath her jaw, the rock of his fist in the socket of her eye.

And in the mornings hearing him gathering empty bottles, sweeping up broken glass, putting the furniture back in place she would ache for him to hold her. Ache for him to sit on the bed and take her hand, for who but he could understand? And so she would call him there where, savaged by guilt and remorse and desperate for her summoning voice, he waited. And he would come and sit with her and take her hand and would hold her kindly questioning gaze in his broken, welling eyes. Then he would go and make her a cup of tea – patiently spooning the bag around till the boiled water had drawn out all the flavour – and would cool the damp tea bag to place on her swollen eye, bring her a fresh warm flannel.

Enshrined among plumped-up pillows, breathing in the perfume of the frangipani he floated in a cut-glass bowl by the bed, enveloped in the haunting Gregorian Chant LP he played for her on the hi-fi, she felt – ridiculous as she knew it was! – somehow blessed.

His ministering would be gentle and penitential and last as long as she could bear to witness his self flagellation; then she would absolve him.

* * * * *

'Lord have mercy on us
Christ have mercy on us
Graciously hear us Jesus
From all evil Jesus deliver us
From all sin
From thy wrath
From the snares of the devil
From the spirit of uncleanness
From everlasting death…'

Instead of coming on this wild goose chase Patrick could have gone to Amsterdam, as he had that first university holiday when he had wandered about the *Oude Kerk* where scarlet lights, slung across the canal, reddened the water and *Raamprostitute* with Panda eyes sat like dolls in ultra-violet display windows offering franchised sex. What surprised him most were the tissue boxes. That eternal damnation could be diminished to a trifle on a tissue so publicly displayed he found incomprehensible.

Reared on muffled confessions to pale priests and intercessions to the Virgin, the machinations of this profound mystery (which one of the brothers at school had named in Latin, rolling the word around his upper teeth with a large fissured tongue before pronouncing it with a long sibilance and a closing clap of capacious lips – 'Sexum!') had from an early age kept his mind imaginatively occupied. Noting that, whether one had cribbed one's homework or had had sex with one's married neighbour or her daughter or both simultaneously; whether indeed one had murdered a whole village or done nothing at all, one was, in the eyes of the church, a miserable sinner, he determined to explore some, at least, of the shores of damnation. For though the wages of sin might be death, the same, it seemed to him, could be said of life itself.

Patrick's first real sexual encounter had been in Durban's Point Road.

It was not the fleshy bulge above the stocking tops, not the swell of melon-big breasts, not the stiff hayrick of hair but that small all-in-one gesture that had done it. In one simple movement, she had tilted her neck, raised her chin, run the moist pink tip of her tongue around immense pencil-lined lips dark and lustrous as black grapes, winked a purple eyelid – the lashes like awnings – and in a promise-filled twinkle caught his eye and so had instantly convinced him that, unwittingly or not, he had entered into a contract and was morally obliged to follow the plump double-u of naked flesh pendulating beneath the leather mini up the stairway to damnation. That this was a commercial deal and she a businesswoman of some experience, who had already run through the services she had to offer, did nothing to lessen the pressure he felt to impress her, to please her, to win her approval. He failed utterly.

He still had visions of her smirking face with the pink bubble gum ballooning from her mouth like an indictment. And then she had taken an amused pity on him, and, at no extra cost, showed him other darker things. He had bellowed like a beast.

'*In nomine Patris et Filii Spiritus Sancti.*'

And now, sitting here in the fuliginous light of an oil lamp reading the missal and muttering the words that had been an integral part of his upbringing and hearing in his mind the murmur of the monks and the swish of the serge robes and the smack of their sturdy leather sandals on cool, grey slate he felt the words fill him up.

'*Mea culpa, mea culpa, mea maxima culpa.*'

* * * * *

And sometimes on a week night a high, wild cry would flare up and the children would lie stiff as spoons, anticipating the tearing and the ruin. And so, Lynne feared, were their lives forever skewed and the small aching fists, once grown to adulthood, diverted to lovers as yet unknown, to children still to be begotten, as the grown-up body, tied to the mysteries of the mind, would one day assume its own imagined autonomy.

She flattened out her features, feigned dismay in wide defensive eyes, and hissing 'Daddy didn't mean it' through a swollen mouth, stood erect watching the world through walls of bullet-proof glass.

She did not feel any shame. More it's inverse, a kind of hard-earned hauteur that came from the sense of having passed a test, having been allowed to move up into a higher plane. It was as if what she had previously endured had merely admitted her into the novitiate of the sisterhood, one of the multitudes of women, who wore their brave vestments – long sleeves, neck scarves, large dark glasses – whatever the weather. For, excepting for its predicted and extravagant Christmas blossoming, violence knew no season, no class. But what had been rained upon her that time had been of a higher order, had, she felt, set her on the initiatory path of the *sanctum sanctorum* of the martyrs and the saints. And saints as she knew do not call for help.

Friends said:

Take the children and leave.

Just get out.

You will find a way.

You are not the cause.

You can't fix it.

You are not alone.

But…

Love!? That's not love, that's a sickness.

But if God tempers the wind to the shorn lamb how faithless then the lamb that sets off for the pastures of the dispossessed where the wind never blows and the grass stays forever green. There was sanctity in silence.

In the end it was he who decided.

That morning when she awoke she lifted a hand and, with the nerve-rich tips of her fingers, gingerly explored the contours of her face: hovering over the skin around her right eye, palpating the distended mass, gently pressing the scant flesh along the ledge of her jaw, finding the chiming pain in the bone beneath. She ran the vault of her right instep down the hard slender shinbones of her left leg encountering the sudden mound of pain and began to sob. The boys were spending the weekend with her mother. She reached a slow arm out to where the broad slope of his warm back should have been – and wasn't. The house was silent. She lay still, straining her ears but could hear no sound of him.

She lifted herself slowly from the bed, went to the bathroom. Her face was curiously off centre. Where her eye had been, a windfall mango had swelled and split open exposing a downward slant of ripe yellow pulp. There was swelling too just below her right cheekbone.

There was no way walking into a door knob ('tall door, tall story!') or colliding with a lamppost ('a lamppost!') or any of the other small, inadequate explanations women like her used, would this time pull the wool over the cold eyes of her colleagues. It seemed to her sometimes that the averted eyes of those who knew nothing about her really, the swift glance of strangers who poured their judgement like acid over the raw open wound of her marriage, caused her more anxiety than the physical pain she suffered.

He packed his bags and hugged his boys and saw in the taut thin line of his mother-in-law's lips that, at last! he was doing something right.

Weeks went by.

She missed him terribly.

* * * * *

'Grant to us, we beseech Thee, almighty and merciful God that we may obtain the invisible effects of that which we have shared by communion in Visible Mysteries, through our Lord…'

He went for long walks, sometimes encountering a neighbouring farmer who, even when the rain was steadily falling, would greet him 'Grand day now!' and he wondered whether *he* whoever he might be who had – to use the word common to cattle breeders in the area – 'inseminated' his mother had walked this road, whether *he* had seen these valleys with their frayed wadding of mists, the silver blades of water that slit the distant mountains, whether *he* had heard the gathering wind in the trees like the thrumming of bicycle wheels on tar, had smoothed a hand over these dry stone walls, breathed in the pulsing brine of this stretch of bog.

He had forsworn his favoured Jameson and other spirits but went occasionally to a pub to assuage his loneliness in pints of black stout, and began to imagine evidence of his genetics all around: the way that man standing before the leaping fire swished his palms past each other just as, when enthusiastic about something, he did; the way another closed his eyes when pulling on his cigarette, as he had frequently done; the way a third threw his head back when he laughed as, he told himself with a chuckle, he never did!

He tried to go to confession once but feeling his knuckles gathering in a fist, was driven by a sudden compulsion to rip open the screen and lay into the priest, the embodiment of this deep, entrenched power that had, so he felt, sullied his very existence.

One morning Patrick watched the mists lift off the land and it seemed to him that the dust cloths protecting polished wood had been whipped off just for his benefit as a sudden shaft of light cut through to light up the green brilliance of a brief, bright field for his eyes alone. And later when he went down to the lake behind the cottage where marsh marigolds and yellow flags grew and wild swans nested (they mated for life he had been told) and felt the thin sun warm his back and threw idle stones into the stillness and, watching the ripples growing out from the dent he'd made in the skin of the lake, felt that his mind, like a mounted telescope at some tourist viewing site, had shifted, so that he was looking in a new direction.

That evening he heard the chug of a tractor, saw against the rind of light that rimmed the hill, the farmer pulling a trailer load of hay, saw the farmer's wife and children sitting on top of it and heard, in the curious way that sound travelled, high above the noise of the tractor, the children calling.

'Dahdee! Dahdee! Dahdee!' and heard their mother say,

'Would ye whist now! Daddy can't hear ye.'

'Dahdee! Dahdee!'

'Whist now Daddy can't hear ye.'

'Dahdee!'

'Daddy can't hear ye.'

And when they had gone and all was quiet he heard the twittering of swallows.

And through his sleep that night the echo of the cry, the call of the blood: Dahdee!

9

The scrap metal man has added a stainless steel kettle to the old exhaust, the discarded pushchair, the army-issued tin hat and the door of a thrown-out bar fridge. He'll have to prize the door apart, take out the firmly bonded padding and scrape all the innards out. Scrap metal had to be clean and of a single type before it could be weighed. Taking car bodies apart to separate the metals is a tedious job.

On the pavement outside Utopia Scrap Metal *rugged men in ragged clothes sit around on bald tyres and the exposed springs of old car seats working at the metal with chisels and hammers, screw drivers and pliers, keeping themselves entertained, laughing and chatting and flirting with the women who pass by.*

But see that patio set by the side of a rate-payer's house? The scrap metal man noticed it the day I died – the last time he had come around this way. It might then have earned him enough to buy another pair of sturdy, second hand army boots, but since it's been left out in the rain all this time, the metal has corroded and now is good for little more than tinting the hydrangeas blue.

He nears number 33 where the extended Coloured family live. The people here know the scrap metal man, know him even better since that fatal day. Were he thirsty, which he is not, he could ask for water here, sure that it would be served straight from the fridge and in a proper glass on a saucer. He could, if it were necessary, even ask to use the toilet. Since the public conveniences were pulled down to make way for the freeway being built alongside the railway line, people who have nowhere really to 'go' worry more about these matters. In the townships there was frequently just one toilet for dozens of families. Long queues would form in the mornings and often people who had to go to work would dose themselves with maizena stirred in liquid and, on the week-ends, take castor oil.

It was the same with water: one tap, long queues. Though 25% of the population might live under these conditions they used only 5% of the available water. And yet the offensive smell of pungent, unwashed bodies that so repulsed white nostrils had somehow miraculously disappeared.

As always the family who live in this sprawling house have left the big gate open. And the little boy? He has just started creche. 'Your child, my child' they say in Africa. 'I will look after your child as though it were my own.'

And so it was that day as the sky slowly closed down.

#33

Prophets of the Front Yard

In the old days, you had a job, says Mal Jan van Langsaan in his too-short trousers and *Proudly South African* cap, you had him for life. Now, if you not kicked out before you takes the greaseproof off your sarmies, you're *mos blerrie* lucky. 'Strue's Bob!

Cling wrap! says Uncle Abdul, lowering his ginormous backside onto the curved concrete bench like a crane off-loading an overstuffed couch onto the wharf.

Wait a bit, wait a bit! says Uncle Ismail. Monday mornings Fatima – may God have mercy on her soul – folding the new greaseproof around my *snoek* and chutney sarmies like she was making the bed in the honeymoon suite at The Mount Nelson.

End of the week it was wrinkled like a *vrot* granadilla.

A clapped out passion fruit, *ne*, says Mal Jan poking a bony finger into Uncle Ismail's frail chest whose passion, the men often joked, had borne no fruit.

Friday night, says Uncle Ismail – who's got a beard like one of Danielle's socks the cat peed on – I'd *mos* twist it up and put it in the kitchen drawer…

That's now a really strange place to put it! says Mal Jan.

…to light the blue flame stove with, says Uncle Ismail.

Ouch! *Eina*! says Mal Jan. Everyone like laughs.

Klomp V*uilbekke*, says Ma with a little half smile, wiping the round concrete table with a lappie.

What's the world coming to? asks Uncle Abdul chirping the remote on his white Camry parked outside our front door and turning to the *chommies* who gather like any time of the day around the table under the mango tree.

Daniel Manual, who wears a black beret to hide his bald patch, reckons he's like related to Trevor Manual, South Africa's first black Finance Minister.

Se voet! says Mal Jan. He's *mos* whiter than a whitey's *poephol*. 'Strue's Bob. He's *blerrie* lucky he's a *bleskop* otherwise you could see he's got no kinks in his hair!

Mal Jan reckons that Race Classification meant that some government person could like stick a pencil in your hair and if it didn't fall out you were a Nonnie, a Non-European. He reckons his Auntie Gertie spent a fortune on *Cherry Peach Hair Straightener* and 'tried for white'. But, *ag* shame man, he said, even if she like jumped up and down in her little Cuban heels, the pencil stayed put like it was concreted in.

What's the world coming to? says Uncle Abdul. Today you've got more chance if you're properly black through and through.

Wait a bit! Wait a bit! says Uncle Ismail like a *tjorrie* trying to start.

Here we go! says Daniel Manual polishing his big thick-framed glasses. Terence reckons he doesn't need glasses. Just wears them to look like intellectual. Same with the beret.

Since his wife, Auntie Fatima, died Uncle Ismail – who used to live in Cape Town – has been living with us. It seems like it's been about a hundred years. It's because of him not having children of his own. Allah did not bless us in that way, he said. But Ma reckons Fatima told her he had like difficulties in that department and was, in any case, just too *blerrie snoep*. She had to turn the sheets and wear the same old pom pom slippers till they were *morsdood*. *Foeitog!*

Uncle Abdul uses after-shave and like dyes his hair. He lives in a smarter part of town but he says you don't get much conversation with the *larnies* so he's always driving around to us 'for a bit of a chin wag.'

'The Prophets of the Front Yard' Ma calls them. She's not sure whether the conversation is always suitable for us kids, but she enjoys having them around. Brandon, our little brother, does too. They bring him Liquorice Allsorts and like bounce him on their knees and go 'vroom-vroom' when he 'kick-starts' his little motor bike.

The trouble with the world today, says Uncle Abdul, tapping a finger like a fat cigar on the edge of the cement table, is Think Tanks. The big shots spend too much time in them and get water on the brains.

Strue's Bob! says Mal Jan laughing like a donkey having an asthma attack.

The trouble with the world today, says Daniel Manual, is that deep down people are really superficial. They're fodder for money-making machines, that's all. They can't think for themselves. And with the Think Tanks and Brain Storms, 24/7 what happens? The thinking compartments get flooded and all the common sense runs out. Mark my words!

Wait a bit! Wait a bit! says Uncle Ismail.

Here we go! says Daniel Manual.

Uncle Ismail was like born in the year of the Revolution. Jason – who's 14 and top of his class – wants to know if it was the French or the Russian one but says, never mind, he's been revolting ever since. Ma says Uncle Ismail may be *vol fiemies* but family is *mos* family.

Uncle Ismail's great great great great great ouma and Ouma Gail's great great great great ouma were like sisters. Ma says they were born in Malaya and came to the Cape on a slave ship. Gloria says nothing's changed; women are still slaving today.

Terence is our big brother. He is 17. He finished with school and his girlfriend at the same time. Now he is like looking for a more suitable girlfriend. Ma says he must now look for a job, suitable or not. But Terence, who has started wearing a do rag around his *kop*, says no, he *is* working. On his rap.

Uncle Ismail has eyeballs like marbles rolled in Vaseline. Daniel Manual says he's probably got cataracts.

Irwin – who's in Matric and wears his jeans with the waist *under* his bum – wants to know why people don't like explain words and things anymore. Ma says if he wants to know something he must look it up.

The only thing Irwin wants to look up, says Jason, is ladies' dresses.

Jason reckons he once saw an *ou* in a wheelchair who was a stand-up comedian. The best joke ever, he said. Now, *he* like wants to be a stand-up, wheel-chair or not. He's always making up jokes. Everyone thinks they are really pathetic and shout 'Sirroun Jason!' even if he is sitting down. He says it's *lank* good training for stand-up.

Irwin looked up cataract in the dictionary. 'Cataract: a large, rushing waterfall.'

He reckons Ouma's got cataracts too. When she's on the toilet it's like Victoria Falls. She doesn't close the door properly because she says 'You can *mos* hear I'm in the lavvy!' Gross! You'd think she could like sit a bit forward to put the silencers on.

Because of the Minister of Education learners in Matric have to do a science project. Like research something. Or something. Irwin thinks maybe he could do some research to see at what angle a chick must lean forward to like have a silent pee.

Girls wee and boys pee, chirps Brandon.
Because why?
Because boys have got a penis!

Ja, we pee miss, Mal Jan sniggers, that's *mos* why us *ous* must put the seat up!

Ag sis man! says Danielle, stretching her legs out to check her new takkies. She's in Grade 7. People say she has like beautiful sea green eyes but Jason says they are just sad and the colour of snot. He'd be depressed too if he had eyes that colour.

Irwin's getting quite good at what Daniel Manual calls 'consulting the dictionary' so now he's like invented this word game. You use any word from any of the 11 official languages and if it's got a double meaning you shout 'Ping!' and score a point. Spelling doesn't count, just the sound. Irwin says the word for that is 'fonetic' but it's not in the dictionary. Daniel Manual says that's because he like looked in the wrong place. It's PHonetic.

Irwin looked 'penis' up in the dick (Ping!) tionary. 'Penis: the copulatory organ of a male mammal.'

In case you didn't know it, says Terence, a mammal is an animal with titties, know what I'm saying?

I haven't got no titties! says Brandon.

Bet you don't know what copulatory means? says Jason.

So tune us, Einstein! says Terence.

It means that if you put it into a chick who's younger than 16 they cop you later. Ping!

Is this dude for real, know what I'm saying? asks Terence, stroking his just-beginning beard between his thumb and index finger. But you can see he's like impressed.

The dictionary sits on the sideboard next to the photograph of Oupa in the red fez with the tassel that he got for going to Mecca for three days in 1952. Gloria, who's 19, says it's not fair: she has to get a student loan and go to university for like three years to maybe one day have a photograph of her in a hat with a tassel on the sideboard.

Ma says anyways how's she going to fit a mortar board over her *doek*.

Gloria's doing like Gender Studies. Terence reckons she must be lank *dof* to take so long to learn bull-cow, stallion-mare, dog-bitch…

The dictionary's been in the family for like centuries. It used to start with 'aardvark: *South African*' which is really *kwaai*. But now it starts with 'balderdash' on account of the cover and some of the pages missing. It sits on top of the *Kritzinger Afrikaans-Engels Engels-Afrikaans Handige Woordeboek*.

Balderdash: confused speech or writing; a jumble of words, Irwin read. He reckons it's what the Prophets sitting around the table speak. He thinks maybe 'balderdash' is like the English word for *kak*.

Ouma Gail, Ma's mother-in-law, lives us with us too. She's always got a big snot rag hanging out of her sleeve. That's because she's like always sniffling. She's still mourning our dad, her son. He was shot dead in a carjack. I find it hard sometimes too. I know it's harder still for Ma. He was her husband. But she doesn't like dwell on it. She says it could be worse. One of us could also have been killed. But I know she still misses him a lot. We all do.

Ouma Gail spends most of her time going to the lavvy or lying in bed farting. Ma says 'farting' is like a rude word. Polite people say 'passing wind'.

Wind? With the old *toppies* it's like 'Gail Force' and 'Hurricane Ismail!' says Jason.

The gas that comes out of people's bums is like a natural gas called methane. Jason reckons with the OAPs it should be called 'Fossil Fuel'.

Terence is like going to write a rap about it. He reckons there's so much methane going to waste they should come up with a plan to like store it to use instead of coal.

'Strue's Bob! says Mal Jan – whose got a bum like to two Marie biscuits. The *troepies* on the border used to go *bossies* sometimes. Then they'd make '*n ou* pull his *broek* down and er…er…pass wind…while they stuck a lighter by his *poephol* and watched the flames shoot out.

It's partly all the cows farting that's causing global warming, says Terence. Know what I'm saying?

That's why we should all be vegetarian, says Gloria.

That's illogical, says Terence. If people stopped eating cows there'd be more of them farting. And all these animal rights people aren't like helping either. Elephants let helluva big ones go, know what I'm saying? The reason they've found gas off the west coast is all the whales down there farting. And all the tourists watching them, farting too.

Terence is thinking maybe he'll design a bag you can fit over your bum to like store the gas. But he'll need volunteers to test it.

Check the chicks in Diesel jeans, says Jason.
Because why?
Because they've got lank efficient internal combustion!

Terence reckons he wants Gloria to be a volunteer.
Because why?

Because, he says, she's always eating beans and lentils and stuff and that makes more methane even than meat, know what I'm saying?

Terence tunes us his rap:

> Wanna know how an *ou*
> Can just keep on the go?
> We pack the means
> Inside our jeans
> Chowing curry and beans
> Don't need no petroleum
> No linoleum no mausoleum
> If you really give a fuck
> Go ditch dat fuelish rut
> Kick some serious butt
> And get your ass in a sling!
> For energy conservation
> Ain't no better thing
> Than farting for da nation
> Brrrap Brrrap Brrap!

The chorus, he reckons, is like a whole bunch of *ous* blowing raspberries.

What's lino got to do with it? says Danielle.

Sis! says Gloria.

Daniel Manual reckons he can speak Khoisan. No one knows if it's true. Because no one else can speak it.

Irwin reckons if Daniel Manual can speak a Khoisan language he should be in a museum like Sarah Baartman who was Khoisan. She was like in the Museum of Man because of having a big poes and a ginormous backside.

In that case, says Terence, they must put me in the Museum of Ladies, know what I'm saying?

Because why?

Because of my outstanding private parts!

Men are always going on about their private parts in public, says Gloria.

Gloria doesn't join the prophets often because she reckons you never know where the conversation can lead.

What about the *Vagina Monologues?* asks Terence.

The Regina Moan-alongs, says Daniel Manual looking over the top of his glasses, is a lot of ladies standing on a stage talking about their gentiles.

South Africa's new motto, which is actually written in Khoisan, is 'Unity in Diversity'.

The old one was 'Unity is Strength' which like sounds the same. But Daniel Manual says the Unity was only about the whites – the English and the Afrikaans – united to be stronger against the blacks. The diversity is like about everybody.

What's the world coming to? says Uncle Abdul.

An agreement with Beijing! says Daniel Manual leaning on the cement table and like pressing the tips of his finger together. Mark my words! While the West is going to the dogs, China is going to every country in Africa!

The Chinese peoples are *mos* monkeys, says Mal Jan. They work for peanuts.

No, they're clever, they make things and sell them at a fixed exchange rate, says Daniel Manual.

Cheap rubbish! says Uncle Abdul. And all the carbon dioxide they're pumping out that's causing global warming!

No doubt about it! says Daniel Manual. But if people didn't want this rubbish they wouldn't make it. As long as there's a demand they'll supply. People shop for 'Made in China' junk Saturday and wonder why they lose their factory jobs Monday.

And anyway the Chinese invented lots of things long before anyone else. Paper. Printing. China.

Is it? *So waar*! says Mal Jan with his clapped-out donkey laugh.

And other countries, says Daniel Manual running a finger inside the collar of his black polo neck, invented the jet engine, the silicone chip, laser surgery. And what did we invent?

The Kreepy Krawly! chuckles Mal Jan with a bony thumbs up.

No doubt about it, says Daniel Manual. And how many garden boys did it put out of work cleaning the master's swimming pool!

The worst thing ever invented, says Uncle Abdul – who divorced his wife a few years ago – was not the atomic bomb. It was the knitting machine.

'Strues' Bob, says Mal Jan. *Ouma en oupa sit op die stoep; ouma brei en oupa poep.*

Ja wat! says Uncle Abdul, resettling his backside. Once upon a time a woman used to keep her man company and her knitting in a basket on the stoep so she could pick it up and click away listening to him sorting out all the world's problems and laughing at his *grappies*. And then along came a salesman and next thing she's sitting inside all the blooming time tearing her hair out and her man left with nothing but 'help yourself!' for supper.

Wait a bit! Wait a bit…! says Uncle Ismail, his eyeballs going wet.

Here we go! says Daniel Manual.

…Fatima never served that.

And then, said Uncle Abdul, the machine was just sitting there in a box on top of the wardrobe and she's *mos* buying jerseys in town and on HP *nogal!*

No doubt about it! says Daniel Manual. Higher Purchase means, in the end, the price is higher than if you purchased it straight away. And in the meantime they introduced built-in-abseil-lessons so, before you're finished paying for the thing, it's stopped working.

Know what's the second worst thing every invented? asks Uncle Abdul.

Pantyhose! says Jason.

The microwave! No more smell of cooking. And a lot more cancer of the bosoms, says Uncle Abdul.

Wait a bit! Wait a bit…! says Uncle Ismail.

Here we go! says Daniel Manual.

…from when I got off the bus there was the smell of Fatima's *boboti* and *geelrys* coming down the street to meet me.

Now, says Uncle Abdul who lost his job in the catering trade (for cooking the books, says Jason), a man's dinner is coming out of the freezer as he comes in the door. And thirty seconds later it's coming out of the microwave onto the TV tray. That's no way to treat a man after a hard day's work.

I don't see no hard work! says Ma plonking a plastic two-litre Coke bottle of ice-cold water on the table. Sitting around talking gets you nowhere.

With permission, says Daniel Manual leaning back and pressing his finger tips together again, it was sitting around talking that saved South Africa from a blood bath. Mark my words. CODESA, the TRC. Only one thing wrong with the TRC…

Whitey! says Mal Jan. For him it was just The Toti Recreational Club and Rights of Admission Reserved.

No doubt about it, but more important: we didn't take a patent out on it, says Daniel Manual, and now everyone is using truth and wreck-a-silly-nation gratis and for free. Mark my words! The Americans would have patented it as 'Intellectual Property.'

And called it Weapons of Mass Discussion! says Jason

What's the world coming to? says Uncle Abdul. You know what we should definitely have taken a patent out on?

Nelson Mandela! says Jason.

Ja, says Uncle Abdul. Remember how *gatvol* he was with the 39 American pharmaceutical companies trying to sue our government for breaking patent rules so we could have cheaper AIDS drugs. They only gave up because they could see it was bad whatyamacallit – PR.

Auntie-retro-wireless! says Daniel Manual. But what we should also have taken a patent out on is…

Dagga *ek sê*! says Mal Jan.

No doubt about it! says Daniel Manual. Marry-Juana You think the fat cats are going to see it in laboratories in Europe and America and not jump on the bandwagon. Here it's a natural race-horse. There's thousands and thousands of acres growing *legally* for the farmer-cuticle industry. They use it under a fancy name to make drugs and make them so dear that people who need them haven't got enough money to buy them!

The fat cats make billions out of it but a *ou* who grows *boom* in his own back yard *mos* lands in jail, says Mal Jan. On TV they showed policemen *donnering* dagga plants the *old toppies* out in *bundu* were growing to make a little bit of money.

What's the world coming to?' says Uncle Abdul.

No good! says Daniel Manual. And it was the columnists who turned the Cape Coloureds into *dronkies*. Got them all picking grapes on their wine-yards and instead of paying them proper money paid some of their wage in brandy.

O brandewyn laat my staan, sings Mal Jan, swaying from side to side. And they *mos* coming home *babbelas* every night! 'Strue's' Bob!

Daniel Manual reckons he saw on the TV where people in South America couldn't like make a living growing the food they were exporting to the United States anymore because the American government subsidised their own farmers so they could grow food cheaper and sell it cheaper. So the Mexican farmers looked around to see what they could grow that the Americans *would* buy…

'n Boer maak 'n plan, Mal Jan interrupts with an athletic wink.

And what did they find? asks Daniel Manual. A huge market for cocaine. So Mexico and the other Latin America countries started growing coca. And what did the Yanks do? Flew to Mexico and the other countries, illegally of course, and sprayed poison on the farms. And it killed the coca plants, yes, but also the food they were growing for their own people.

Yaysus! says Mal Jan. And the Mexicans are supposed to be the crooks!

No doubt about it, says Daniel Manual. And there's this other thing they have in school now where you have to come up with an idea for a business. It's called on-top-manure-shit. You lose your job and now you must come up with a business plan and beg the bank to do you a big favour and get you into debt for the rest of your life. And they know 96% of new businesses fail in the first two years! Mark my words!

What's the world coming to? says Uncle Abdul.

Wait a bit! Wait a bit! says Uncle Ismail.

Here we go! says Daniel Manual.

….Fatima had this idea of using *rooibos*…

Rooibos! says Daniel Manual, banging his fist of the table. More big-shot crookery! Right now big companies are fighting over the name. The name *we* called it. A company which had *niks* to do with the business registered the trademark in the US and then sold it to another American company who reckons people must pay them to use it. The court cases are costing hundreds and thousands.

They say an idea can like come to you any place, any time. This one came shooting up right outside the front door: a little plant with four leaves with patterns like Ma makes with a fork on her butter icing. It was like a miracle. Dagga on the doorstep! Irwin says if it had popped up somewhere else we could have like put a box or something over to keep it safe. He had to think of a way to protect it before Ma came home.

Geniuses always get their best solutions (Ping!) in a bath, Daniel Manual says. He told us about this Greek *ou* who like gave up trying to figure something out and went to have a bath. The problem went clean (Ping!) out of his head and then he started shouting 'Erica! Erica!' Erica was his wife. Or maybe like just his girlfriend. 'Erica! Erica! I've found it!' No one could remember what he found. Terence reckons it was probably just the soap. But it's supposed to show that, when you're not like looking for it, the answer just comes.

So Irwin filled the bath and lay there to see if anything would like come up. Only his dick did. He stared at it for ages. It looked like a rose. And then suddenly he had it! The answer was right in front of his nose. 'Chantelle! Chantelle! I found it!' Chantelle is like his girlfriend.

The thing was not to hide the plant but make it look as though it was supposed to be there. He jumped out of the bath, wrapped a towel around himself and picked like three of the little roses and their leaves growing by the door, put them around the plant and told Ma it was because a chameleon had died there. Ma said she had no idea he was so sensitive. He tuned the *chommies* the situation.

Daniel Manual said the plan was sound and no doubt about it. He reckons there were these guys who had to transport sheets of glass. But it didn't matter how much bubble wrap or HANDLE WITH CARE stickers they used, the glass was like always getting broken. They were so shattered (Ping!) in the end they didn't pack the glass at all, just like slid it down the sides of the bakkie. And it never broke again.

Because why?

Because everyone could see it had to be like handled with care.

So now the plant, transplanted when Ma was asleep, is growing there between the shed and the fence.

Irwin reckons cannabis comes either in the male or female sex. He read on the internet that you can tell a dagga plant's sex by looking at 'the sexual organs nestling in the crotch.' He's hoping for a girl.

No doubt about it, says Daniel Manual. Because gold and diamonds are underground, it's easy to control the business. But when you've got something growing any old place, mark my words, you've got to use different cat-ticks. Make people think it's bad for you, and then ban it. Meanwhile, says Daniel Manual, the real criminals drive around behind tinted windows selling mandrax so they can afford to send their children to 'varsity' in Rava's and 4x4's.

Dagga is like alcohol, makes people *boos*, says Uncle Abdul.

No ways! says Terence. You won't get a Rasta abusing his wife and kids and breaking up a joint (Ping!), know what I'm saying.

Daniel Manual reckons if people were really healthy the farmer-cuticle industries would like go bankrupt. They get *our* ingredients cheap to make expensive medicines and make a fortune for themselves selling the drugs to those who can afford them while we *vrek*.

I think I know what I'm going to do for my project next year. I'm like going to research dagga. You can make rope and clothing and paper from it. KwaZulu Natal has the perfect growing climate for it. I reckon ordinary people should like have the right to grow it. And from the money they make they can build proper houses and schools. And if they like use it and all other natural remedies they won't even need more hospitals.

Terence says he'll work on some lyrics with words like need and greed and weed. He says I can call my project the same name as he's calling his rap 'Profits of the Front Yard.'

The dagga plant has already got more leaves; they're like so perfect it's scary. It's weird how a simple thing has got such power.

A few letters of the alphabet can make you *poep* yourself too, says Mal Jan. Like A N C used to make whitey go even paler.

It's called in-dock-tree-nation, says Daniel Manual. If you want power, give people something to be scared of. That's why the Nationalists got people terrified. It's what lots of governments do all over the world. Always have. Always will. Mark my words! But when the ANC came to power all the big shots supported them – Anglo American *nogal* – because they could see where the money was and where it was still going to be and where it was going to stay. And not go to the people who suffered under Apart-hate. And they use the newspapers to make the man in the street…

Get run over! chirps Jason.

…extra *dof*, says Mal Jan nodding like he knows it all.

No doubt about it! says Daniel Manual adjusting his glasses. Everywhere in the world the media lie to people to try and make them believe whatever the big shots want them to. It's called Prop-a-gander.

Stuffed or not, laughs Jason glancing around to see if anyone else gets his joke. It's time their goose was cooked!

Irwin's been working on the AIDS rap:

> **Tourist pack it**
> **big shots wear it on a jacket**
> **But da little red ribbon**
> **just don't hack it.**

'Strue's Bob! says Mal Jan. Red ribbons for AIDS, pink ribbons for one kind of cancer, yellow for another, maroon for something else. They're pushing ribbons for Africa and us walking around dolled up like poodle doodles. And then there's all those days! AIDS Awareness Day, Tree Day, Civvies Day. One day for this thing and another day for that! They use up all 365 days and there's none left for an *ou* to do what he likes in.

The schools too, says Uncle Abdul, are messing around with this AIDS thing. The *laaities* must now go home and tell their parents to use french letters. School children were only taught *'n bietjie* reading and *nog 'n bietjie* arithmetic because the Nats reckoned the Bible said black people must be 'hewers of wood and drawers of water.' For ever and a day.

It was the same for us *ous*, says Mal Jan. I only learnt the three R's: Reading, Writing and Arithmetic.

And fok-all spelling! says Jason.

Terence tunes us his rap:

What are men dreamin
pumpin semen
know what I'm meanin?
It's not lurv day making
it's not lurv day faking
it's orphans for da nation's undertaking.

That's what I want to know, says Mal Jan. How come, when everyone knows you can get AIDS – and *nogal* make *klonkies* with AIDS! – if you don't use a french letter in traffic, how come...

TRAFFIC?' everyone shouts.

Ja, man, you know mos um, um intercourse, he mumbles going red and looking down at his bony knees.

Daniel Manual throws his head back; he's laughing so hard his false teeth like rattle. Maybe that's why they're making... making...making drivers get plastic-coated licences! A Prophylactic for Traffic!

The *chommies* sent Irwin to fetch the Afrikaans dictionary and Daniel Manual like looked up 'intercourse' and there it was: the Afrikaans for intercourse was *verkeer*. Then he looked up *verkeer* and there it was: the English for *verkeer* was traffic. Then he looked up '*FIKS*' – which is Afrikaans for AIDS – *fiks*: strong, fit, healthy.'

Yaysus! says Mal Jan, There's *mos* the answer! If you use er…er…

A condiment! Daniel Manual laughs.

If you use a *dinges*, Mal Jan flicks the back of his hand across the open page, you won't get strong, fit and healthy! Here it *mos* is in black and white. So that's why peoples is not using them!

What's the world coming to? says Uncle Abdul.

Mark my words! says Daniel Manual.

Irwin did like some more dictionary research.

They don't have penis in Afrikaans either, he says. They've got penetrate and penicillin and penitent but no penis.

The Afrikaners *mos* must have a Pee-Mis, says Mal Jan.

Irwin looked up what girls' private parts are called and then the English translation for the word: it was 'poetry.' Cool eh!

Irwin is like writing this poem 'Chantelle, life without you is hell.' Terence says *Ja*, that's probably where she'll tell him to go.

The dictionary was published in 1976. Daniel Manual says that's when school children in Soweto rioted because they didn't want to learn Afrikaans.

They had a point, no doubt about it, says Uncle Abdul.

Irwin has nearly finished his lyrics:

> **Be no need**
> **for Nevarapine**
> **if dere never had been**
> **a penis near her**
> **be no children**
> **needin rearin**
> **if dere pa**
> **never had *naai*'ed dere ma.**

'Strues Bob! says Mal Jan. Lots of AIDS and *fokall* jobs.

It's all this *Science* and, with permissions, *Poepology*! No doubt about it, says Daniel Manual, that's why there're so many people without jobs.

'*I* can give the lot of you jobs!' says Ma coming out with a basket to bring the washing in off the line.

Ag Ma! what you give is just work. With a job you get holidays and…

But Uncle Abdul is like pressing his big fat fingers on the table and slowly raising his ginormous bum.

The Camry makes a clicking sound. Home James!

The *chommies*, chuckling nervously, get up.

Typical! says Ma. Just say the word WORK and you won't see them for dust!

10

I got up early the day I died. For two or three hours I worked on the letter that had for so long been on my mind. It was still no more than a rough draft and I put it in the pocket of my apron and went down to the vegetable garden. I would think about it – and the farm I had so dearly loved – while I weeded.

The price of scrap metal is set internationally, so is the price of mohair. When George began to assist father in the running of the farm he, of course, like many of the younger generation, insisted on investing in all the latest machinery eventually needing just one 'boy' for every 1500 hectares. The men – 'boys' of course regardless of age – lost their jobs and with them the houses where families like Lawrence's had lived for generations. The farmers prospered: large cars, swimming pools, satellite dishes and with them high electric fences and intercom systems.

The dog chained up in the big yard is barking again. I used to hear him when, even as a puppy, he was kept outside howling in the night when the weather was wet and he ached for the supple warmth of his mother's belly and the rhythm of her blood. I used to lie in the dark and listen to him and wonder what was best: to be put down to rest in peace or to cry alone in the rain. But it's the children I worried about and what they were learning about care and love, what they were learning about suffering and indifference.

The monkeys had been at the mealies again. I could see their teeth marks down the cobs they'd ripped open and I saw where the dragon fly had laid her little wormy eggs. And she so beautiful. Like a brooch mother used to wear: stripes on the abdomen, the thorax purple and blue, and, on the black wings, red dots. So beautiful, so utterly beautiful that you'd want to preserve it. But you can't, not without killing it. And when it's dead, the colours fade.

Then I heard, somewhere in the far distance, the curiously sad and circussy tune of the ice cream van and remembered Walls *ice cream! Then the little tune was overlaid suddenly by the telephone ringing: a two-beat repetitive ring and a couplet of silence, the sequence coming at me, coming at me, again and again. I had been trying to sort out my affairs; it was probably the solicitor or someone like that phoning. I wasn't in the mood for speaking to them. I felt for the letter in my apron pocket.*

#29

Bullet Holes in Angel's Wings

Dear Tanya,

Since you have kindly agreed to be my executor I want to explain why I did what I did in my will. I know you think of me as your maiden aunt (great aunt!) so I hope that you won't be too shocked to find that there's more to me than meets the eye! I trust that *you* will one day find true love – if you haven't already! – and that you will be happy.

I'd better start I suppose with a man called Elliot. Poor Elliot. I often wonder how different my life would have been if Father and George (my brother, your grandfather of course!) hadn't interfered.

I was heading for the shelf – as they used to say in those days of women who had reached twenty-five with no marriage prospects – and had met Elliot through the Hitching Post in the *Farmer's Weekly*. A bit like people now meeting through the computer I suppose. I am not ashamed of that. It was difficult for people like us who lived in isolation to meet in any other way but it also meant that the most casual of introductions was overloaded with significance. We wrote to each other and then started corresponding regularly and when father and George went to do business in town and collect the post there were three or four letters for me at a time. George teased me unmercifully. After some months Father and Mother discussed matters and Father wrote to Elliot inviting him to come and visit us on the farm. Things went rather well and he stayed for several weeks.

Father liked him because he too had a farm (which, considering father could barely stay away from his lands, his animals, for a single night, should have alerted him) and asked intelligent questions and listened to the answers and because he was attentive to mother – rising when she entered a room, pulling out the chair for her – and was appreciative of her cooking. George liked him because he made him feel superior. Mother liked him because – though he refused third helpings! – he was a nice person. I liked him because I had convinced myself I already loved him.

His mother had died a year previously and he lived alone and, I suppose, needed a wife to run the home. He spoke to father and when he left there was an understanding between us. We made our plans by mail. Since his farm was a long day's journey away, too far to merit more than a single trip, it was decided that we would come up and he and I would be married there in the church in his nearest town. Father had announcements of marriage printed. Mother and I made my wedding dress and supervised the baking of the cake. I spent a lot of time writing down recipes and adding to the items I kept in mothballs in my Hope Chest, where girls like me would keep the household linen and embroidered tray cloths and crocheted antimacassars in the hope of one day marrying and needing such things!

Father and George sat in the front of the Chevrolet, mother and I in the back with the wedding cake propped between us and the dress draped on the window ledge. It was night when we arrived but Father said later he could see immediately that we had been duped.

I awoke the next morning to the smell of burning coffee. The men had gone to the lands. Mother was sitting on a bench in the sun. She took my hand and drew me down next to her and stroked my forearm not saying a word. I felt uneasy.

When the men came back, Father had pink spots of anger on his cheeks, George scowled, Elliot seemed aged. He brought cane chairs out for father and George and himself sat on his haunches.

Father declared that Elliot was a liar and a blackguard and he would not under any circumstance allow his daughter – whom he dearly loved – to make her home in this 'hovel'. George in his usual domineering tone told Elliot that he was an insult to the farming profession, and that no sister of his etc., etc. Mother sniffled into a scented hanky. The upshot was that Father said he, personally, was calling the whole thing off and forbade any further contact between us henceforth. Elliot said that perhaps I should make the decision. George said how dare he speak to

Father like that. Father said, 'She is in no fit state to decide anything. One day she will thank us.'

We drove home in silence. Father wrote letters to those to whom he had sent cards. Mother tucked mothballs between the folds of the wedding dress and packed it away. George ate the cake.

I don't know whether Elliot ever wrote again. I received no letters. And when the telephone rang the two longs and two shorts that was our ring on the party line I was never summonsed. No one mentioned Elliot.

I spent all day alone in my room and refused to 'join the family' for meals. I could not understand how they could go on eating all that copious food as though nothing had happened. Or how they could go to church in town and sit in the pew that bore our name in a little brass holder.

It was strange to me too that everything in the house stayed just the same: the old wind-up gramophone on which, smiling, Elliot and I listened to father's old records of Richard Tauber and Tino Rossi, the chair he had always sat on on the stoep, even the ruched satin cushion.

The only time I went out of the house was to go to the toilet, the long drop where no one had thought to replace the old sheets of *The Farmer's Weekly* with something less remindful. I hardly ate and got very thin.

But if I thought I was unhappy then I had no idea of what was to come.

Father said that I would get over it. That I would meet someone else. (!) That what I needed was to get out of the house.

I don't know how long it was but one day I did get up and go for a walk. Just down to the river. I was shocked to see how dry everything had become, how desolate everything looked but I remember thinking that at least Nature had had the decency to present the veldt appropriately.

I did feel better for having gone out and every day walked a little further into the koppies. I took a book with me – *Wuthering Heights*! or was it *Pride and Prejudice*? – and sometimes a picnic lunch, just an orange and a stick of biltong and stayed away for many hours.

One day on one of my walks I was surprised to see a young Coloured man and a little boy down by the river. I recognised the young man instantly. He was wearing a khaki bush hat but I could see the scar on his temple. And then of course there were the eyes, so brown, so beautiful. He was one of the *bywoners*, 'those who live alongside', and whose families had lived on the farms in the area for generations, and who had provided labour for the white farmers who had taken over. But why am I telling you what you already know?!

Lawrence used to come and play with George and me when we were little. I remembered the last day he came. We had turned a diesel drum on its side and the idea was to stand on it and move your feet so that the barrel would roll along under you, building momentum. The person who could make the barrel go furthest was the winner. But that day George who, as usual had put himself in charge and was bossing the two of us around, had fallen off rather quickly and landed with his face in the red dust. Lawrence and I couldn't stop laughing. George was furious.

And then it was Lawrence's turn and George pushed him hard so that he fell. And as he fell a piece of rusty metal poking out of the top of the drum had cut his temple. The blood spurted out alarmingly. I screamed. It was usually mother who came running from the kitchen, screen door slamming, apron flying to sort out our playground troubles but that day she was off somewhere seeing to the hens. I put my arm around Lawrence and dabbed at the cut with the sash I pulled from my dress and I remember being surprised that the flesh beneath his skin was as pink as mine and the blood as red.

It was Father who came to see what was going on. I told him George had pushed him but it was Lawrence Father scolded. He told him that people should stick to their own kind and that he was not to come and play anymore, that he didn't want to see him around here ever again. George stood there nodding as Father spoke, and grinned triumphantly as Lawrence walked away holding my scrunched-up sash to his wound. I felt sad as I watched him go. He was my friend.

I always remembered what he had said earlier that day when we were happy – that feeling the drum turn beneath one's feet was like feeling the world go round.

So here we were twenty years later. I was both delighted and shy, and a little embarrassed, to see him but there is always something special about meeting up with people who knew you in your family setting when you were little and fresh to the world and knew nothing of the complex strands that bind families together and the things that rub against these strands to make them fray and snap.

(If, in telling you this story, I tarnish the memory of your grandfather and of your great grandfather, I apologise but I can only tell it in the way I know.)

That day down by the river Lawrence told me that after that incident he had been sent to live with his elder married sister in town and had passed standard eight and was working for a cabinetmaker and that he loved working with wood, the feel of it, the smell of it and the way the wood sometimes swirls – like Walls chocolate and vanilla ice cream is what he said!

He had married but his wife had died in childbirth, the child – the little boy he was with – had survived and lived with his *ouma* here on the farm. Lawrence came as often as he could to visit him and yet I, having always stayed so close to home, had not seen him in all these years. It showed me what strange lives we led!

I could see the pain of his loss was still with him and when he asked me about my life I had nothing really to say. We arranged to meet again.

It seemed to me that Nature was again playing her part for that same afternoon the drought broke and the smell of the rain on the baked earth seemed to fill the world with joy. I naturally made no mention of my encounter with Lawrence and his little boy, Paulie, a delightful child full of curiosity and invention.

One day we sat on a koppie while Paulie made roads between the stones and played with a *tok tokkie* beetle and looked down on the farm and watched Father and George like little ants tinkering with the tractor. It was then that I told Lawrence of Elliot and how unhappy I had been and speaking to him, out there in the fragrant knobbled veldt with the cicadas singing and the mountains ranged one behind the other in soft purple piles, I felt as though an angel had come and lifted a burden from my shoulders.

Father said he was glad to see that I had taken his advice to get some fresh air and that it was quite remarkable how much good just getting out of the house had done me. His tone made me suspect that George had been spying.

I had always had 'my' horse. I had never been much of a horsewoman but I now realised that riding would allow me greater freedom and as Bess and I learnt to understand and trust each other, my confidence grew and soon I was saddling her up every day and staying away for long happy hours. Father remarked that it was unbecoming for a woman to sit astride a horse. Mother worried about my complexion. George ranted that if 'this' carried on they would have no chance of marrying me off. That is the way they spoke in those days.

For myself I felt that I could gallop to the ends of the earth, if – a small inner voice told me – Lawrence were there. The veldt was green and the animals fattening. There were tiny *leeubekkies* and sudden daisies among the pastel stones and the air was spangled with birdsong. There were larks and *bokmakeries* and butcherbirds, there were *mossies* and wagtails and small sunbirds dropping like stones from the mimosa trees. I had a friend again.

He came often to the *bywoner* house where his *ouma* lived and when he did I tried always to meet with him and Paulie. Lawrence was interested in everything to do with Nature and was able to answer all the little boy's questions and teach us both many things. It was from him I learnt that each star is 4 million miles away from its nearest neighbour, and the tongue of the whale is eight foot thick. I also learn that it was the Russians who had invented ice cream. Sometimes I took a picnic for the three of us; Mother remarked that my appetite had improved beyond all recognition!

Those few months were the happiest of my life.

And then one day there was a cloud burst, and in no time the red earth had turned to mud, the dam had broken its walls and the river had rushed and washed right over the bridge. I knew when I heard the phone ringing, two longs and two shorts, that the call was for me. George summonsed me angrily to the phone: 'Some Hottentot wants to talk to you.' I knew immediately that something awful had happened.

It was a friend of Lawrence's phoning from town. Paulie had disappeared; Lawrence had already left for the farm and had asked the friend to call me. The rain had eased off but it would not in any case have made any difference to me. I ran to the stables, saddled up and already had one foot in the stirrup when George grabbed the bridle.

'Where the hell do you think you're going?'

I didn't answer but kicked my heels in Bessie's flanks and shot off. George was shouting. I will not repeat what he said. I still find it too painful.

'Go Bess go!' I screamed. The rain mingled with the tears that drenched my face as we galloped through the mud.

When I got to the little house, Lawrence had just arrived. Paulie had been playing in the puddles outside with the other children and had somehow wandered off. They had looked everywhere for him. Lawrence took Bessie; there was a better chance of finding him on horseback. I stayed in the little house and had *bossies tee* with *Ouma* who knew she said, *in my bene*, that something was terribly wrong. We talked of what a sweet child Paulie was 'just like his dad' she said and then she went into the next room and I heard a wardrobe door open and she came out with an old manila envelope. 'I kept it for the young *mies*,' she said. I opened the envelope. Inside, washed and ironed many years before, was my sash. Few things have touched me as much.

The men returned despondent. I still can smell their chew *tabak* and their greatcoats drying by the old black stove. Two long hours passed before we heard the sound of hooves in the distance. Slow hooves. My heart fell.

He was already dead when Lawrence found him. His foot had hooked into a tree root at the river's edge and he had fallen face down into the water.

Lawrence was distraught. Holding the body of his little boy, he sobbed like a child, and asked what kind of a God it was who could put such suffering on him. Again. I will never forget the anguish in his eyes.

The police came and I asked them to inform Father of what had happened and tell them not to expect me home until the following day.

We laid Paulie out and I stayed in that little house amongst the keening relatives singing and weeping all through the night.

When I got home the next day Father and George had faces like thunderclouds.

'It is their misfortune, not yours. Let them get on with it,' Father said.

'Yes, it has nothing to do with you!' George said. Had a rifle been handy I would have shot them both, I think.

Watching the little white coffin being lowered into the ground in the cemetery, 'their' cemetery, singing from the hymn sheet that shook as I tried to hold it firm between my hands '…no more childish griefs or fears, no more sadness no more tears…' I knew that everything would now be different.

Those were fragile days. I did not want to impose myself on Lawrence and he did not want to put me, as he later said, 'in an awkward position' but somehow through the maze we found a way of reaching each other and I realised then that I had not before had the slightest idea of what love was and that the attraction to poor Elliot was based on nothing more than a desire to get away from the stultifying existence of home.

I think perhaps that death, or the imminence of it, as in war time, peels away the usual reserves of inhibition and self-protection and exposes the softer inside part in the shells we build around us and so we are vulnerable and within this shared vulnerability comes a desire to give to each other, to meld, to fuse. When I was with Lawrence I felt the soaring of my sprit like a line of pure light leading straight to heaven. Our souls breathed together when we kissed.

Father was bewildered by the disappearance of the docile daughter who always did as she was told and wondered where this strong-willed woman had suddenly come from and said perhaps I should have been allowed to marry Elliot after all.

'Oh yes?!' I shouted, 'You told me that one day I would thank you. That day has come.'

Mother sniffled into a scented hanky.

I found now that more than anything in the world I wanted to bear Lawrence a child, not only because of his loss, though for that reason too, but because I wanted to be with child by him, for him, for us, for, in a way, my country, my world.

What did I care about convention, the law, when it seemed to me that the universe itself backed my desire? All I cared about was him and our love for each other.

I wanted to be with Lawrence forever. The more Father reprimanded and Mother sniffled, the more George shouted and said *Sis!* and all manner of dreadful things, the more I wanted to be with him. One Saturday night, overwhelmed by love and desire and unable to sleep, I lifted the wedding dress out of its mothballed box; my hands were shaking as I put it on and every muscle in my body tense as I crept out of the sleeping house to the stable.

It was gone midnight when I arrived at the little house. Lawrence too had been unable to sleep and, hearing the hooves, was waiting for me. He took the reins and I sat behind him as we galloped into the night, wishing that it could be into far-away and forever. It was (still is!) the most wonderful night of my life. Lying together on his coat on the ground as the world slowly turned looking up into a cold sky, thick with stars I felt I had never before know what stars are, what silence is, what anything in its essence actually was.

'We'll put a stop to this before it is too late,' Father said when I returned as the dawn household was stirring.

I just smiled.

My room was kept locked at night.

Bess was taken away.

George was instructed not to let me out of his sight.

Through sealed notes passed through 'the girl' I managed to keep in touch with Lawrence as we struggled to find a way to be together.

He had told me once that, caught in a crevice, a *dassie* will swell its body so that the hunter cannot pull it out. I had not in my mind planned it that way but it seemed that that was what my body was doing. It was trying to save me. I did not yet know how cruel they could be.

I was eating like a horse.

One day when we were in the dairy separating the milk from the cream Mother remarked that I seemed to be gaining weight. I said nothing. She looked at me hard, my body silhouetted against the blue sky at the wide open door and then she cupped her chin in her hands and said 'Oh God what have you done! Lord have mercy!' and ran out across the backyard.

Father kept me locked in my room all day. George stood outside the door telling me that I'd broken mother's heart, taken years off father's life. That I was a disgrace to the family name. Father and Mother talked late into the night. The telephone rang many times.

I don't know what they did to sedate me but I remember that the doctor came and, after that, everything was hazy. All I know is that a few days later I was waking up in a hospital bed in Port Elizabeth, bereft and in pain. The tears running down my desolate cheeks, I felt cold and confused as though I was swimming a slow breast stroke with wilted limbs under a heavy weight of arctic water and couldn't, or didn't want to, reach the surface.

I longed to feel the hauling grip of Lawrence's hand. Longed to feel his tautly muscled arms around me. His soft warm skin. His breath on my face.

I thought of how I used to hold the hens on the block while mother chopped their necks and how the headless bodies flapped out of my hands and ran around without direction and then I thought of how I used to pluck them and how mother cleaned them, pulling the organs from the cavity with a sucking sound and a film of dark blood on her hands and I couldn't stop crying.

Every morning I woke up disappointed that I was still alive.

Eventually when I was pronounced strong enough for the journey they took me back to the farm.

They didn't need to lock my room for I was too feeble to do anything but lie there with curtains drawn listening to the skinny voices of the children hanging in the wide air, their laughter bubbling across the lucerne lands, sobbing for the child, our little tadpole, they had ripped out from inside my body, pining for the man I loved.

One day I heard shouting at the kitchen door.

'Bugger off!' George yelled, 'You are breaking the law!'

And then I heard Lawrence out in the yard. 'I love you, Rose,' he called! 'I love you!' His voice, which was always so deep and lovely to me, seemed to diffuse into a thousand tiny fractures like a little hurt boy and the tears just flowed. I had no energy to get up or do anything besides tug at the curtain in the hope that he would register the movement and read my mind and the silent lips he could not see, ' I love you too, Lawrence!'

He came again a week or so later.

This time I was sitting on my bed.

'I love you, Rose! They can't do this to us!'

'Shut up, you bastard!' George, my constant keeper, shouted. 'Leave her alone! She wants nothing to do with you.'

I pulled at the door. But it was locked.

I pulled at the window. But it too was locked.

I tried to shout out but my voice was weak.

Then I saw the pewter vase of purple everlastings that stood on my dressing table and somehow gathered the strength to pick it up and hurl it at the window. I stood back and watched the glass shatter and fall as if in slow motion.

Lawrence ran towards the window. Our eyes met for just a moment but it was all we needed; nothing would destroy our love.

George chased him off yelling, 'If you persist with this nonsense you know what'll happen. I'm warning you.'

Then he turned on me 'Are you mad? You could have hurt yourself!'

'Hurt myself!' I shrieked, 'Hurt myself!' I flung myself down on the bed and the world cracked apart.

It was one of the 'girls' in the kitchen who told me that Lawrence had disappeared. It was the radio that told me some weeks later that the remains of a man, thought to be those of a young Coloured man reported missing, had been found on a farm in the Karoo. He had apparently been mauled by a leopard. A month or so before a group of men had, they said, tracked a mountain leopard down. George had personally fired the fatal shot. Father told me that as though I should be pleased. I did not ask why they had not brought the trophy home.

The things I have heard lately on the news confirm what I have long known, that cruelty has no bounds.

They didn't do proper investigations in those days. Not on 'them'. But I knew that if they had they would have found among the bones on the little koppie overlooking the farm house, evidence of a bullet in the back.

I never spoke to George again.

Father set up a trust account so I could make a new life for myself hundreds of miles away. The only time I returned was for mother's funeral. It was then that I found that, just before her death, she had inherited another farm '*Ververgeet*' – Long Forgotten – from a distant, childless relative. Presumably with Father's approval, she left this farm to me. It had for some years been managed by a third party and through the solicitors I simply kept the arrangement going.

When Father died he, naturally, left the family farm to George. To me he left a lump sum of money he had invested.

Although over the years my heart has ached for those blue skies, those hot dry plains among the mountains, I could not bring myself to go back to that place of pain that I loved so much.

I trust you will understand why I leave '*Ververgeet*' and the money to those named in the will. Aside from anything else,

Lawrence's family have worked long and hard in this part of the world. They deserve to own at least some small part of it.

May it serve them well.

This house I leave, of course, to you.'

Perhaps I'd said too much. I didn't want to cause undue upset. 'You broke your mother's heart,' was what they'd said to me.

They were still so clear the sea green curtains around the bed and the nurse with her tight starched belt and her upside down watch and her upside down mouth and the view of the sea from the window. The sea-green sea. A D and C. Dilation and Curettage was what I heard them say.

The telephone had stopped but that strangely hypnotic little tune was coming closer. The ice cream van was coming up the lower part of the street.

The scrap metal man heard the moment of stasis as the driver's foot in its worn flip-flop pressed the clutch to the hot floor of the cab and geared down to take the incline. Was alert to the danger.

The phone was ringing again.

It kept coming at me, coming at me. And now it was ringing in my head, two long shrills and two short, two long and two short, and now it was a slow sombre single note, over and over. A deep metal resounding that repeated itself again and again in my head. It felt as though my skull had become a belfry. A bell was tolling in my brain. I flung the trowel aside.

When I got to the house the ringing had stopped but, hearing the little merry-go-round song so close, the memory of ice cream flooded the soft sides of my mouth and alerted the thousand taste buds attentive on my tongue.

I opened the gate and heard the rush like strong water running over rocks, and saw the child tadpole-eyed, come free-wheeling down the street, saw the scrap metal man running with the weight of his trolley pulling at his arm muscles, heard the thud of discarded boots, heard his whistle, pitched to the universe, piercing the sky, alarming the stars, saw the trolley shoved onto the grass verge, saw where his temple had caught on the protruding rod, saw the blazing windscreen and… The child! The child! I heard the sound of braking on the tar, hard, and the little ice-cream tune, loud, and I plunged across and plucked him swift, threw him swift, out to the grass verge, and I heard him yell long and lustily. He was alive! The child was alive! This time I had saved a life! And oh the joy of it!

And then I felt, briefly, the ice-cream van reverse and the scrap metal man reach towards me and put a hand under my head and reach his other hand to me and I took it and saw thick cuticles, like old putty on old panes and I looked up into caring brown eyes looking warm into mine and I saw other brown eyes brimming and smelt the memory of chewed tobacco and wood smoke, of worked muscle and sunshine plaited into grass matting, of merino dip and diesel, of horse droppings and herbaceous heat and of unutterable kindness.

I saw the dandelion clock explode and heard the icebergs shift.
And the sky slowly closed down as I heard the driver say
'She came flying out of nowhere!'

Out of nowhere, out of a derelict Whites Only Ladies Waiting Room in an abandoned station by a desolate siding, where – in the middle of a journey whose purpose I had forgotten – I had been discarded many years before. Out of the still blue gloom of an empty hall where the windows were shuttered and the door bolted. Out of the loneliest loneliness imaginable.

Now there is movement, now there are people, now the windows are opened wide and the light streams in and I am flung up and out, scattering bright, wet diamonds in a parabola of sparkling air.

Space curves, the horizon is elastic, time does not run out. The earth sits in the hollows of a spongy universe leaning in against itself, spinning at 800kms hurtling around the sun at 100 000 kph. There are 140 billion smudges of frayed batting, 140 galaxies like the Milky Way each with 100 million stars.

The tardy light that bends from the daytime rush of stars that daylight has blanked out, leaps into our eyes a thousand days after leaving the sun.

Arm yourself with wonder, mantle the world with soft delight. Unbundle the river, break open the sky, see from the inside of the fly's eye, shine through the glow-worm's skin. Such minute ordering is incomprehensible

In the universe you are nothing. But the amazing thing is that you so gloriously are; the architecture of your cells so explicit, the profoundness of your soul so ineffable.

Since the universe shifts continually outwards nothing can ever be called 'whole,' or anything be final.

Untether the stars in your eyes, hold onto the memory of light, amaze the angels. The day is not yours to seize but the moment! that you can inhabit with nerve ends poised for the unimagined extraordinariness that's there within all ordinary things.

Beneath the casual sky I exhale your breath.

Don't weep for me.

Acknowledgments

Aden and Jada Rose for their
distinctive and all-embracing hugs.

Sophie for her stalwart mothering
(of me too) and for knowing
when to use – and not use –
semi-colons; commas, and full stops